PROLOGUE

I never fancied myself in love before. I have worked as an Elite Warrior for over seventy-five years, keeping the innocents protected from the vile creatures that roam this earth, vampires and people alike. I never had time to think much about settling down, because after two hundred years on this earth, I lost faith in ever finding my destined mate. Don't get me wrong, I have had plenty of women warm my bed, but never more than once. I can't afford to give them any chance of developing feelings, because if you aren't a mate, then there is no life for us.

Jill was unexpected. By helping my Elite brother, Jax, with his mate, I stumbled across my own. She is like the brightest star in the darkest of nights, a beacon that calls out to my soul, and the angel that has captured this vampire's heart. Why the fates chose her, I will never know, but I am forever grateful that they have. Now, I just have to convince her, my angel with her long, thick, silky waves of hair and those soft doe-brown eyes that makes my heart melt when she looks into mine, that we are meant to be.

We were moving in the right direction finally, her getting over the whole "vampire" thing, when she was taken from me, along with Jax and Cassie, Jax's mate, by a man that thought to have her as his own. Two months I had spent searching for her, for them, with no success and when I thought all hope was lost, Jax and Cassie came home. They had escaped, but Jill was not so lucky.

The man who had abducted her was the head of the Hunters, a group of regular men who hunted vampires, not caring if they killed the innocent or not. To them, we were all killers and needed to die. Hunters do not see us as the humans that we are, with a slight difference in our DNA, because we need blood to survive, we are automatically considered monsters who drain the life out of people. That is far from the truth for most of us vamps, we drink the blood of animals, from blood bags and on occasion, a willing female during a one-nighter, but never do we drain anyone dry.

The bastard had hidden Jill away on Cousins Island, which is part of Yarmouth, Maine, to keep her away from me. Jax had figured out the location after his mate had overheard a phone conversation between Stephan, a new Elite recruit, and Jason, the head Hunter. It was a shock to find out that one of our own was a spy. Stephan had begged for his life, pleading that he did it to save his own, but it meant nothing to us. We take care of threats our own way and a spy in our midst is one of the biggest threats of all.

Taven, our head Elite, took care of the matter himself, since he was the one to bring Stephan into the Compound. Thankfully, the rest of the new recruits checked out and are able to move forward within the ranks, but not before the blood battle between the Elite and the Hunters.

We found Jill on the Island and after the long battle, I was able to bring her home. Killing Jason on the battlefield that day gave me satisfaction, but it wasn't until we brought Jill home and realized the damage that had been done to her emotionally and physically, that I wished I had drawn out his death! The spark that she once had is now gone, along with her free spirit and love for life. The smartass comments that would fall from her mouth, especially when her and Cassie were going at it, no longer bless us with their presence; her light is gone.

It took about a week after her return before she would talk to anyone but Cassie, and the only reason she talked to Cassie right away was because of Jax and Cassie's baby daughter, Jill's namesake. The only emotion she really shows is when she has Jillian in her arms. She loves that baby girl so much. She is slowly coming back to us, but I am not sure if she will find her way back to me. She hasn't spoken about her abduction except to put me at ease by informing me that she was never fully raped, "fully" being the key word.

It's been six months now since her ordeal and I have not been able to hold her in my arms since the day I carried her home. It's been excruciating, but she is slowly warming up to me again. She smiled at me for the first time a week ago and even went so much as to lay her hand on my arm for a brief second. I have never been a patient man, but for Jill, I will wait an eternity, if need be, but praying that I won't have to.

ONE

DUNCAN

I'm just throwing on a pair of sweatpants after my shower when I hear her screams in the room next to mine. I fly to her room in vampire speed to find her sitting up in her bed, trembling. Afraid that she will shrink back at my touch, I just sit on the edge of her bed, "It's okay, Jill. It was only a nightmare. You are safe here at the Compound, nobody is going to hurt you ever again."

This has been our nightly ritual for the past six months and that is why I had her room moved next to mine. She is my mate and responsibility, regardless of how she feels about it. She wouldn't talk to me for three whole days after I had moved her things over to this room, but as her nightmares continued, she had a change of heart. She can no longer live by herself, worried that she will be taken again, and even though Cassie wants her to stay with them, her nightmares won't allow it. There are nights like tonight where her screams will wake up the whole house if she stayed with Cassie and Jax, but with Jillian, Jill doesn't want to inconvenience them, so she agreed to stay at the Compound until she no longer had them.

Tonight's dream must have been a bad one, because the next thing I know, she is throwing herself into my arms, tears streaming down her cheeks. It feels so good to have her in my arms again, even though it is under these circumstances. I hold onto her tightly and let her cry it out until she can't cry anymore. Once she realizes that she is in my arms, though, she slowly pushes herself back and away from me.

"I am so sorry, Duncan. I don't know what came over me. I guess it was a pretty bad one tonight."

"Don't ever apologize, Jill. This is what I am here for, to help you get through this."

"Why, Duncan? Why are you wanting to waste your time with someone that is damaged?"

"You are not damaged, angel, only fractured. You will heal in time."

"It's been six months, Duncan. They don't seem to be getting any better!"

"You went through a horrific ordeal, Jill! You can't expect to get past that so soon. If you ask me, I think you have done a damn good job coming as far as you have!"

She won't look at me, so I take a chance and reach out, gently lifting her chin so she will look at me. I can see the struggle she is having with not pulling away, but she never moves. My heart breaks for her and I feel utterly helpless, not knowing how to help her.

"You may not want to hear this Jill and I don't want to frighten you, but I am one hundred percent sure that the fates brought us together to be mates. Now, whether or not we act on that, does not matter to me right now. My main concern is helping you get your life back, so I am not going anywhere."

"You could never frighten me. It's just so hard to be touched by anyone and I hate that I am hurting you. I may never be able to get that part of myself back and I refuse to hold you back. You should just forget about me and move on… be happy; that's all I want for you."

"You don't get it, angel. There is no moving on for me! We only get one mate in our lifetime, and you are it for me!"

"I see," she sighs and lays back down, turning her back towards me, "I'm going to try going back to sleep. Thank you for checking on me."

"Goodnight Jill. I am right next door if you need anything." I walk out of her room and go back to my own. I am seething with anger towards the son of a bitch that did this to her. I punch the cement wall by the door, cracking it and causing pieces to fall to the floor. I can use a good sparring right about now, but I don't want to go too far in case she has another episode. Instead, I hit the floor and start doing push-ups.

I hear a knock at my door, "Duncan, can I come in?" Taven asks.

"Sure."

"Hey Buddy, what's going on?" He examines the damage to the wall.

"Sorry, just let my anger get the best of me."

"Do you want to talk about it? I heard her screams again."

I stop and jump up really quick, grabbing the towel from my shower to wipe the sweat from my brow. I am not really in the mood to talk to anyone right now, but Taven means well, and he is a good friend, I can't just turn him away.

Hesitating, "I just don't know how to help her. It's been months and even though she is socializing a little more, the nightmares seem to be getting worse. She won't talk about it, not even to Cassie. What did that bastard do to her, Taven?"

"I feel you, man. I'm not even her mate and it frustrates me that we can't seem to help her. She is always skittish when one of the men walks into the same room, like she is waiting to be attacked again."

I think about his words and an idea comes to me. It may not be the answer, but it may help a little. "What if I teach her how to defend herself?"

"You mean, like train with the men?" Taven crinkles his brow.

"Well, maybe eventually but start her off with just training with me and work her way up. Maybe if she learns to defend herself and feels like she can take care of herself, then she can start to heal. I honestly don't know, but it's all I got."

"It actually sounds like a great idea, Dunc. Talk to her tomorrow about it and see what she thinks."

"I think I will. Thanks for the talk Tav, it helped." I smile at him. Things start to look up and the anger subsides for now.

The next morning, I get up early and go for a run before going down to breakfast. Jill has made it a habit to eat just as everyone else is finishing up and heading out. It's her way of avoiding everyone, if possible. So, I decide to take my run first, shower and then grab a bite, knowing that she will be there, eating alone.

She doesn't disappoint. Jill sits at the table, casually eating her French toast and reading the newspaper as I walk in. She stops in mid-bite and watches me move around the kitchen, grabbing a plate and some utensils.

"Good morning, angel. Did you sleep any better after I left?"

"Actually, I did. Thanks for asking, Warrior." She emphasizes the name.

"Warrior, huh? I might get used to that name." I chuckle. She has asked me to stop calling her angel, but I can't help it, so now she has decided to start calling me by a nickname apparently.

"You are running behind, aren't you? You usually eat early and then get your run in. I hope I didn't make you oversleep."

"Actually, I have already had my run and my shower. I thought I would try and catch you after everyone had cleared and before you head out."

"Oh," she put her guard up, "Why were you wanting to catch me?"

I set my plate and coffee down on the table and sit down across from her, "I thought that maybe, since you are still on your leave of absence from work that you might want to do a little training."

"Are you saying that I am getting fat?" she accuses.

Laughing, I shake my head, "No honey, there is not an ounce of fat on you!"

"Then why would I want to train. I hate sweating and I have never liked exercising."

Hesitating, not knowing exactly how to broach the subject, I decide to just jump right in, "I thought, maybe, you would like to learn some defensive techniques. You know, so you can kick some ass if you ever need to." I smile.

She perks up a little when I say the last part, "Who would be training me, and would I be with all the others?"

"I will be doing the training, that is, if that is okay with you. As for the others, no, we will train in private, where nobody is watching." I see the frightened look that comes across her face before she quickly removes it, "Hey, you do know that I would never harm a hair on that beautiful head of yours and I certainly would never make you do anything that you don't want to do!"

Blowing out a sigh, she looks at me, "I do know, deep down, but I can't help my reactions."

"So, what do you say? Are you in?"

"You promise no strenuous exercises?"

"I promise, nothing strenuous, for a while anyway." I wink at her.

"I suppose I could give it a try. When do you want to start?"

"How about you meet me in the weight room in about an hour. The guys will be sparring at that time, and we shouldn't be disturbed."

"Okay, it sounds like a plan. I'm going to head back to my room and change, see you in a bit."

She walks out of the kitchen a little happier than when I found her. It went a lot better than I thought it would go and now I am feeling better about the whole situation. I think this may just be what she needs, especially in getting her confidence back. I finish my own breakfast and go in search of Taven to let him know that I will be occupied for a few hours, in case he needs me.

JILL

Last night's nightmare was the worst! When will they stop? All I want is to get my life back and to feel normal again! I hate having to look over my shoulder every minute of every day. I know I am hurting the ones that love me the most, but I don't know how to stop feeling like I am being watched or that Jason is going to jump out at any moment and take me again. Jason is dead! I watched it happen with my own eyes...

(FLASHBACK)

I remember being inside the house and hearing shouting outside, so I peek out of the upstairs window carefully. Jason always warned me to stay away from the windows, so I do, otherwise, there will be hell to pay. That day, though, aside from the shouting, something draws me to look out. As I peer through the crack in the curtain, I see Jason and his men running towards the woods, armed with crossbows and knives. I look towards the woods, and I see the Elite emerging from the trees, wielding swords and knives of their own, Duncan was leading them. I couldn't help but cry out in relief. They have found me! With tears streaming down my cheeks, I watch as the Elite start cutting down Jason's men, even though they are outnumbered at least two to one. Duncan, swinging his sword, severs the arm of Mika, the second in charge of the Hunters, and Jason's best friend. He drops to the ground and Duncan continues on, as if looking for someone. He is headed in Jason's direction. I watch as Jason raises his crossbow and pulls the trigger, embedding an arrow into Duncan's thigh. He doesn't even flinch, but continues on, cutting down another of Jason's men who comes at him from the side. Jason raises his crossbow once more and shoots, hitting Duncan in the shoulder this time, and yet, it still doesn't stop him! Duncan brings the hilt of his sword down on Jason's head, causing him to stagger, but not fall. I can see Duncan is saying something to him, but I can't hear, and I can't read lips, but then I see his sword pierce through Jason's gut and out of his back. Duncan yanks the sword out and Jason falls to his knees. He looks up and sees me staring out the window right before Duncan brings his blade down, severing his head from his body. The battle continues for quite some time, some of Jason's injured men run, but all of the Elite are still standing. That's when Duncan looks up and locks eyes with me. He smiles and runs for the house. The next thing I know, I am in Duncan's arms, and he is carrying me down the stairs and out of the house. I am still in shock that they have found me. I can't speak. All the way back to the compound Duncan holds me in his arms and all I want to do is wrap my own around him and hold on tight, but I can't.

(END FLASHBACK)

Now that I think about it, I don't think I ever said thank you to any of them. They all saved me that day, well physically anyway. Emotionally, I am totally fucked up! How do I ever thank them? A simple thank you isn't going to do. As I ponder over this, I change into some workout clothes and grab my sneakers from the closet.

There is a knock at my door, and I hear Cassie on the other side of it, "Auntie Jill, someone is here to see you!"

I smile and fling the door open. I love spending time with little Jillian, she is such a joy! "How's the most beautiful girl in the world today?" I ask her as I am stealing her from her mother's arms.

"I am doing fantastic, thanks for asking!" Cassie replies.

Rolling my eyes at Cassie, I give my attention back to Jillian. I can't help but wonder if I will ever be blessed to have kids someday. The rate I'm going, not even being able to stand the touch of anyone, it's looking like it's not going to happen. I'll just have to be content with loving up on this little girl.

"What's with the workout clothes? I didn't even know you owned any." Cassie asks sarcastically.

"This is my only pair. Remember about a year ago when I went through the stage of wanting to be more fit? Yep, bought these and they have been sitting there ever since. I just took the tags off them." I can't help the chuckle that slips.

"So, why are you wearing them now?"

"Duncan is going to start teaching me defensive moves."

"Wow, that is a great idea! Maybe I should join you. I am sure the guys would love to watch Jillian for a bit. I had to sneak her in so we wouldn't get bombarded before we got to see you!"

"Well, all the men are in training right now, so it's quiet. Why are you here so early anyway?"

"Miss Jillian has missed her Auntie and Jax needed to speak with Taven. Something is going down I think, but he hasn't told me what yet."

"I have a little time before my training, so I can visit with my favorite little girl." I turn my attention back to Jillian, "Wow, has she grown again?"

"Yep. It seems like every day she is bigger than the last, but Dr. Howard says that she is in all the right percentiles for her age. She is even sitting up now!"

"That's awesome! Next, she will be crawling and soon after that, she will be walking and getting into everything."

"Don't remind me! So, anything new with you? I wish you would just move in with us, so I can see you every day."

"Nothing new and you know why I can't move in with you. I am still having my nightmares. In fact, they seem to be getting worse! Last night was a bad one."

"Oh honey, when will you talk to me about them? I can't help you until you do."

"I am not ready to talk about it. I am trying to forget about it and talking about it isn't going to help me forget."

"You know, they say that once you get it all out in the open, it's easier to move on."

"I know what they say, Case, but I don't think it will help in my situation."

"Hey, you never know until you try!"

"Drop it Cassie, please."

"Okay, okay, I will. For now, at least. So, want company during your training?"

"Honestly? I am hoping for some alone time with Duncan. He has been so sweet and patient with me, always there when I need him. I want to try and have a decent conversation with him, show him that I do appreciate everything he has done for me. I just don't want him to get his hopes up about us."

"Jill, you two are destined mates, you will be together. It is just a matter of time, and healing on your part."

"I don't want him pining away over me, Case! It isn't fair to him!"

"He has no other choice, unless he decides that he never wants to share his life with someone or have a family of his own! You are it for him, when are you going to get that?"

"Ugh, that's pretty much what he said last night when he came to check on me after my nightmare. I actually jumped into his arms; I was so scared! I felt like I was home for a moment or two, until my senses caught up to me and I had to push myself away from him. I want to be with him, but another force keeps pushing me away!"

"Well, maybe spending more time with him and learning how to protect yourself will help out in the long run. I miss my bestie!"

"I miss her too, believe me! I had better head out before I am late. Let's make plans to do dinner sometime soon."

"Great, sounds like a plan! Have fun with Duncan." She says as she winks, taking Jillian out of my arms.

I kiss the top of Jillian's head and say my goodbye's.

I walk into the weight room and halt. Duncan is here, doing pull-ups. I take a moment to molest his body with my eyes, roaming over his shirtless torso. He is magnificent! I feel a stirring down in my lady bits, but then it's gone as I realize that he has stopped and is now standing there, staring at me with an amused smile on his face.

"Am I early?" I blush, knowing that he caught me staring at him.

"Nope, you are right on time. I was just getting some stretching in before getting started. You need to do the same."

"I can't do a pull-up to save my life!" I say incredulously.

He laughs. God, I love the sound of it! "I am not going to make you stretch like that, Jill. We will start with more simple stretches. Come here and I will show you some simple ones."

I walk over to him, and he has me turn around, "Do you mind if I touch you and show you the proper positions?" He asks before laying a finger on me.

All I want is for him to touch me, but my psych doesn't let me do what I want, but I nod my head 'yes' anyway. He brings one of my arms up and tells me to spread my legs wide apart, placing my other hand on my thigh. He then has me bend, stretching my raised arm over my head, "Reach until you feel your muscles stretching right through here." He instructs as he slides his hand down my naked side, sending tingles throughout my body, "Hold it for a few seconds and then do the same for the other side."

This goes on throughout all the stretches, him touching me and sliding his hands down my body. I feel wetness pool below and then he jumps back and tells me that it's enough. I turn around and he is standing there, straight as a board, his nostrils flaring.

"Is everything okay? Did I do something wrong?"

He relaxes, "No, you did great. Let's get started." He says in a gentle tone, and we begin my first training session.

TWO

DUNCAN

I am smart to wear loose fitting shorts to the training session, because I've been semi erect throughout most of it. When I see Jill standing there in her dri-fit leggings and sports bra, all other thoughts go out the window and all I can think about is tearing what little she has on, off! It doesn't help that she is looking me over like I am a piece of meat. The stretching is the worst! I almost throw her to the floor and ravish her the second I smell her own arousal from my touch. She wants me just as much as I want her. If only we can get past the wall that is keeping us apart!

Aside from that, I think the training has gone well. We train for well over two hours, her not wanting to leave until she has perfected the moves that I taught her. Not sure if it's her will to protect herself or what, but she is a very fast learner. If she continues like she did today, she will be well on her way to getting her life back, and hopefully, me getting her back into my arms.

I stay behind another hour to get some of my own workouts in before heading back to my room to shower. Jill is coming out of her room as I am getting to my door and once again, my arousal hits as she stands there, seeming to be captivated by my state of undress. I smile and lean up against the wall, crossing my arms over my chest.

"Like what you see, angel?"

Clearing her throat first, "You are very fit." She blushes and looks up at me.

"Don't stop on my account. I can stand here as long as I need to until you have your fill." I tease.

She ignores my comment and steps closer, "I want to thank you again for everything that you are doing for me. Also, I never thanked any of you for coming and saving me that day. I am forever in your debt." She looks down at the floor.

I straighten myself out and carefully pull her into a hug, holding her as tightly as I dare, "I will always come for you, angel. Never doubt that." I plant a kiss on the top of her head. Then it happens, I feel her arms slide around my waist and she hugs me back. My heart leaps at this baby step. I loosen my grip on her and pull slightly away. She looks up at me and smiles. Reaching up on her tip toes, she places a feathery kiss upon my cheek and then steps back.

"Well, I better let you go and shower, you are all sweaty." She wrinkles her nose but continues to smile.

"Thank you for that, and before I forget, you did a great job back there. You are going to be my star pupil."

"I am your only pupil, Duncan." She chuckles and walks away.

I enter my room and head straight for the shower. I turn the water on cold and step under the spray, hoping it will take care of my little problem.

I go looking for Taven after my shower. Finding him, Kole and Xavier all in the conference room sets off the warning bells. I close the door behind me, "What's going on?" I ask.

Taven hesitates before answering me, "Sit down Duncan, you are not going to like this."

I take a seat and wait to hear what they have to say, "I received this early this morning and have been trying to figure out how to tell you about it." Taven slides a sheet of paper over to me.

I quickly read the scribbled handwriting and then I read it again. I try to stay as calm as possible.

"Duncan, she is perfectly safe here. We will keep round the clock guards with her. He is just blowing off steam." Kole is trying to calm the maddening rage building within me.

"I have already talked to Jax this morning and he is moving Cassie and Jillian to the Compound this afternoon." Taven confirms.

In my hand, I hold a note from the mother fucker that I let live, minus an arm. He says that due to the circumstances at hand, he has no choice but to take revenge of the murder of one Jason Kennedy and the other ten men that lost their lives the day of the battle, trying to "protect" an innocent. He says that the so-called innocent is no longer considered one, since she willingly left with us and that they will take retribution on anyone that has mated or has sided with such vile monstrosities.

"We cannot tell Jill about this; she is suffering enough. We will take care of this as quietly as possible." I reply in a calm voice.

"Is that such a smart move, not telling her about the threat? She needs to be protected 24/7 at this point." Xavier expresses.

"I will not lose my mate over this! I made head way this morning and I refuse to set her back!"

"Duncan, think about it. If you keep this from her and she finds out, she will never forgive you for keeping it from her." This coming from Kole.

I sigh, "I know this, but how do you think she will take it, knowing that her nightmare isn't over yet?"

"That's why we end this once and for all, everyone gets taken out!" Taven slams his fist down.

Not knowing what else to do, I agree. Making sure they know that it is I who will talk to Jill about this and no one else. The three of them agree with me and I leave them to go find Jill. Can't a girl catch a break? Why? Why is this happening to her? Hasn't she been through enough?

Jill finds me before I can begin to search for her, "Hey warrior, do you have a few minutes?"

Loving her nickname for me, I smile, "I always have time for you, angel. What's up?"

She looks around and then pulls me into the nearest room, which happens to be a bathroom, "I'm going to try something before I lose all my nerve or before I think too much into it."

I just look at her questioningly, waiting. She grabs hold of my face and brings it down to hers, her lips claiming my own. I am stunned and it takes a few seconds to realize what is happening. She is kissing me! I don't move except to open up for her when her tongue demands I do so. She moves her arms around my neck, and I cautiously place my hands on her hips, but just barely. I want her to know that she is in charge.

I feel like a high school kid, making out for the first time. Her touch causes my arousal to spring forth just as she moves in closer. She gasps as it grazes her stomach, and she pulls away. Dammit! The last thing I want to do is scare her, but she surprises me once again as she lightly runs her hand over my growing hard on. I am in total shock with this sudden change in behavior from her, but I revel in her touch regardless.

"I want to please you, Duncan. Just don't make any sudden moves to touch me, okay?"

"I would love nothing more, but I want it to be a mutual experience for our first time." I say as I move away.

Disappointment shows in her eyes before it turns to embarrassment, "Hey," I say, grabbing her chin and looking her in her eyes, "There is nothing to be ashamed or embarrassed about. I love that you are willing to do this for me, but I can never except it until I know that I will be able to return the favor."

"What if that never happens?" Tears brim her eyes and threaten to fall.

"It will, eventually, and I will still be here. Why don't we go back to your room, I need to talk to you about another matter, if that's okay."

"What is it?"

"It's not something I want to discuss in a bathroom." I chuckle.

Nodding her head, she opens the door and walks out, heading to her room. I am nervous as fuck. Not knowing if this is going to set us back or what, but the guys are right. This isn't something that I can keep from her.

Jill invites me to sit beside her on the bed. I am not sure if that is such a good idea, but I do it anyway. Her room smells like wildflowers, just like she does, not helping to calm my still aroused shaft.

"So, what is it you need to talk to me about?"

"I am going to be totally honest with you, Jill. You have been making great headway with putting your life back together, but I am worried what this news may do to that, to you."

Looking confused, she just sits there and waits for me to continue.

"Taven received a letter early this morning. It was from one of the Hunters that survived the battle." Jill's face pales. "They want revenge, because we took out their leader and ten other men. He says that because you chose to leave with us, he no longer considers you an innocent and since Cassie willingly mated with Jax, they are coming after you both."

Jill stares off in shock, "You have nothing to worry about, we won't let them get to either one of you. Jax will be moving Cassie and Jillian into the Compound this afternoon, too." I try to calm her.

She looks back at me, "Who wrote the letter?" she asks.

"Does it really matter?"

"Maybe not, but I want to know. Who was it?"

"It was signed by some Mike guy or something like that."

"Mika?"

"Yeah, I think so. Why, what's wrong?" I ask her as she becomes paler and starts to shake.

"You can't let him, of all people, get to me! I will kill myself first, if he does!"

"Of course, I won't, baby. What are you not telling me?" The fear in her eyes is so real, it scares the shit out of me! I pull her into my arms and hold her tightly as her body continues to shake.

JILL

This can't be happening! Just when I thought I was beginning to get my life back, it crashes back down. The arms wrapped around me is the only comfort through all of this turmoil in my life. I cannot and will not let Mika ruin me! He has done enough damage, no more will I let him scare me. Now that I am back with Duncan, he will give me the strength to fight! First, I need to get over my fear and tell him everything.

Taking a deep breath, I turn my attention back to the man holding me, "Duncan, I think it's time that I tell you everything, but it hurts to think back on it, so it may take a bit for me to get it all out. You need to promise me that you will let me tell you everything, before you react. Otherwise, I may not be able to finish."

"You don't have to tell me anything if you are not ready, but I promise I will listen until the end if this is what you want."

"It needs to come out. It's just that it's painful and I am embarrassed. I am worried that you won't want me anymore."

"Nothing could ever make me not want you anymore, angel, nothing!"

"Please just keep holding me until I am done."

"I've got you, baby. I'm not going to let go."

Taking another deep breath, I start at the beginning, "I was brought to that house after they abducted me and Cassie. I thought she was there too, but when I asked Jason if I could see her, he told me that she was not there, that's when I really became scared. He kept rambling on about how he was in love with me and that in time I would forget all about you. That you have me under some kind of influence or mind control. He kept me locked in the room that you found me in, and everything was fine that first week. I was brought food, water and whatever else I asked for. I thought that if I just bided my time, he would let me go." I was so wrong.

"It was well into the second week when he started visiting more, trying to talk to me. He would sit for hours, carrying on a conversation as I just stared at the wall. I wasn't even allowed to look out the window. The first time I defied him, and he caught me, he dragged me away from the window by my hair, slammed me into the wall face first and blocked me from moving by shoving his body up against my back. That is when he first tried kissing me, too. He had leaned down to kiss my neck, but I threw my head back, slamming it into his face and giving him a bloody nose. Needless to say, he was pissed, because he turned me around to face him and then punched me so hard, I was thrown to the floor.

That would happen every time I would decline his advances. Finally, he decided to call Mika into the room. He told me that he was disappointed in me, because I was willing to give it up to a vampire, but that he wasn't good enough for me. So, he was bringing in the big guns and that he was sure that Mika would break me. He gave Mika permission to do whatever it took to make me change my mind… anything except have sex with me. He said that he wanted that saved for himself. Mika grabbed me and smiled at me with malice, and I knew right then that I was screwed.

A couple weeks had passed with Mika belittling me and making me feel insignificant. He even went as far as putting a choker that you use for dogs around my neck and walking me around on a leash. I was so humiliated. That is when I shut down completely. I thought that if I just mentally left my body, then it wouldn't be so bad. It worked that way for a couple of days, but it enraged Mika. Apparently, Jason was seeing it as a set back and threatened to fire Mika, but Mika begged for one more chance and Jason gave it to him.

Mika took things to a whole other level. He told me that the more I fought him, the worst it would be on me. I couldn't see how it could get worse, besides for raping me, but Jason had already warned him that he couldn't have sex with me. I found out quick that there were other ways to rape someone without having sex with them." I shudder at the memory and then Duncan's arms tighten even more around me, and I can feel him shake. I don't dare look up at him at this point, so I continue, determined to get it all out.

"At first it started with grabbing my chest and twisting my nipples when I wasn't quick enough to do his bidding. It quickly escalated to ripping my clothes and using a whip across my bare ass hard enough that I now have scars. One day, I lay there crying, because it hurt so bad, and it pissed him off even more. That's when he started using his fingers and jerking off to him finger banging me. He would bring other guys in to do the same, leaving a mess all over me and making me clean it up once they were done. They abused me in such a horrific way that I had no choice but to do their bidding.

It was the morning of the battle when Mika finally told Jason that I was ready for him. He could have told him sooner, but I believe he was enjoying torturing me. Jason was excited at the news and had locked me up in the room, because he wanted his "alone" time with me. That is when you attacked him and his men. When I saw you take Mika's arm off, I prayed that he would bleed to death. I guess not." I don't realize that I am crying until I move my head and feel wetness on Duncan's shirt.

I wipe my eyes and glance up at him. He is staring across the room, a tick in his neck and now shaking uncontrollably, "Duncan? Please say something."

He slowly turns to me and plants a kiss on my forehead, "Can you excuse me for a few minutes angel? I don't want to leave you at the moment, but I don't want you to see what I'm about to do next either." He moves away from me, stands, and walks out of the room.

What the fuck? I finally tell him what happened, and he walks away? My anger rises and I get up and follow him to give him a piece of my mind! I round the corner and see him slam out of the back door, so I start to run so I can catch up. Before I even get to the door, I hear a loud roar and then an even louder crash. I shove the door open and stop in my tracks. There is Duncan, his back to me, and beyond him is a car smashed into a freshly fallen tree. I hear multiple footsteps running towards me from behind and turn to see half the Elite skidding to a stop at the site before us.

"Jesus, what the fuck happened and why is my car smashed in a tree?" A pissed off Kai asks.

They all look at me, as if I'm the one that did it. Holding up my hands, "Don't fucking look at me! Does it look like I can pick up a car and throw it at a tree?"

"What's got him so pissed?" Taven asks.

"Pissed isn't even the word I would use!" exclaims Max.

"I finally told him what happened while I was in captivity." I look towards the ground, not wanting to see the accusing looks that they may give me.

"Oh fuck!" Is all Taven says.

Duncan is back and standing in front of me, tilting my head up so I will look at him. "Don't ever feel guilty about anything that happened to you or for how angry it makes me. None of this," he looks at his damage, "is your fault. Do you hear me?"

I want to cry, and I think he notices, because he picks me up, cradling me in his arms and takes me back inside and to my room. I don't know how to feel right now. Here is this vampire, who can not only pick a car up and throw it, but also has the strength to knock a tree over with it, and yet he handles me with so much care, never hurting a hair on my head! Why am I holding back on letting him love me, when I now know that my feelings for him go beyond anything I have ever felt before?

I know what I need to do. Everybody has been telling me that it is bound to happen, but will I be able to stand being touched so intimately, even by Duncan? I want so bad to make our mating official, but I don't know if I can just yet. Maybe give it a little more time.

THREE

DUNCAN

I want to destroy everything in my path and kill every last Hunter! How can they call us monstrosities when then have done unimaginable things to an innocent woman? I knew it was bad, but never could I have imagined it being that bad! Now I truly understand why she has been so distant towards everyone, towards all the men. How could she trust any male near her ever again? She is my mate, and we may never be able to make it official, never have children. All that doesn't matter to me, I want to be with her, even if it means being celibate the rest of my life. As long as I have Jill and I can keep her safe and protected, it's all that matters.

Jill stirs in my arms and pushes herself away but doesn't go far, "Duncan?"

"Hmm?"

"Will you kiss me?"

Wait, what? She is asking me to kiss her? How can I do that, knowing what she has been through? Why does that matter? Just kiss her already! "I would love nothing more, but are you sure?"

"I am very sure. I want you Duncan, and we need to start somewhere."

"Okay but know that you can stop me at any time."

"I trust you, warrior."

That did it for me. I lean in, grabbing the sides of her face and claim her lips with mine. The kiss is a gentle one, but she wants more as she opens her mouth for me, and our tongues collide. She crawls onto my lap and straddles me, wrapping her arms around my neck. I'm worried that my growing arousal will stop all, but she moans instead, and I can feel her warmth through her jeans. She grabs hold of my hair and pulls at my head, as if trying to get our lips closer, but they are already fused together.

Next thing I know, I am being pushed back onto the bed and Jill is still straddling me, only now, her hips are gyrating against my full blown hard on. I may need to stop this or else I am going to come in my own pants. That will be a huge mess!

Jill pulls away first, but only to kiss her way down my neck. "Angel, you have no idea how this feels to me."

She sits up and looks at me with desire burning in her eyes. She yanks at the bottom of my shirt and pulls it up and over my head with my help and then sits there, running her fingers over my rock-hard abs and pecks, while biting her bottom lip. My cock is aching to be freed and to plunge into her warm depths. She brings her mouth to my chest, sprinkling wet kisses across the width of it and working its way down to my stomach. She doesn't stop there, though, her fingers quickly undo my button and zipper, and she jumps back as my cock is released. Wide eyes look at me before a smile splits across her face and both her hands wrap around my big girth.

I lay my hand over both of hers, stopping them before they start rubbing me, "Are you sure Jill? I am afraid that I may not be able to stop if we start this and I don't want to ever hurt you."

Her brows crinkle as she thinks, "I am tired of living in fear because of that son of a bitch! If I don't try and get my life back, then he has won. I am trying really hard here, I don't want to be a tease, because I want you so damn much! Just let me take the reins and we will see what happens."

"You are killing me here, baby, but you got it. I'm all yours, have at it!" I smile.

I don't need to tell her twice, because she definitely goes at it! Pumping my dick in her hands and massaging my balls, I am ready to explode! Then, there is a knock on the door.

"Jill are you in there?"

"Go away!" Jill yells.

"Come on Jill, we need to talk about this!" Cassie replies, apparently thinking that Jill is upset over the letter.

"We can talk about it later!" She growls as she continues sliding her hand up and down my dick.

"No, we need to talk about this now!"

I put my hand over Jill's mouth as she is about to respond, "Cassie, can you please go away for now?" I chuckle at Jill as we here a gasp outside the door.

"Is that you Duncan?"

"It sure as hell isn't anybody else!"

"Oh my God, I am so sorry. I will just stop back later." We hear her giggle.

Jill and I both yell back, "Thank you!"

Footsteps lead away from the door and with my vampire senses I hear Cassie mumble, "It's about fucking time," and I can't help but to smile.

"Where were we? Oh yes, I remember now." As her mouth comes down over my engorged cock.

I have gone to fucking heaven! Her mouth's warmth sends tingles throughout my body, and I have to grip the bedding, so I don't grab hold of her head and help her. She is doing an amazing job on her own! I bite down on my lip and cut it with my fangs that extend on their own. My vampire wants to come out and play, but I must hold him back, she is far from ready for that.

I feel my balls start to pull up, "Um angel, if you don't stop, I am going to explode in your mouth and I don't want that to be the first place that I come."

She giggles and continues, picking up speed and swirling her tongue around. I try to pull out, but she holds firm, and I erupt down her throat. She takes it like a champ and swallows continuously until the last drop is out.

"Why you little vixen!" I pant and look at her. With an evil smile upon her face, she pretends to wipe some cum off her mouth and suck her finger.

I roll her over onto her back, "Is it my turn now?"

I see a little fear reach her eyes and I want to punch myself for being so inconsiderate! I want nothing more than to give her pleasure, like she has done for me, but I will stop if that is what she wants.

I go to roll off her, but she stops me, "Aren't you going to undress me first?"

My heart slams into my chest at her words, knowing that I still need to take it slow with her, I claim her lips first. Pulling her shirt up as I ravage her mouth, only breaking from them long enough to bring it up over her head. Next, I find the clasp and her bra is off within seconds. I can feel her creamy breasts against my chest, I want so bad to caress the mounds, but I don't want her having flashbacks of any kind by using my hands. Instead, I work my tongue down her neck and continue until I reach the silky buds of her nipples. I don't suck, just lick at them and blow on them until they are as hard as my dick is. Her hands in my hair tell me that she is loving the attention, but I am greedy and want more, so once again, I move lower, licking all the way down.

I reach her jeans and use my teeth to bite off the button that is keeping me out. I can smell her arousal and the wildflowers within it. Her jeans are off in a heartbeat and the only barrier now are the blue lacey panties that match the bra, now laying on the floor. I lick her heat through the thin material, and she moans, thrusting her hips at me. Unfortunately, the panties will not make it out in one piece, as I grab them and tear them off her.

I start on one leg and rain kisses down her thigh, raising her leg, I give her calf the same attention until I reach her foot and then her toes.

I then work my way back up her other leg, not stopping until I reach her heated core, and what a lovely core it is. With just a landing strip of hair, her lips glisten with her wetness. I look up at her and she is staring at me under hooded lids. I don't take my eyes off her as I slowly lap at the wetness that her lips are offering, making her hips jerk from the sensation. I take my time, paying special attention to the part that was brutalized by another, trying to take that memory away from her.

She's moaning in desire as my mouth makes love to her pussy, my fingers massaging her clit. She's panting as her body responds for more and I give it to her, sliding my tongue up into her wet warmth and fucking her until she can't hold back anymore, and her juices cover my tongue. I have never tasted anything like it, I crave more, but it will wait for later. Right now, I want to feel her walls around my cock as I slide home. I gradually make my way back up her body as I kiss every inch of her flat, creamy stomach and then her tits and ending with her mouth.

"You taste so delectable, baby. I am already craving more, but right now, I want to be inside you. Are you ready for me?"

"I have been waiting a long time for you warrior. Don't make me wait any longer!"

With that being said, I angle my cock at her opening and gently push my tip in. Fuck, she is so tight! I pull out, just to push back into her another inch, keeping this pace until I am seeded all the way in. Good God, I need to stop for a second before I spill my seed already.

"I could die right now, angel. It's like I have finally come home." I say before I take her lips with mine. The kiss grows passionate as I start to move inside of her. Her legs wrap around my waist, and I grab one, lifting it higher, causing me to go deeper yet!

"Oh God Duncan, you feel better than I thought!" She starts taking the tempo a little faster until I am slamming into her, watching her tits bounce with each thrust. I feel her pressure building as my cock thrusts in and out of her suctioning walls. I reach between us and squeeze her nub, taking her over the edge.

"Oh, oh, oh, Duncan, FUCK!" she screams at her release which in turn, rips mine from me and I explode like Mount St. Helen, ramming into her until the last drop is out.

I collapse on her but keep most of my weight on my elbows as I kiss her lips softly until she is done shaking from her orgasm. Moving to my side, I take her with me and stay embedded in her warmth. I am not ready to leave her just yet.

"Are you okay, love? I didn't hurt you or anything, did I?" I move a piece of hair off her face and tuck it behind her ear.

"Never. You could never hurt me, warrior." She passes out from exhaustion. I smile to myself, and my last thought is how I never would have expected this from her this morning. My angel has fight in her, she is going to be okay.

JILL

I wake up, not knowing what time it is, but it doesn't matter, because Duncan is still here and still inside of me. Hm, I could get use to waking up like this; studying his gorgeous face while he sleeps. His long lashes are closed over beautiful brown eyes, he's got a strong jaw line and his sandy blonde hair that hangs to his shoulders, but I can't forget about his physique. Washboard abs with just a trace of hair leading to his treasure, and what a treasure it is! I can't help but wonder how I got so lucky to have found him, but I am not letting him go. I will do whatever it takes to keep him with me.

I am aroused again from just watching him sleep with his cock still inside of me. I start moving my hips, so his cock slides in and out of me.

"Mm, you can wake me up like this any time, vixen." He gives me a cocky smile.

We continue to make love on our sides, just taking it slow, "You like this don't you? Your guy using my sleeping bag to keep warm." I joke.

"I do very much! You have ruined me for every other woman." He teases.

I laugh and then something comes to mind, "Duncan, will you show me your fangs?"

"You want to see my fangs?"

"Yes, I have never seen them before, and I want to see them."

"Why do you want to see them?"

"Because I want to see how big they are and see what they look like before you sink them into me."

He cocks his brow at me, "Are you asking me to bite you?"

"No, I'm telling you to bite me after you show me." I smile.

He smiles back, extending his fangs. They are big and beautiful. My finger is drawn to them, and I slide a finger over one, fascinated by it. I turn my head and offer him my neck.

"You do realize that my bite will cause extreme pleasure for you? So, hold on tight angel, cause it's going to get wild!" Before I can respond, his fangs pierce my skin, and he sinks right into my jugular. Desire burns through me, and I am spiraling higher than I ever have before! He starts thrusting into me harder until finally, I burst. I swear I see fireworks with each pull he takes from me, causing my orgasm to be never ending, and Duncan to spill into me with his own. I start coming down as he retracts his fangs, licking his bite mark.

"Holy fuck, Duncan. You need to bite me every time we make love!"

"Once you agree to become my mate, it will be like that for the both of us." He smiles warmly.

"It's not about agreeing to become your mate, it's about me getting over the fact of drinking your blood. I want more than anything to make it official, I just have a tiny problem with blood."

"You can get over any obstacle that comes your way, babe. I can wait as long as I know it will happen someday." He kisses me gently and pulls away, "Now, we should return to the land of the living. It's already 6pm."

"Oh God, Cassie! Shit!"

"What about her?"

"I am not ready for her to bombard me with a hundred questions." I giggle.

"Ah yes. You have fun with that. I need to find Taven and see what kind of plan we can come up with for our little issue. You should go get some food, since you missed lunch."

As if on cue, my stomach rumbles, "I guess you are right. Will you sleep in here with me tonight, Duncan?"

"Of course, I wouldn't want to sleep anywhere else, love! Let's get moving." He pulls out and I feel empty.

I head straight for the kitchen, following the delicious smell that is drawing me in. As I walk in, four pair of eyes all land on me, two of those pairs are crinkled from smiling. Dammit! I was hoping to eat first before having to deal with Cassie's smartass comments. Now, I have both her and Jax to deal with and probably Kai and Max as well, if Cassie has said something.

"Pay up bitches!" Cassie holds her hands out to the guys and they each lay a twenty down on her hand, reluctantly.

"What's that all about?" I ask.

"Oh, you know, they all bet that you two would be "busy" for the rest of the night, but I knew you would come up for food!" She winks at me.

"Nice, I could use the cash while I'm on leave!" I snatch the sixty bucks out of her hand, causing the men to erupt with laughter.

"Hey, that's mine!" Cassie squeals.

"Think of it as a lesson learned. Never bet on my sex life!" I smirk as I open the fridge.

As Cassie sits and pouts, Max informs me that there are leftovers in the oven that he was saving for us. I go over and pull out the pan of lasagna and breadsticks and prepare them to be reheated.

"So, where is your other half, Jill?" Jax inquires.

"He went to find Taven to talk about a plan of action."

I hear chair legs scrape and I turn to see all three males head for the door, "Damn, do I smell or something?"

"Since you asked, we can smell the hot sex all over you!" Cassie laughs.

"Are you fucking serious?" She shakes her head yes and taps her nose.

"Vampire senses, remember?"

"God, how embarrassing!"

"Oh stop. We are all happy for the two of you! So, did you do the bonding ritual?"

I shake my head no, "Not yet, I am still queasy about the whole blood thing, but I did let him bite me." I smile mischievously.

"You didn't!"

"Yep, why not? He is a vamp, and he needs blood, that's the least I can do for him with everything he has done for me."

"So, how are you taking this new threat? Be honest with me." Cassie looks at me worriedly.

"I was scared, at first, but now I am just fucking pissed! The fact that he wants to take it out on us is beyond infuriating! He is just pissed that he can't torture me anymore."

"Jill, I am so sorry!"

"I'm okay, really." For the first time in months, I really do feel okay, more like my old self again.

"Are you ever going to be able to talk about it?"

"Duncan knows everything and honestly, you all were right. It did help to get it out."

"You told Duncan before you told me?" She looks hurt.

"Case, he is my mate and I needed to tell him, so I could move on and start my life with him. Please don't take offense."

"Guess I need to get use to not being your one and only, huh?"

"It's like you and Jax. He finds out things before I do, doesn't he?"

"You are right, I'm sorry. Are you feeling better enough that you can continue with helping me plan the wedding?"

"Oh my God, I had completely forgotten about that, I am so sorry!"

"No worries. We pushed it back, because I needed my bestie to be part of it. It's now scheduled for June, on our one-year anniversary of meeting." She smiles, "It worked out better this way anyway."

"That's only two months away!"

"Plenty of time. It's not like we have anything else to do right now. At least it will keep us busy."

"Well, let me go shower and we can get started. By the way, where is my namesake?"

"The guys tuckered her out and she needed another nap. I'm going to pay for it tonight though. She will be up until midnight!" She frowns at the idea.

"You better bring her to me as soon as she wakes up. I miss her little chubby cheeks!" I can't wait to have kids of my own, Duncan's and my own, but definitely not so soon as Cassie and Jax did. I want time alone with him for a bit. Thank God, I got on birth control after getting back here. I didn't want to take the chance of being taken again and getting pregnant if they ever raped me. I know I am safe now, but I also know how fertile female mates are for vampires. He would probably have me knocked up after our first time together! That's pretty much what happened with Cassie.

No, I want to be mated and married, before we start having kids, but we will definitely be getting a lot of practice in making them before we do!

FOUR

DUNCAN

I'm in the Conference room when Jax, Max, and Kai come walking in, all smiles. Jax slaps me on the back of the shoulder as he walks by, "I don't know what you did Dunc, but keep up the good work!"

"Do I dare ask what you are talking about?" I'm a little confused.

"Your girl is finally on the road to recovery. Her smartass comments are beginning to come back! She even swiped sixty bucks from my woman for betting on your sex life." He laughs.

"Who was she betting against?" I ask in annoyance.

All three of their smug grins dropped from their faces, "And what, exactly, was the bet?"

"Bro, we were all rooting for you two to be in her room the rest of the night and Cassie bet that Jill would come up for food. I guess we all know what was more important, ha ha!" Kai seriously doesn't know how to keep his mouth shut!

Max slaps Kai on the back of his head, "Ow, what was that for?"

"I suggest you not say another word when it comes to mine and Jill's sex life, if you know what's good for you." I bring my vamp out in warning.

"Shit man, I was only joking, sorry!"

"Hey Taven, looks like you might as well give Jill your twenty as well!" Jax laughs.

I spin around and glare at Taven, "Hey, you would have been in on the bet too if it was one of the other guys, Duncan!" He says in his defense.

The sad part is that it is true. We all like betting on everyone in the Compound, so I guess it's only fair that it's my turn, "Can we please get back to the matter at hand?"

We call all the other Elites in and spend the next few hours talking strategy and planning for different types of attacks. Jax, Kole and I are off watch/search detail, because we need to stay with our mates and Kole is needed for all IT purposes. Otherwise, everyone else is assigned details and shifts, except for two others that are on private details at the moment. The five new recruits come in handy, bringing our numbers up to twelve abled men for this special assignment. I hate that I need to stay back, but Jax and I are the best ones to protect our mates. We will do anything to keep them safe.

By the time we are done, it is almost ten and Jill has already retired to her room. I enter quietly, so I don't wake her, but she isn't in her bed. I hear water splashing coming from the bathroom, indicating that she is taking a bath. My arousal is quick at the thought. I knock on the door and wait for her answer.

"Is that you, warrior?" She giggles at her nickname for me.

"Yes, babe, it's me. Just wanted to let you know that I am here."

"You can come in you know. It's not like you haven't seen any of this before."

"If I come in now, we won't be coming out for a while." I chuckle. As much as I would love to watch her soak in the tub, my cock would never behave.

"Not even to wash my back?" She pouts.

"Ugh, you are going to be the death of me!" I respond as I walk in. There she is, leaning back and relaxing, bubbles fill the tub, but her nipples stand out above them. I let out a growl as my arousal turns to full blown hard on.

"If this is truly too much for you, you can wait in the room while I finish up." She is playing with one of her nipples the whole time she speaks.

I stomp over to the tub, undressing as I go. I settle myself behind her lovely ass and lay her back against my chest, whispering in her ear, "Can I help?" while watching her fingers play.

"Be my guest, I have two you know"

I begin to play with the other one as I kiss up and down the column of her neck. She starts to moan from the nipple play and my soft kisses, but then I happen to notice something in her other hand and question her. "What in the world do you have in your hand?"

"Oh this? Have you never seen a vibrator before?"

"Not one like that! What is that on top of it, a little rabbit?"

She laughs, "That, my boy is a clitoris stimulator. It vibrators your clit while the shaft is in the hoo-ha. It's very gratifying."

It takes me a minute, before everything clicks. "What the hell are you using that for when you have me? Am I not doing it for you? If that is the case, I will let it out full force. I was holding back for our first time!" I defend myself.

Jill laughs hysterically, "Settle down big boy, you are amazing! I was just feeling a little frisky and I didn't know how long you were going to be."

I grunt at her excuse, my ego still feeling a little deflated. Then I think about what she was doing while I was away and it kind of turns me on... a lot! "So, how does that thing work anyway?" I know how they work, but I want to see her demonstrate it for me. God, that's so hot!

"All you do is turn it on like this." A loud vibrating noise echoes in the room.

"Yes, but how is it used? Show me," I whisper seductively.

"You just want to see me play with myself."

"Is that so bad? Your man wants to see you in action." I smile.

"Oh really? Are you going to finish me off too?"

"Baby, I'll do whatever you want me too!"

Both hand and vibrator sink below the surface, making ripples in the water. The bubbles are long gone, and I can see clear as day. I watch as she inserts the rubber shaft into her pussy, while the stimulator attacks her clit. My own shaft pressing into her back as I watch in fascination. Both my hands come up and play with her nipples, causing moans to escape her lips. Her hips begin to move, and I now know why I heard splashing water. Fuck, this is such a turn on, watching your girl play with herself. I am going to have to remember to bring her toys out for play time! I squeeze her nipples one last time and she climaxes.

I pick her up and carry her to the bed, laying her so her ass is at the edge. Lifting her legs up in the air, I slide my cock right into her without any warning. She squeaks in surprise, but she starts rotating her hips, letting the pleasure take over once again.

JILL

My legs are in the air as he is thrusting into me, touching every nerve ending inside of me. I am trying to match his strokes, but it's hard in this position. He brings his hand to my clit and starts rolling it around and rubbing it, causing pressure to build.

"Don't come, Angel."

Wait, what did he just say? I am already almost there, he's crazy! Just as I was about to explode, he stops… everything. "What the fuck? I was almost there!"

"I told you not to come, so I stopped." he chuckles.

"You are such a fucking tease! Come on, Baby, please make me come now!" I plead, trying to gyrate against him.

"How bad do you want it? I can bring you to climax slowly," he says as he starts stroking long and slow, "or I can take you there fast!" He starts slamming into me hard and fast.

"Oh my God, just like this!" He is ramming into me so hard; he needs to hold my legs so I don't slide across the bed.

"Or would you rather me take you like this?" He flips me over into the doggie style position and continues to thrust fast and hard. Bringing his hand around, he pinches my nub and my juices explode, soaking his cock.

He pulls out and uses my cum to lube my ass. "Do you want me here, Baby?"

"I've never tried it, but do to me what you will." I pant.

I feel pressure when he sticks his tip in and I tighten up. "Relax, Baby. It won't work if you are all tense." He instructs me.

I try to relax but there is more pressure as he pushes in another inch. Next thing I know, he is grabbing the vibrator that I didn't know I still held, and he turns it on. I feel him insert it into my pussy and then slide it out, just to push it back in. It makes my muscles relax and he is slowly entering my ass another inch. He continues until his dick is fully planted. He starts to thrust both his dick and the vibrator, filling up both my holes. I have never been this full, it is insane and I love the feeling!

Picking up the tempo, I slam my ass into him over and over until I feel him swell even more, right before he spills his load deep in my ass. He leans over me and I feel a pinch at my neck as his fangs sink in. I am there, desire swirling through me and I come… hard! Screaming his name over and over as he drinks from me. Finally, when I think I can't take much more, he pulls his fangs out and then his dick, but leaving the vibrator in. He watches as he plunges the toy in and out of me until, once again, I let go. This time, he removes the toy and shoves his tongue in its place, savoring the taste of my essence.

The next morning, I head to breakfast with everyone else instead of waiting. Taking back my life isn't as hard as I thought it would be, once I put my mind to it and stopped the pity party I had going on for myself. I actually enjoyed the constant chatter of the guys, teasing each other over this and that. I sat there just smiling at their banter while I ate.

Duncan walks in after his run and spots me at the table. He makes his way to me and plants a kiss on my head. "Glad you could join the land of the living, Beautiful."

"I had to start sometime and I'm glad I did; your boys are hilarious!"

"Yeah well, they have their days." He chuckles.

"I'm going to go change while you eat, so we can start my training." My chair scrapes as I stand and I reach up to give him a kiss before heading out.

He slaps my ass, "No going easy on you today." He informs me with a smile.

Shaking my head, I take my leave and head to my room. I am almost to my room when I hear a big explosion. Hitting the floor, I look around to see if it was inside the building, but I don't see anything that indicates that it was. My name is being called with a panicking tone and I look behind me to see Duncan flash to me.

"Are you okay? Are you hurt anywhere?" He is looking me over frantically.

"I-I'm okay. What was that? It sounded like an explosion."

"That is exactly what it was, but I'm not for sure where it came from."

Just then, Kaid comes running in from the front of the Compound. "Some fucker just blew up two of the cars parked out front!"

Duncan helped me up from the floor as all the Elite crowded into the hallway. Jax and Cassie, carrying Jillian, come down the hallway. "Jesus, what the fuck is going on?" This coming from Jax.

"A couple of cars were blown up out front." Duncan informs him.

"Not sure whose cars they are, but the owners are going to be pissed! Good thing they couldn't get into the gates or it could have been the Compound!" Kaid says.

"This isn't a coincidence, there is just no way! Those mother fuckers are starting a war!" Jax is fuming. "Has anybody found out where they are hiding out?"

"Not yet," Taven answers, "but I expect to know by the end of today!" He looks around at everyone. "I want a couple of you to go out and help with the carnage, but keep your eyes out, they may still be in the area. Kole, I want you to go check video footage and see if we caught anything from the surveillance cameras from the front and the sides of the Compound."

"I'm on it!" Kole throws over his shoulder as he is already walking towards the Tech room.

I'm standing there in disbelief. The balls Mika has to pull something like this! He definitely has a death wish, because the look that Duncan and Jax exchange between one another, is one that I hope never to see again. I hold Duncan tighter as a chill runs up my back.

My training session got pushed back to early afternoon. Once everything was all clear, Duncan had me meet him in the Weight room. Both Jax and Cassie were there as well. The guys had decided to teach us women how to wield a knife and showed us all the kill spots to go for. After an hour of that, they took us to the shooting range that was located underground. Cassie and I are handed a small hand gun and are shown how to load and unload it, how to put the safety on and how to hold it properly. I have never been a fan of guns, but desperate times call for desperate measures.

For the two of us that have never shot a gun before, we weren't too bad. Of course, my aim was better at close range, hitting the kill zones, but I still would be able to injure someone at far range as well. Cassie, was a dead shot either way, go figure, she has always been good at almost everything.

The guys gave us holsters and instructed us to carry the weapons at all times. I was kind of nervous, continuously checking the safety to make sure it was on. The last thing I need is to shoot myself in the foot! Cassie didn't mind carrying at all. She's always been a bad ass in my eyes, I am surprised that she didn't take up carrying one when it became legal. Now that she was a mother, she was really protective and so she was comfortable with carrying it, but I worry for her. She is a super klutz.

According to Duncan, Kole did find footage of two men lurking around the Compound in the early hours of the morning, but he couldn't get a facial recognition on either one. They knew where the cameras were and so kept their faces hidden well. The search was still on for the Hunter's whereabouts and it wasn't looking good in finding it by nightfall.

Taven set up watch detail around the Compound and once again I felt like a prisoner, not being able to leave. It isn't as bad as it was with the Hunter's though. They are doing it for our safety and not the deranged self-gratification that Jason and Mika had done it for. Besides, I have Cassie with me now and Duncan.

Spending our confinement playing card games, watching tv and movies, and of course, sexual interludes with my hot as hell vamp, the time wasn't as boring as I thought it would be. Three days of this and I haven't once broken down like I thought I would. Duncan was very attentive to all of my needs.

Cassie and I got quite a bit of the wedding planning done and all that was left was her dress fitting, the cake, and the menu. Jax had guards for the seamstress, baker and food vendor who needed to come to us. I was in heaven when the latter of the three came. I love food and taste testing all the delicious items was a dream, but I couldn't help but wonder if this would be over by the wedding. Cassie was hoping for an outdoor ceremony, but it will be too dangerous if these assholes are still running around.

I was so deep in thought that I didn't hear Duncan come up behind me. I jumped when he went to put his arms around my waist. I ducked and moved to the side, grabbing his arm and twisting it behind his back, just the way I was taught. "Shit! Don't sneak up on me like that, Warrior!"

"Good to know that you are a quick thinker." He chuckled.

Slapping his arms away as he once again tried to encircle my waist, "Don't try buttering me up after scaring me like that!"

"Oh, come on sweetness, I didn't mean to scare you. It's not like I tip toed over to you. What were you thinking about?"

"Just wedding stuff. Thinking of what we will do if the Hunters are not dealt with by then. It will be too dangerous to have the wedding outdoors."

"What? You don't have faith in the Elite? We will do everything we can to make sure it's safe enough. After all, it's not every day that our men get married."

"I have complete faith in all of you! It's just that it's supposed to be a happy day for all to enjoy and not have to worry about an attack."

This time when Duncan reaches for me, I let him wrap me in his arms. "We will get them soon. I want this all behind us so we can finally start our lives together as well."

His comment got me thinking on a whole different matter, "Duncan, in all this time that we have known each other, I have never asked you about you. So much has happened that we just never got around to asking about each other. Hell, I don't even know your last name!"

Duncan chuckles, "Duncan McPherson, at your service."

"McPherson huh? You are Scottish then." I smile.

"Yes, born and raised in Edinburgh. I was born August 2, 1791 and turned in October of 1818. My family were farmers, our land was one of the biggest in the area. I had bought the land beside my parents, planning on expanding together. My parents had wanted me to travel and meet someone to settle down with, but that was no interest to me. My sister use to tease me that nobody would ever want me if I waited too much longer." He chuckled at the memory before his smile faded. "I was out buying more livestock when I got jumped. At first, I thought it was a robbery, but then I saw her fangs. I'm not sure if it was her plan to leave me for death or if she wanted to turn me. I never saw her again. I went back and just pretended that I stayed longer trying to find myself a girl, too appease my folks. Nobody was ever the wiser.

Then about six years later, Edinburgh's great fire happened, my parents and sister were among the dead. I ended up selling everything and moved from one place to another, never staying longer enough to call it home. Then about seventy-five years ago, I met Taven, and now here I am."

I could tell that he didn't want to talk about his family anymore, so I let it be. "Wow, you are ancient!" I couldn't help but laugh. "Good thing age is just a number to me!"

"Hey, I look damn good for a two hundred and twenty-seven-year old, wouldn't you say?"

Cocking a brow at him, "Conceited much?"

"Nope, just stating the facts. How about I show you what an ancient guy can do!" He claims my lips in an all-too consuming kiss. Wrapping my arms around his neck, I respond back, desperate for his touch in every way.

FIVE

DUNCAN

It's been three weeks since the explosion in front of the compound and we are no closer to finding the Hunters. I have to give them credit, they are good at hiding, but everyone makes mistakes. It is only a matter of time before they make theirs. Meanwhile, the women are becoming stir-crazy, not being able to leave, and causing massive bitchiness. Jax and I don't dare bring it up but try to ease them as much as possible.

As much as we dislike the idea, Jax and I decide to get the women out of the house for the day. Jill is ecstatic when I tell her of our plans to go to the coast and spend the day at the beach and shopping at the store fronts on the strip. Not that neither of us guys want to spend time shopping, but if it makes the women happy, then we are all for it!

I pack up the SUV and we leave Augusta behind us. We thought about going to Jax and Cassie's cottage in Bar Harbor, but I am sure that the Hunter's know about it and are watching it, so we drive south. It is a beautiful day for the beach life, taking in the sun, playing a little beach volleyball, and of course, swimming in the ocean. By late afternoon, Jill is pretty red from all the sun she took in, so we decide to pack up and find some dinner, shopping as we search for a restaurant.

The women were loading our arms up with all sorts of goods, from sundresses, scarves, jewelry, hats, pretty much everything but the kitchen sink. Jax has a scowl on his face and that alone makes my day. As long as my angel is having a good time, I can handle anything.

Finally, after an hour and a half of shopping and twenty shopping bags later, we settle on a little Chinese restaurant. We pick a corner table in the back, as always, so we can watch everybody coming and going. The women are oblivious to our watchful eyes or else they would be upset that we are working instead of just enjoying ourselves.

"I'm going to go use the restroom." Jill announces as she stands up. I look around and see the 'Restroom' sign on the other side of the restaurant and down a hall. I don't like that it's out of my line of vision, so I concentrate on my hearing senses while she is gone.

I pick up on another woman's voice. "Why, aren't you a pretty little thing! Are you from this area?"

"Why thank you! No, just here for the day." I hear Jill respond.

"Me neither. My husband and I are from Northern Maine. We are here on vacation for the week. It's so pretty here!"

"Yes, it is. I can't believe I have never been here before." Jill seems relaxed enough, but I'm not taking any chances, so I continue to listen.

"So, I saw you sitting with your friends in the corner. Is that good-looking male with the ponytail your man?"

"Duncan? Yes, he is and the other two are my best friend and her fiancé."

"So, where is it you said that you are from?" Something in the woman's voice changes and I think Jill picks up on it. I can hear her heart rate go up.

"I didn't actually. It was so nice to chat, but I better get back out there. Enjoy your stay."

I'm relieved that she is coming back to the table, but it is short lived, because next I hear her shriek, "What the fuck are you doing?" Then all is quiet except for a thump, like a body falling to the floor.

I'm up and out of my chair so fast, heading to the restroom. I slam open the women's bathroom door and there is a woman, with dyed flaming red hair, in the process of texting someone. I see Jill slumped on the floor, a syringe lying next to her. The woman goes to scream, but my hand is around her neck in a second, trapping any noise.

"Who the fuck are you and why is my girl unconscious on the floor?" I am fuming.

All I get are gurgling sounds, so I loosen my grip just a bit. "Some guy paid me to inject her! That's all I know, I swear!"

"Shit, Jill!" Cassie and Jax are here now and Jax locks the door.

Turning back to the stranger, "So, where did you meet this guy that paid you?"

"I was coming down the street when he approached me." She explains.

"What did you inject her with?" I demand.

"It's just a sedative, but I knocked her out after injecting her, because it takes a little bit to go into effect."

"Well, sorry if I don't believe your bullshit story, so you are coming with us for the time being! Jax, go out and pay for our meal and then come back so you can escort the 'lady' to the SUV."

Jax leaves to do my bidding and is back a moment later and escorting the woman out the back door. I pick Jill up and walk out behind him, settling Jill in the front passenger seat.

I pat down 'Red' to make sure she has nothing else on her and put her in the back seat between Jax and Cassie, "You have your gun, don't you?" I ask Cassie.

"Of course."

"Good, take it out and keep it on her in case she tries anything." Cassie looks like a natural as she holds her gun pointed at the woman, no sign of distress or anything on her face.

We are making our way out of town when the woman's phone buzzes. Jax grabs it from her hand and reads the text that has come through.

Hey Baby, what's taking so long?
Did you get the bitch?

"You didn't know the guy, huh?" I ask, looking through the rearview mirror.

"Fuck you!" was her only response.

"Jax, text him back and tell him that there was no chance to do it, but make sure it sounds like her. Check their previous conversations." I instruct.

"You actually say this to each other through text messages? That's fucking gross!" Jax makes a gagging sound, while swiping down on the screen.

"Do you mind vampire? Those are private!" The woman sneers.

"Watch how you speak to my man, bitch!" Cassie shoves her gun in the woman's side.

"He ain't no man, he's a monster and you are just as bad for being with him!"

"Cassie, keep your calm and don't let anything she says, get to you. We need her alive." I turn my head to see her response as she nods her head in understanding.

Jax speaks up, "So, Jenny here will be expected back by noon tomorrow."

"Ah, nice to meet you, Jenny. Mind if I call you Jen?" My sarcasm comes out.

"I have something better, don't talk to me at all!" She says snidely.

"And we have a wanna be badass I see." Cassie rolls her eyes.

We are about five minutes away from the Compound when Jill starts to stir, "Hey baby, how are you feeling?"

She groans and brings her hand to her head, "Like I was out partying all night with Cassie! My head is killing me! What happened?"

Cassie took the liberty, "This fake ass red-headed bitch injected you with a sedative and knocked you out!"

"Just an abduction attempt is all." I wink at her.

Jill swings around on Jenny, "Did that piece of shit, Mika send you? He is a sick fuck! Why are you mixed in with the likes of him?" She is raging with anger.

I was just pulling into the gates when Jenny answers, "You're just saying that, because he wouldn't fuck you when you begged him to!"

I have never seen anyone angered as much as Jill is by Jenny's response. Jill flies into the back seat and starts pummeling the woman. Cassie holsters her gun and just sits back and smiles. I slam the SUV into park as Jax is jumping out, trying to get away from fists flying. I jump out, laughing and shaking my head, as I reach into the back and grab Jill. She continues to kick her legs out at Jenny as I'm pulling her away. Jax jumps in and grabs hold of Jenny then leads her into the house.

Jill is still seething and trying to break free as I keep her wrapped in my arms, "Shh, angel. Don't let her get to you. Of course, the fucker would turn it around on you. Do you really expect better from him?"

She stops fighting, but continues to pant, trying to catch her breath, "You're right, I'm sorry. I need to be better than them."

I tilt her head up to me, "Do you feel better?" I smile as I ask.

"Actually, I do." She chuckles and then brings her hand to the back of her head and winces.

"Let me look at that, babe." I turn her around and examine her head. Finding a huge lump on the back of her head makes my own blood boil, "We better get some ice on this." Grabbing her hand, I head into the Compound.

Max is in the kitchen cleaning up after their supper, "Hey guys, didn't expect you back until later."

"Yeah well, we ran into a little trouble. Do you have any ice packs by chance?"

"No ice packs, but I'll put some ice in a baggie for you. What happened?"

I proceed to tell him about this evening's events and by the time I finish, he is pissed, "Now he has women working for him? What a fucking low life!" Max looks at Jill, "Did you really go ape shit on her? Man, I would have loved to have seen that!"

"Calm down. We are all upset over this whole situation, but we have to keep our heads in the game. We do have the woman in custody and if she doesn't talk then Jax is willing to use his mind control abilities to get answers. We have finally caught a break." I exhale.

"I think I am going to go lay down and try to get rid of this headache." Jill states.

"I'll walk with you and stay for a bit before I go to the interrogation room." I stand with her.

"You don't have to, babe, I'll be fine. It's more important to find those mother fuckers than it is to baby me, go."

"Okay, but text me if you need me."

"I will, now go!" She chuckles.

I leave her standing in the kitchen, holding the ice to her head. I will find the assholes and God help them when I do!

JILL

I go to my room to lay down for a little bit and next thing I know, it is four thirty in the morning and Duncan is sleeping beside me. The ice bag, now only water, is laying on the nightstand next to the bed. I snuggle in closer to my warrior and he tightens his hold on me, I can't help but grin. My hand up against his bare chest, I feel the muscles beneath my fingers, and they move on their own, tracing every crevice lining each muscle.

"Keep that up, sweetheart, and you are going to find yourself on your back with your legs up in the air." He mumbles.

Now that is something I can work with; I think to myself as my hand slides lower until it cups his arousal. In a flash, he has me on my back, my legs up over his shoulders as he thrusts into my damp opening. A moan slips out as I throw my head back with the sheer bliss of his cock inside me.

"I warned you this would happen if you continued playing with fire, angel!"

I can't speak, all I can do is moan in the pure pleasure that this man brings to my body. I bite my lower lip as I feel my climax build. With my legs up in the air, his cock reaches my entire depth each time he slams into me.

"You like that, huh?" He asks as he begins to play with my nub.

"I want more, give me more!" I finally cry out.

"Oh, you want more? How about this?" He ups his tempo by turning on his vamp speed and oh my God, I have never been fucked as good as I am right now!

"OH, MY GOD, YES DUNCAN… JUST LIKE THAT!" I see sparks as I explode, wave after wave crashing down on me.

Before I can fully recover, he picks me up and flips over so I am riding him. He continues to fuck me, not slowing down and once again I'm being thrown over the edge. He dips a finger in my ass, and I scream out in ecstasy, slamming myself down on his dick, over and over, until he erupts, his cum filling me up. I crash down on his chest, spent.

"Holy fuck, I love you, Duncan!" The words slip out before I can stop them. Shit! Did I honestly just say that to him? Oh well, the cat's out of the bag now, besides, I speak the truth. I love this man, this vamp with all I've got.

He kisses the top of my head, "I have been waiting a long time to hear you say those words, angel. I love you too!"

I look up at him in the early morning light and see the love shining in his eyes. I claim his lips as he starts making love to me once more.

After our early morning sex session, we shower and then head for breakfast, but it's still early enough that the others haven't come down yet, so we find something quick and then hit the weight room. I am getting stronger every day and my techniques are pretty damn good if I may say so myself. Duncan and I spar one another and even though I get my ass whooped every time, I am much improved.

Duncan doesn't take it easy on me. He says that by coming at me full throttle, I learn faster, and even though I wanted to beat his ass that first week, I can't thank him enough. I did learn so much faster. I am doing so well that even Taven compliments me and says that I may be able to join the Elite someday if I choose to. Of course, Duncan didn't like the sound of that, not because he didn't believe that I could do it, but he doesn't want me to have to face the kind of danger that they do. Ugh, such a guy thing!

I may not have the strength of a vampire, but I am quick on my feet and that is what helps me this morning when I trip up my man for the first time. I whoop and holler and jump around, fist pumping with excitement. Duncan just sits there watching me with a smile on his face.

"Great work, little one! Don't think I will let you do that again though!" I run over and jump on him, knocking him over. It soon turns into a make out session until the first few men come walking through the door, whistling at us, "Get a room!" they yell. I get to my feet and head for my towel to wipe down.

I flick Duncan in the ass with it, "Last one to the shower gives the message and no cheating!" I call over my shoulder as I run out the door. I know he will let me win, because he loves giving me massages, but I'm not going to complain.

I jump into the shower first and he follows, washing my back and massaging it at the same time. He insists on washing my whole body every time, but I'm only allowed to wash above his belt line, except for when we have time to explore further. Today isn't one of those days though. We need to get down and check on the prisoner. She still hasn't said a word as of yet.

We are heading to the interrogation room within a half hour and Jenny is still sitting there, her head down on the table fast asleep. I slam my hand down on the metal table, causing her to jump up. Her eyes wild with fright until her senses come to her and she realizes where she is at, and she glares at us.

"You might as well let me go, because I'm not talking."

"Oh, we don't free criminals… ever." Duncan informs her.

"But I'm a woman, you can't treat me like this!"

I step in, "I am a woman, but you chose to treat me far worse. Did you not?"

"You don't count, because you sleep with these vile creatures, so you are considered one of them!"

I couldn't hold back. I go off and punch her in her jaw, causing her head to jerk to the side.

"Easy, baby. We aren't done with her yet. You want to find Mika, don't you?" Duncan calms me and I step back.

"You won't get that information from me, so you are wasting your time!" Jenny's jaw is already starting to swell.

"Oh, you will give it to us, even if it isn't willingly." Jax steps into the room.

"W-What do you mean?" she stutters.

"Well, Jenny, some of us 'vile' creatures have special abilities, and I am one of them. I can control your mind and make you tell us whatever we want to know."

"No!" she whispers, "They will kill me!"

"None of them will be living once we find them, so you are safe." Duncan states.

"For now." I throw in.

"So, what's it going to be Jenny. Are you going to tell us what we want to know or am I going to have to take it from you? And before you decide to try and dupe us, know that I can also tell when you are lying." Jax informs her.

"Do what you want, but I'm not talking." Man, she is stubborn.

"Fine, suit yourself." Jax walks over to her and lays his hands on her head. He stands there for a few moments with his eyes closed, different features dancing across his face as he concentrates. Jenny starts crying, making it hard for Jax to get clear pictures, so I pull my revolver out and point it at her skull, safety still being on, but what she doesn't know, won't hurt her. It does the trick, and she shuts the fuck up.

Finally, after a moment longer, Jax's eyes pop open. "Got it!" he says with an evil-like grin.

"Great work, bro! Go inform Taven and the others while Jill and I lock this bitch up." Duncan instructs.

Jax flashes out of the room, leaving us behind with Red, "Thanks for letting us pick your brain. You now get to sleep it off in your own little cozy cell." I say sarcastically.

"Why can't you let me go?" Jenny whispers.

I squat down next to her, "What were you planning to do to me, Jenny. If you had succeeded in my abduction, Mika would be using me again, for his own little perverse fantasies. Just like he did last time. Hell, I might be dead by now, who knows! You, Jenny, are getting away scot-free compared to what would be happening to me. So, count your blessings, because if it was up to me, I'd beat you to an inch of your life and then leave you for dead. Or better yet, I'd let the true vile vamps drain you until you are almost dry and then leave you, to turn into what you seem to hate the most!" I stand back up and turn, looking up at Duncan. He is standing there with pride in his eyes, so I smile and wink at him.

"Damn, that was so fucking hot!" They are his only words as he grabs the prisoner and takes her to her cell.

SIX

DUNCAN

Mika really isn't the brightest tool in the shed. He has actually taken up residence in our old Compound that we abandoned when Jill, Cassie and Jax were kidnapped by Jason. Maybe he thinks it will be the perfect place, because we won't look there, but he does not take into account that if we do find them there, we know all the ins and outs of the structure. Aside from any new surveillance and alarms that they might have installed, we can get in there with our eyes closed. As for anything new, Kole can take care of that. He is the best IT guy out there.

We spend the day planning while waiting for nightfall to come. Jax has seen that the Hunter's numbers have grown since the last battle. There are now about fifty Hunters to our seventeen, but again, we have to leave a few behind to protect our mates and Jillian. Taven decides to call in a few more friends from the southern part of the state to help out, bringing our team to twenty-seven. We can manage a two to one ratio with no problem.

Jenny's phone has been going off since noon time, when she didn't show up, but we decide not to respond to any of the messages. Jill finds me in the Armory while I'm suiting up. I can tell she is worried about all of us, but me especially. Wrapping my arms around her, I hold her close, "Don't you worry about me, angel. I will take care of the bastard once and for all and I will come home to you; have a little faith."

"I do have faith, but that doesn't mean that I am not going to worry until you are back. Please be very careful, they are sneaky shits, and I wouldn't put it past them to have a trap set up for you. I don't think they chose the old Compound because they are stupid. Keep that in mind." The crease in her forehead deepens.

"We have put that into account as well, but I am hoping that it is the latter." I kiss her forehead.

"Duncan, when you get back, I want you to know that I am ready to make our mating official. I should have said it sooner so we could have done the ceremony before you left. I hate that I have to depend on Cassie and Jax's connection to know that you are okay."

"Oh angel, if anything brings me back, it's knowing that we will finally, truly be mated. I love you more than life itself and I will make sure you will be safe from this fucker, once we are done!" I claim her lips in a deep and passionate kiss, not wanting to let her go, but reluctantly doing so.

"I love you Duncan McPherson, my warrior. Come back to me."

"Your wish is my command, my lady." I smile down at her, kiss her forehead and turn, leaving her standing there, watching me and the Elite go off to battle.

We are all spread out around the old Compound, each having our own position, waiting for Kole to give us the go ahead once all surveillance and alarms are down. Seven minutes later, I get the okay. I quickly radio the team with the go, and we are off. There are four exits to get in and out, five men take each door and the other seven stay outside until needed, in case we had any runaways.

We make a clean sweep of the place, but it is empty. What the fuck? There are signs that they have been here, and just recently. Shit! I don't like this feeling that I'm getting in my gut.

"Everyone back to the Compound ASAP!" I yell over the radio.

Jax comes running over to me, "Cassie just informed me that the Compound is under attack! We have to go now!"

We leave five guys behind to get the SUV's back and the rest of us take off using our vamp speed, it is much faster than any vehicle. The whole time, my thoughts are of Jill. Scared shitless of what will happen to her if that fuck face gets his hands on her again! Then there is Cassie and little Jillian, Jax must be going insane right now. We are the ones that have everything to lose, maybe that is why we are way ahead of the rest when we turn the last corner and take in the fiery site before us. Without losing a step we zoom through the burning gates, just as they are about to collapse.

Once we are in, we stop dead in our tracks. Even though fire burns all around the Compound, the building itself isn't on fire, but we can hear screaming and banging coming from the inside. The rest of the men show up and just as we are about to go running inside, there are battle cries coming from all around us. We are trapped, or so they think!

Jax and I go after the five men that are blocking us from getting to the women and baby. Knife in one hand and my sword in the other, I go all in, slicing open one of their chests before plunging my knife into his neck. The next one points his crossbow at me, but I spin, kicking it out of his hand and bringing my sword down, severing his head. Jax has made quick work with two others and that leaves just the one, which we both turn to at the same time.

"Fuck this!" the guy says and tries to run.

"I got this, get your ass inside!" I yell at Jax, and he takes off, disappearing within the Compound.

I catch the guy by his hair and fling him up and behind me. He comes crashing down in a heap onto the pavement. I'm not taking any chances; I take his head as well! Looking around first to see if I can see Mika, I don't, so I speed off towards the front door.

Gunfire sounds as I enter and I duck, not knowing where it is coming from or who the target is. I glance around and see nobody. Making my way to where I hear crashing, I hear Jill's pissed off voice.

"You fucking dare come into our home and think you are going to take the mates of two of the strongest vampires? Man, you better hope my vamp don't catch you! It will make that swollen eye I gave you feel like child's play!"

I can't help but let out a laugh, "That's my girl!" I continue following her voice.

"You do realize that Mika sent all you ass wipes to do his dirty business, because he knows you all don't have a chance against the Elite! What's his plan? Why is he trying to have all his men taken out? Oh, what's the matter, cats got your tongue?"

I hear something slam into a wall and I turn the corner just as a guy slumps to the ground. I look at my angel at the same time she spots me, and she comes running to me, jumping into my arms. I catch her, slamming my mouth to hers, so happy that she is unhurt.

"I leave you for a half hour and you trash the place, sheesh!" I smile down at her, but then I feel a sharp pain in the middle of my spine, and I can't stand any longer. My knees buckle and I go down, taking Jill with me. I hear Jill scream my name and then gunfire, but that is all before everything goes black and I fall into oblivion.

JILL

Duncan is kissing me and accusing me of trashing the place one minute, and then he is falling to his knees, taking me with him. I see the arrow protruding out of the middle of his back, "DUNCAN!" I scream, tears springing to my eyes, but then I see a figure standing in the doorway. Mika! Without even blinking an eye, I pull my gun from its holster, taking the safety off, and aim. He slams into the wall from the impact of the bullet, but I only get his shoulder. I aim again, this time lower, and bullseye! He screams bloody murder and grabs his dick.

"You fucking bitch! You will pay dearly for this!" He limps away, but I can't stand the thought of leaving Duncan, so I let Mika go. Hoping this time, he bleeds to death! I return my attention to Duncan.

"Baby, can you hear me? Please say something, anything?" I get nothing. I feel for a pulse, it's still there, but it's faint. I don't dare pull the arrow out, I may do more damage than good. I start screaming for help, "Hold on, warrior, you can't die on me! Do you hear me? Don't you dare die on me!" I do the first thing that comes to me. I find a shard of glass from a broken vase and slice my wrist wide open, bringing it to Duncan's mouth, "Drink, baby, please!" There is no movement, so all I can do is hope that enough of it slides down his throat on its own.

Xavier comes running in and slides to a stop. I look at him, my tears streaming down my face as I hold my wrist to my vampire's mouth. "Please, Xavier, do something. Save him!" I plead. He rushes over and picks Duncan up.

"Wrap your wrist before you lose too much. Now!" he demands, "I'm taking him to the medical ward, meet me there."

I nod my head and then rip a large strip of my shirt off to staunch the blood flow. Man, I really cut deep! Once I tie off the homemade bandage, I race to the medical ward. Raven is already there, thank God, and I watch as they pull the arrow out of Duncan's back. They then shove a feeding tube down his throat and start feeding him blood through the tube.

"I-Is he going to be okay?" I stammer as I grab his hand.

"Only time will tell, Jill. The arrow nicked his heart. You were smart to not remove it right away. Xavier told me what you did," he nods at my bandaged wrist, "you might have saved his life by getting blood into him right away. Let me look at the wound."

I watch as Raven unravels the makeshift bandage and blood spills out. "Damn, how deep did you cut?"

"I don't know, I wasn't thinking when I did it! I was more concerned for him!" Fresh tears spill down my cheeks as I look back down at his pale face. The man I love is laying here, maybe dying, and they want me to worry about myself?

"Jill, we are going to have to stitch you up right away, before you lose any more blood!" Raven pleads with me.

"Well, then do it right here. I'm not going anywhere!"

"You cut yourself too deep and did too much damage. We need to put you under in order to fix it." Raven is frantic.

"Find another way, because I'm not leaving him!"

He is hesitant before he speaks again, "There is only one other way and that is to drink vampire blood."

"Well then, what are you waiting for? Go get me some!" I am so annoyed with him right now. Here I am sitting with my love who may die and I'm feeling a bit woozy, while Raven argues with me! He finally leaves me alone, but only for a minute. He is standing beside me again, a bag of blood with a straw sticking out of it, in his hand.

"Are you sure, Jill?" He cocks a brow at me.

"Of course, I'm sure!" I snatch it out of his grip and start slurping it down. It has a cinnamon taste to it, almost how Duncan smells, weird, but it actually tastes good.

"I grabbed one of Duncan's back up blood bags for you. I don't think he would like you drinking anyone else's blood." He snickers. He is right, Duncan would freak out on him if he did, "You should start healing in a few minutes, but in the meantime, keep the bandage on."

"Okay, thanks Raven."

"Holler if he shows any signs of waking up. I'll be in my office in the corner."

I don't know how long I have been asleep, but I wake up to a finger grazing my cheek. I open my eyes and a pair of gorgeous brown eyes are smiling down at me. I jump up and yell for Raven. Duncan winces at the loud noise.

"Oh, I am so sorry, baby!" How are you feeling? Are you in any pain?"

"Water would be nice, I'm a little parched."

I run over to the sink and fill a glass, spilling some, trying to hurry back. Raven joins us, a grin on his face, "I should have known that your ugly mug would survive! I see you took the liberty of puling your own feeding tube out."

"I'm not easy to kill, not when I have a ravishing mate, waiting for me and I'm not an invalid." He squeezes my hand.

"You scared the hell out of me! Don't ever do that to me again!"

"Sorry, love. I was only trying to protect you."

"Actually, you were trying to maul me instead of watching your own back!"

"Well, I hope someone took the son of bitch out! That hurt like a bitch!"

"I tried, but he got away. I'm sorry. I'm hoping he bled to death, though. If not, he is going to wish he had!"

"Why is that?"

"Would you want to live if you had your dick shot off?"

Duncan spits the water he just took a sip of, out and gave a hearty laugh. "You shot his boys? Now that I wish I could have seen!" he smiles proudly at me.

"Actually, I shot him in the shoulder first and when that didn't stop him, I aimed lower and hit my target." I shrug.

He laughs some more, "I almost feel sorry for the chap!"

"I wouldn't. It was Mika." I informed him.

The amusement leaves his face, "You mean to tell me that he got that close to you?"

"Yes, and you are not going to like this, but I am pretty sure I pissed him off even more by removing his dick. He said that I was going to pay for shooting him. I would have gone after him, but I couldn't leave you." I threw myself at his chest, but softly, not wanting to hurt him.

"It's okay, angel. We will get him." He wrinkles his brow a moment later, "What is that?" as he points to my wrist.

"I didn't know what else to do, so I cut myself and tried giving you some of my blood."

Raven steps up at this point, "I am pretty sure she saved your life for acting as quick as she had. The arrow nicked your heart, Duncan. If she wasn't there, you would be dead by now."

I reach over and tear the bandage off. Creamy white skin has replaced the torn opening.

"If she cut herself, then why isn't there a scratch on her?" Duncan looks confused.

"Because, I had her drink a bag of your blood." Raven reported. "She wouldn't leave your side so we could put her under to fix the damage she had caused. She cut too deep, severing her artery." He scolds me.

Duncan is not a happy camper with this news, "Don't you ever endanger your life like that again!"

"Oh, you can almost die from protecting me, but I can't do anything to try and save your dying ass?"

He calms down a bit, "You know what I mean. You should have gone with them so they could fix you."

"They did fix me, better than what they could have by operating!"

"I see that. So, you finally drink my blood, and I was not awake for it?" He pretends to be hurt.

"Stop being a cry baby! As soon as you are better, we will be mated, and I'll drink from you all of the time."

"I'm better now, Doc!"

Chuckling, Raven points a finger at Duncan, "No mating rituals for at least 24 hours! Let yourself heal completely."

"You are cramping my style, Doc!"

"I'm serious Dunc. No mating for now!"

"Don't worry Raven, I'll make sure that I don't drink his blood until you clear him." I let a giggle slip past, earning me a frown from my warrior.

"Well, I'll leave you two alone for a few minutes before I inform the others that you are awake. For some reason, you have quite a bit of friends who want to see you." Raven smirks at his own joke.

I look back at Duncan and then crawl into bed with him. He inches over to make room, but I see that it's uncomfortable for him to do so.

"Just stay where you are, I'm okay."

"Have I told you lately how much I love you?" He says while staring into my eyes.

"Yes, you have, but you can tell me again, because I will never get tired of hearing it." I hug him tightly to me and as I drift off to sleep again, he whispers in my ear, "I love you, my little angel. More than words can ever express." I feel him kiss my head and then I am out.

SEVEN

DUNCAN

The following evening, I sneak off to Raven's office, hoping he has a few moments to look me over and give me the all-clear. I have been waiting months to make Jill my mate officially and now that she is ready, I don't want to wait any longer. I have been acting like a teenage boy waiting to lose his virginity. You know, the ones that don't ever see any action, because they are the underdog, but then it's finally going to happen? Yep, that's me! I've waited two hundred years for this, and nobody is going to stop me from making her mine!

I set our training session for tonight so Cassie can get my room all set up. I want it to be special for her. There are ten dozen roses being delivered in about forty-five minutes, while Jill is being distracted. I've also ordered chocolate, strawberries, whipped cream and champagne. I don't like the latter but will drink it for her. I would do anything for my angel.

Raven isn't in his office when I get here, so I send him a quick text. He replies back right away informing me that he won't be back for another two hours. UGH! I text back, saying that I will be going ahead with my mating ceremony without my checkup and all he says back is 'good luck buddy'. Pfft...seriously! I don't doubt he is just yanking my chain about the whole twenty-four-hour wait, that asshole!

Jill is already warming up when I get to the gym. I switch to the gym for our training sessions, because she is excelling well. I don't like that she is interested in joining the Elite, not because she is a woman, but because she isn't a vampire. We take on adversaries that are sometimes stronger than we are. She does not belong out in the field, but I leave that argument for another day.

Standing here in the doorway, leaning against the frame, I watch her do her stretches. She's got curves that any woman would die for, and that ass? Wow! Her tits are a whole other story, the way they fill out her sports bra, I am surprised they carry one that supports those girls! They fit in my hands perfectly, and I've got some very large hands.

She catches me admiring her, so she bends over, stretching her hamstrings and giving me a full and glorious view of her backside. My swelling cock is telling through the gym shorts I am wearing. The devious smile she gives me at the growth in my shorts, does me in, so I lock the door and I charge across the room, picking her up so she has to twine her legs around my waist, and walk over to the large wall mirror. Pressing her back against the cool surface, I wedge my thickness between her luscious thighs and feel her heat immediately.

I claim those beautiful plump lips of hers and she responds by opening up. The taste of fruit from her dinner lingers on her tongue, as I swirl mine around, tasting every crevice. I hear little mewling sounds coming from her, so I keep going. She is rubbing her core up and down my cock, making my arousal unbearable. I reach down between us and very carefully, I tear a hole in her workout capris, so I can have access to her already soaked entrance. Shoving the front of my shorts down, I drive my cock into her causing her to gasp. Her pussy clamps down around me with every plunge, resulting in me teetering on the brink of explosion, but I don't give in to it. My cock is relentless as I plunge into her continuously, using just a tad bit of my vamp speed. I break away from her mouth, expose her tits and latch on to a hard nipple. She throws her head back as she arches into my mouth. My fangs sink down just above her nipple, and she screams as she comes, convulsing as her climax takes over. My own crests, as her pussy walls causes suction and drains me of every drop.

We are both spent as I lower us to the floor to catch our breath. I swipe a strand of hair that falls over her eye and kiss her forehead, "I love you, angel." I whisper with the kiss.

"I love you too, warrior."

"I think we should cancel our training for today. What do you think?"

"What? You don't want me flashing my hoo ha every time I kick out at you?" She smiles.

"Oh, I would love that sight, but I don't think we will get any work done by that happening." I nip at her earlobe, causing her to shiver.

"Well, I know of another workout we can do. It involves wrestling with your opponent, except there are no clothes allowed." She looks at me under hooded eyes, her lips are still swollen from mine, and I reach up and trace the lower one.

"You know, we keep going like this and you are going to end up swollen with my child, because your birth control can't keep up!"

"Would that be so bad? I mean, I'd rather wait a while, but I wouldn't be upset if that were to happen." Her voice is low and seductive.

"Bad? Oh baby, I can't wait to plant my seed and watch your belly grow with my child! I am just being patient for your sake."

"Well, why don't we take this back to the room, and we can practice some more. You know, just to make sure we get it right for when the time comes." I get a wink and a smile.

I grunt and stand quickly, fixing my shorts, before picking her up. I unlock the door and open it. There is Jayde, Kaid, Kai and the five newest recruits standing there, all with shitty ass grins plastered to their faces.

"You didn't get any bodily fluids on the floor, did you? I'd hate to slip and fall." Kai always needing to be the smartass!

"Only if you plan on being close to the mirror. Don't mind Jill's ass print on the mirror either, I'll clean it later." Jill slaps my chest as her face turns red and I can't help but chuckle.

The guys burst into laughter and slap me on the back as I walk by, "That's our boy!" Kaid winks.

Jill uses her hands to cover her face and embarrassment, "That's enough. Can't you see that my woman is uncomfortable?" My smile contradicts the chastising tone.

"Awe, nothing to be embarrassed about Jill. It takes a real woman to be able to please us vamps. It's an honor to have you among us!" Jayde's words have no comfort for her though.

By the time we make it to my room, Jill is fast asleep. I lay her down in my bed and begin to undress her. Laying there, on top of the covers without a stitch of clothing on, I just gaze at her perfection. Thinking to myself how I'm a lucky son of a bitch to have this angel in my life as my mate. I reminisce on the first time I saw her at Cassie's house, almost a year ago now. I took one look at her and knew I had to have her. There was a glow-like aura surrounding her and right then, I knew she was my angel. I have never told her why I call her by that nickname, but there it is.

I kick off my gym shoes and socks before removing my shorts. I slowly crawl into the bed beside her and pull her into my arms, careful not to wake her. My room is filled with roses and a tray sits on one bedside table with the edible foods I requested, and the other table has a tray with goodies that I didn't request, but more than happy to have. Cassie did an awesome job with the set up, I definitely owe her one! I fall asleep with Jill in my arms and her wildflower scent tickling my nose.

JILL

I am encased in warmth as I wake. The feel of large strong arms holding me up against a wall of rippling muscle and a heavy leg is draped over my own. I smell something floral, and I try to focus my eyes. The room is engulfed in candlelight and roses upon roses flood the room. I gasp loudly at the sight as my heart melts. Feeling Duncan stir behind me, I rub my backside against the slab of meat lying tucked into the crevice of my ass and I marvel in the feeling of it swelling from the motion.

"Mm, you can wake me up every time like this." His breath tickles the back of my neck with his words.

"If I wake up to a room like this every time, I will happily oblige." He moves his leg and I automatically lift mine as he slides his pulsing length between my thighs. He just slides back and forth across my now slippery passage. A tremor moves through me from the anticipation of what is to come. Tonight, we will be fulfilling our destiny and becoming mates. To live the rest of eternity by this gorgeous man's side, is not anything I could have ever dreamed. Just a year ago, I was alone, thinking I would never find a man to love me the way I needed to be loved or have a family of my own. Now here I am, loved by Duncan, a vampire, and talking about children and a future.

Finally, he enters me slowly, filling me, and I struggle to catch my breath from the sensation of my body's reaction. Pumping into me at a slow pace, he leans up on his elbow so he can reach my nipple and claims it with his mouth. I moan from the jolt that it gives me as he sucks and licks at the sensitive bud. My hand in his, he works it down my body until my fingers find the nub that is in desperate need of attention.

He lifts his head for a moment to watch me fondle myself, "God, I love watching you play with yourself! You are so fucking sexy, baby!" His cock is picking up pace as he watches with his lust-filled eyes. He returns his attention to my tits as he and I rub at my clit more vigorously. My pressure builds steadily, and he removes his hand from mine to grab my thigh, opening me up wider. He thrusts even deeper and harder as my climax spirals out of control, sending me over the edge and I feel his explosion inside me at the same time.

"That's it, Baby, take it all! Every. Last. Drop!" He pounds into me until he is drained completely.

Before I can recover, he rolls me onto my stomach, stretching me out. He restrains my wrists in cuffs, "Is this okay, sweetheart?" I nod yes. I look to the side and see a tray with my different sex toys and different flavored lubes scattered about. Oh, my God, I am going to kill Cassie! It had to have been her, that little shit! "Oh!" I gasp as Duncan massages his way down my back. "That feels so good, don't stop."

"Honey, I can guarantee that I am far from stopping!" He chuckles. He continues down to my backside and is now placing tender kisses in different areas of both cheeks. I know what he is doing. Those are the places that I have scars from my imprisonment. I start to tear up, but he is moving again, lower, and rims my back hole with his tongue and fingers my clit at the same time. It feels fucking good! I start moving my hips to rub against his tongue and fingers, but he slaps my ass, "Don't move, let me do it!" he demands and grabs my hips, yanking them up so my ass is in the air, my face pressed down into the pillow. Warm liquid runs down my ass crack and he rubs it all around and plunges a finger into my hole. Finger fucking my ass with one digit feels amazing, but when he inserts a second one, I squirm at the fullness it gives me. Pumping his fingers in and out, I start moaning, "Not yet, sweetness, I am just getting started here." He pulls out making me feel empty, but then there is a buzzing sound.

"I'm going to fucking love this! Are you ready?" He didn't wait for my answer before sliding the vibrator into my ass. Shit! I feel fuller now than with his two fingers! He starts to finger my pussy as he plays with the vibrator in my ass, turning the levels of vibration up until it hits the highest one, "Oh yeah, that's the one. Do you like that? You do, don't you? Fuck, I can watch this toy fuck your ass all night! How about we add a little something, something to the mix?"

I can't think straight, my ass is full, and the vibration is hitting every nerve back there. Did he say he was going to add something? What more could he possibly add? I feel it then, the tip of his cock easing its way into my pussy, stretching me like never before. It's uncomfortable, but I groan anyway, because it feels so good!

"Jesus angel, this is so tight, not sure I'm going to fit, but I am sure going to try!" He pulls out a bit and he must have added some lube to his shaft, because it slides in a little easier. He continues pulling out and pushing back in until he is deeply seeded within me.

"Fuck!" slips from my mouth and he stays completely still.

"Do you need me to stop, babe?"

"Don't you fucking dare!"

"Thank fuck, I don't know if I would be able to!" He slides out again, taking the vibrator with him and then thrust both back in and keeps repeating the motion, "That's my girl, take it all. My little sex kitten likes getting fucked in both holes, don't you?"

I'm too immersed in the sensation of being filled that I don't answer. I can't find the words to describe the overwhelming feeling it gives me while being fucked.

"Answer my question or I'll stop." He threatens.

"Yes." I stammer.

"Yes, what?"

"I love getting fucked in both holes at the same time! I'm so fucking full right now, fuck!"

He picks up the tempo and I am now being slammed in both ends, "See what you do to me when you talk that way? I can't contain myself, especially while I'm watching this toy fuck you at the same time! I hope you are ready, because I'm about to blow.... hard! With that comes a roar and even faster thrusting as he empties himself inside of me. The force of his eruption and being slammed in the ass, tears me apart and I scream bloody murder as I come all over his dick.

He pulls the vibrator out and sinks down on top of me, kissing the back of my neck and bringing his hands around to twist and tweak my nipples. "Are you ready to ride me now, baby? I want to see these gorgeous tits bouncing up and down as you are doing the same to my cock."

"I may need a minute, warrior." I'm panting so hard trying to catch my breath.

"Oh no, we are finishing this now. I have waited so long to make you mine and now it's time."

"Okay, your wish is my command." I giggle.

He reaches over and removes the cuffs from my wrists and then I'm flipped around and coming down on his shaft, which is still hard. I am so sore from the pounding I just received, but that doesn't stop me from taking the reins and start riding him vigorously. He is breathing heavy and grunts each time I slam myself down on him. I throw my head back as desire starts to creep up inside and I moan. One hand massaging my tits and his other, my clit, he brings forth yet another orgasm.

He sits up as I continue to ride him and with one of his claws, he stabs his jugular, blood starts to run out. I smell cinnamon as he brings my head towards his neck and without hesitation, I latch on and start to drink. He is groaning in ecstasy with each pull that I take and pumping down faster on his dick. I feel his fangs sink into me and the mixture of us feeding from each other sends me tumbling over. Our explosions are simultaneous, and we ride them out together.

I am not sure when it happens, but I realize that I now have fangs that are sunk deep within his neck. I retract them as he pulls his out and our orgasms are over. I can't move, I can't talk, I can barely breath as he pulls me into his embrace. It takes us both a few minutes to catch our breaths.

"Jill Earnhardt, I promise to love you, cherish you and protect you forever." He kisses my forehead.

"Duncan McPherson, I promise to love you, cherish you and protect you forever." I turn my head up and meet his lips for a soft kiss.

I don't remember anything after that, because once our whole sex fest is over, I fall into a deep coma-like sleep.

I wake up the next morning to find that all of my senses are heightened, but Cassie warned me about this happening, so I'm prepared, but Lord, I didn't expect this! Everything is brighter, I can hear the heartbeats in another room, and the smell coming from the kitchen is delicious! I look over at Duncan, but he is gone and, on his pillow, lays a long stem rose and a note.

Good morning angel,

I am sorry I couldn't be there when you woke up. Taven needed to meet with us men. I will return soon with breakfast, to feed that belly of yours! I love you and don't you dare move from that bed until I get back!

~ D ~

I can't help but grin at his words. Hopefully he is gone for a few moments longer, because I have to piss like a racehorse! I hurry to the bathroom and boy, am I sore all over, but I wouldn't have traded last night for anything! After emptying my bladder, I wash my hands and then look at myself in the mirror. Not too bad after a night of wild sex. I look lower and noticed the two small puncture wounds in my neck. Dammit, he could have at least closed them for me, ugh!

I walk out of the bathroom and right into a brick wall, also known as Duncan's chest. I smile as I look up, but he has an eyebrow cocked and is looking sternly at me, "I specifically remember telling you in my note to not get out of bed."

"And I really wanted to follow your orders, but I didn't think you would have wanted me to piss in your bed." I bat my eyelashes at him.

"Do you know what happens when people don't follow orders? You especially?" He is stepping forward, causing me to step backwards until I hit the wall.

"What, you going to spank me?" A chuckle slips past my lips.

"Exactly!" He throws me over his shoulder and carries me over to the bed, sitting himself down on the edge and then laying me over his knee on my stomach.

"You cannot be fucking serious, Duncan!" I'm trying to scramble off, but he holds firm. Whispering down by my ear, "This is what bad girls get when they don't listen to an order. I'll go easy on you, since I know you are tender after the pounding I gave you last night."

Liquid fire pools at my entrance from his words. He sniffs the air, "Someone loves it when I talk dirty to them. Let's see how you like your punishment." I feel a slight sting on my ass cheek and then another one on the other side, but he rubs them gently before he gives me another round. My clit rubs on his rough jeans with each slap, and it turns me on even more. By the time he is done delivering my spankings, I am sopping wet. He spreads my legs wide and delivers a slap to my pussy. I cry out, but not from pain. He recognizes it and delivers a few more, causing me to cry out with each one.

Once he is done, he lays me on the bed, leaving me turned on while he grabs the tray of food that he brought in. Oh, hell no! I can play my own game. I resituate myself so I'm leaning back against the headboard, my legs spread wide open. I use one hand to roll a nipple between my fingers and the other hand starts sliding through my slippery folds. Duncan turns around and practically drops the tray, catching it last minute. His eyes turn smoldering.

"What are you doing? You need to eat something."

"I think you need to eat something too! You need to keep your strength up."

The food ends up on the floor anyway as he drops it and stomps over to me. He kneels on the bed and then slides his face between my thighs to start his morning meal.

EIGHT

DUNCAN

It's Jax and Cassie's wedding day and since we have had no more threats or mishaps, we are having the ceremony at their cottage in Bar Harbor. We figure it will be safer to have it there than to have it closer to home. Besides, it's where they met and where he proposed to her. I hear it's a romantic thing to do, but hey, I'm a guy and really don't think too much into that kind of stuff.

Jill and Cassie have been busting their asses these past few weeks, trying to get everything in order and just right. Aside from our training sessions, I haven't seen much of my woman, so I'll be glad when this is over, and everything can get back to normal. Well, as normal as it can get anyway. A vampire's life is far from what you would call normal.

The ceremony will be held on their private beach, which is now decorated in black and white, with a pop of orange. Chairs are lined up on each side of the aisle where the bride will walk down with her father and there is a wooden arch at the end, covered in orange and white lilies. Just a simple, yet intimate setting. All the Elite from our Compound will be there along with a few outside friends of Cassie's and of course, her parents.

Taven has hired the outside Elite team that helped with the raid against Mika to be security, that way none of our men would miss the wedding. We are one big family, brothers until the end, so it is important that each one of us are here. Of course, I get roped into being the Best Man since Jill is the Maid of Honor, but Taven is also having to wear a monkey suit as a Groomsman. Cassie has an old school friend, Liz, that she has asked to be a Bridesmaid and every Bridesmaid needs a Groomsman. Taven hates the idea, but you can't turn down the offer when it is one of your best friends asking you.

As I stand at the alter with the guys, I watch as a little boy comes down the aisle, pulling a wagon with Jillian all decked out in a cute little flower girl dress. I was told earlier that the boy is one of Liz's two sons. I can't help but smile at the tikes as they make their way to the front, Jillian all smiles from the attention. Boy, is she going to break a lot of hearts when she is older!

Next comes, who I'm assuming is Liz. A very beautiful woman, but she has nothing on Jill. I feel Taven stiffen beside me and I glance over at him. He is staring at the woman walking down the aisle wearing a black chiffon dress that blows when the wind picks up. She has shoulder length blonde hair and pretty blue eyes. I catch Taven adjusting himself and I can't help but grin.

Jill is next to walk down. My heart literally stops beating when I lay my eyes on her. Like the woman before, she is wearing a black chiffon dress that is strapless, accentuating her breasts, and hugging all her fine ass curves. I lift a finger to my mouth to make sure I am not drooling, and she catches me; a flirty smile appears across her face. She takes her position at the alter and then gives me a once over, cocking her brow and running her tongue over her lips. A lust-filled gaze in her eyes. Damn I knew I looked good, but to get that response out of her? Glad I have this jacket on is all I can say!

Cassie comes down the aisle, beautiful as ever. She is wearing a dress that almost makes her look like a mermaid. It's tight fitting all the way to her knees and then flares out. Jax actually grabbed my arm to keep himself from falling over. I have to admit that she looks hot in that get-up. Jax straightens up and then takes a few steps to retrieve his bride from her father's arm. The ceremony begins as they take their spots in front of the minister.

My eyes keep wandering to my mate, wondering what she is thinking of. She has a smile on her face and her eyes glisten with unshed tears. I know I should go ring shopping, but with everything going on, I honestly haven't even thought about it. I know, not an acceptable excuse, so now I will make it my number one priority when I get back. She deserves a wedding and a whole lot more; I plan on giving it all to her!

The reception follows right after the ceremony, with music, dancing, alcohol and a buffet to die for. Every type of food you can imagine is offered, this being Jax's only say in the whole event. When you live as long as we do, money is no object, we become self-made millionaires. Which is good in this case, since this reception alone, cost a fortune.

It is time for the wedding party dance, so I grab my girl and twirled her around as we make our way to the dance floor. Bringing her into my embrace, I hold her tightly against me. I want to make sure everyone who is attending, that I do not know, knows that this lovely piece of ass is mine.

"Wow not only are you a big bad warrior, but you can also dance! You don't find too many with your skills." Jill jokes.

"Well, you better be done looking for those men, because I am all you need, and you are now mine." I claim her lips for a brief, but passionate kiss.

"Don't be starting that now. We both know how we will end up, with me on my back and legs up in the air." she winks at me.

"What's wrong with that? I can always just bend you over something and take you that way too. That way, we won't mess up your hair."

She slaps my arm, "You be good for at least a few hours! I promise I'll make it up to you later." She rubs herself against me and I give a low growl.

"Tease!"

The reception goes well into the night, everyone having a great time and not one mishap. Well, unless you count Kai showing off out on the dance floor and slipping on someone's spilled drink, but that was funnier than shit. Kai just laughs it off and limps off of the dance floor, a little embarrassed. Other than that, I think it is perfect all around and we can all breathe a sigh of relief. Maybe the Hunters don't know about Jax and Cassie's little get-away cottage.

Jill and I, along with Taven and Liz are the only ones who are staying at the cottage tonight. Jax and Cassie has left for their European honeymoon, leaving Jillian in the care of Patricia and Gary, Cassie's parents, for the two-week duration. Everyone else either stays at the local hotels or make the drive home.

It is nearing midnight as the four of us sit out on the back patio, making light conversation, when Liz announces that she is beat and heads for bed. Taven watches, as she makes her way inside. I'm watching the different expressions play across his face as he watches her leave. He looks my way and sees that I am staring at him.

"What?" He asks with annoyance.

"Nothing. Just wondering what's on your mind. You look a little confused every time you look at Liz, what's up with that?"

"None of your fucking business, that's what's up with that!"

"Whoa, Buddy. I was just asking a question, no need to jump down my throat!"

"Ugh, sorry. I'm just not feeling myself right now, kind of drained myself. Think I'm going to hit the hay as well. See you guys in the morning." He waves at us as he stands and walks into the cottage.

"Wonder what that is all about." Jill mumbles.

"Not sure, but if you ask me, I think he has found his mate." I chuckle.

"Who Liz? Why do you think that?"

"Well, I can sense that she is the right blood type and by the way he stares at her and some of his reactions, it looks like he is going through all the emotions that I went through when I found you and what Jax went through when finding Cassie. It's quite disturbing at first." I snuggle my face into Jill's neck and inhale deeply, letting her essence engulf my senses.

"I guess there is only one thing to do then." Jill pulls away, causing me to snap back to reality.

"What is that angel?"

"We need to make sure that Liz comes around more often." The devious smile spreads across her face and she wiggles her brows.

"Oh man, Taven may kill us for this, you know that, right?" I question with a cocked brow.

"He will thank us in the end, I'm not worried." She states this as she stands up and pulls me with her, "I want to walk on the beach, let's go."

"A little bossy, are we?"

"Well, you don't have to go, but you will if you know what's good for you."

"Blackmail will get you everywhere with me, love." I chuckle and let her pull me towards the private beach.

JILL

As I walk hand in hand beside Duncan on the beach, my thoughts go back to the wedding. Cassie made such a gorgeous bride, and I am so happy that everything went off without a hitch! I finally stopped worrying about the Hunters making a move halfway through the reception. Dancing in Duncan's arms helped to relieve the stress and I let myself relax. He is a very good dancer, just like everything else; he is just the best.

As the idea crosses my mind, I slip my hand away from Duncan's and quicken my pace. I know he can catch me with his vamp speed if he really wants to, but he hangs back. I quickly go to the zipper on the side of my dress and unzip it, letting the material fall and pool at my feet. I look back over my shoulder and see Duncan freeze in place, shocked to see that I have been completely naked under my dress the whole time.

Stepping out of the material, I head towards the shore line, but never make it. Duncan is there, pulling me into his arms, my bare back against his hard chest. I struggle to get out of his arms, only for him to tighten his hold.

"Ah, my little vixen wants to play now, huh? I remember earlier today when you were rubbing this tight little body against my cock! Now, I get to repay the favor." He whispers in my ear as he holds me against him with one arm and brings his other hand south of my belly button. It stops at the place I am most sensitive, and my body responds to what it wants most; my thighs open up to allow him entrance.

Pressure starts to build as soon as his finger slips inside, and his thumb starts circling my clit. I moan and he loosens his grip just enough so his other hand can play with my nipple. I relish in the feel of what this man's hands do to me. Feeling his arousal against my back and knowing that it will not be long before he shoves himself inside of me, I wait in anticipation, enjoying the feel of his finger inside of me, slickened with my juices. He adds yet another finger and I tilt my hips forward to let him have better access.

I am so wet; I can hear the suctioning of my walls as he thrusts his fingers in and out of me. A moment later, I am being forced to the sand on my stomach, only to have my hips yanked up. Duncan rips his shirt off and lays it in the sand, commanding me to lay my head down on it and to not move. I do as he says as I hear him undoing his pants and seconds later, he slams into my waiting pussy, taking the breath right out of me. He continues to plunge into me fiercely, not hurting me, but boy am I going to feel it tomorrow!

It doesn't take long for my body to spiral out of control, taking Duncan with me, but he isn't finished with me yet. Picking me up, he carries me into the ocean, which is still too cold for this time of year. My lungs seize up and I start shivering, but Duncan continues further into the water until he is waist deep. His mouth claims my own and he is lowering me onto his still engorged shaft. I clamp my legs around his waist and start moving with his thrusts. The cold slowly slips away as heat starts to spread throughout my body. I'm panting with the need for my release as I open my mouth and sink my little fangs into his neck, causing him to grunt and pick up his pace. He is now slamming into me with vamp speed as he latches on to my own neck.

I feel his cum exploding into me as my own climax takes over my body. We both retract our fangs as he is still jerking inside of me trying to unload every last drop. Without removing himself, he walks back to shore, grabs his tuxedo jacket and wraps it around me as he takes us back to the cottage and into our room. He is silent the whole way. The last thing I remember is him laying down in bed with me sprawled on top.

I wake up just before dawn, still laying on top of Duncan. I can hear his labored breathing, telling me that he is still asleep. Realizing that his cock is still inside of me, I start to slide off him slowly, trying not to wake him up. It doesn't go as planned and I find myself on my back in a flash, legs up in the air and getting thoroughly fucked.

"Don't ever try slipping off my cock again without letting me come in you first, woman!" He stares down at me.

"I didn't want to wake you." I sputter between thrusts, "Oh, my fucking God, Duncan, you are going to rip me apart! Don't stop!" A few more thrusts and we are both over the edge. Duncan drops beside me, taking me with him.

"Well, all I wanted was a glass of water." I say breathless.

He chuckles, "Sorry baby! This is what you do to me. God, I love you!" He presses his lips to my forehead.

"Don't be sorry, you can take me like that any time, but can I get my glass of water now?"

"Stay right there, I'll go grab it."

Duncan is back in a flash and hands me the glass. I drink it down quick and then head to the bathroom to release my bladder. As I come out of the bathroom, I see a flash of red right before Duncan slams his body into me, sending us to the floor. Next thing I know, I hear glass breaking and an array of bullets hitting everything above our heads. Duncan has me army crawl into the bathroom as he shields me with his body. He checks me over, but all he finds is a scratch on my arm that looks like a bullet nicked me. I hadn't even felt it. It is barely bleeding, but Duncan is flying through the cabinets trying to find a bandage.

"I'm okay, it's only a scratch." It doesn't calm him down, though. My words don't even phase him. He finds what he is looking for and begins to wrap my arm, "Baby, I'm okay. Calm down please, so we can think straight!" This catches his attention, and he sits back.

"I'm going to kill those sons of bitches once and for all!" He says through gritted teeth.

Just then, we hear the bedroom door bang open and Taven's voice booms through the room as he calls out to us. The shooting has stopped, but for how long, we don't know. Duncan cracks the door open and peers out.

"We are fine. Jill has a nick on her arm but that's it. How is Liz?" He inquires.

"Shit!" Is all we hear before Taven flies out of the room. Then we hear a strangled roar coming from the room across the hall.

"Stay right here until I come back!" I nod my head in response.

Once I am alone, I start to shake a little, "Stay calm." I tell myself out loud. The minutes tick by until finally, Duncan returns. He hands me some clothes and puts a finger to his lips indicating for me to stay silent. I dress quickly and wait until he finishes up collecting all the medical supplies he can find. I roll my eyes thinking that he is mental if he thinks my little scratch will need all the items he has now thrown up on the counter. I watch as he grabs a decorative basket that is hanging on the wall and starts shoving all the supplies into it. With the basket in one arm, he grabs me close to his side and shields me again as we make our way out of the bathroom, across the bedroom and out to the hall.

He leads me to the room that Liz is occupying, but doesn't stop until we are inside the big walk-in closet. Taven is kneeling down in front of another body that is sprawled out on the floor. He turns when we enter and I see that it is Liz lying on the floor, covered in blood. I go to scream, but Duncan is there, his hand over my mouth. He whispers in my ear, "She took a bullet to her back and one to her thigh. She is alive for now, but we need to stop the bleeding. Taven has back up on the way, so we need to stay put and quiet until they get here and it is safe to move her. Do you understand me?" I shake my head with understanding and then drop down to my knees beside her.

Taven throws a clean towel in my hands, "Put pressure on the thigh wound and I'll keep the pressure on her back wound." He whispers.

I can see the deep concern in his eyes. He doesn't think she will make it. I can't help but let the tears flow. I have been friends with Liz forever, she can't die! She has two boys that need her! I should have never let her stay, even though the danger seemed to be over, we should have known!

Fifteen minutes later Xavier, Dane, Jayde, Kai and Cooper show up, along with the Elite from earlier who helped with security during the wedding.

Xavier was the first to speak, "We did a sweep of the area, but didn't find anyone. We did find a bunch of casings though. It looks like they were using subsonic ammo." he states.

"Yeah, we didn't hear anything until the shot came through the window, but they were using laser lights and that's how I knew they were out there before the first round came through." Duncan explains.

"Is it safe enough to transport Liz?" Taven asks frantically.

"Yes, we will make it safe enough. Will she make the drive back?" Dane questions.

"She is stable for now. I don't want to give her any blood until the bullets are out, but I will if I have no other choice." Taven states.

"With that bullet in her back we should try not to move her too much. I will go find something that we can use to carry her out." I fly from the room looking for anything that will work. Finding an ironing board in the utility closet, I grabbed it and returned to where Liz is still unconscious, "It's all I can find, but it should work fine."

"Good work Jill, thanks!" Taven nods at me.

With little effort, the men get Liz onto the ironing board and carries her out to one of the cargo vans. I jump into Duncan's SUV, and we were off, headed back to Augusta.

We make it back to the Compound a little after sunup. Duncan has called ahead and talked to Raven, letting him know we are on our way and to be ready for Liz. He is actually outside with a stretcher waiting for our arrival and Liz is rushed right in. Raven tries keeping Taven from going in the surgical room, but Taven isn't having it. He wins the argument and goes in, along with Max and Kole to help assist.

Since I am the same blood type, Raven asks me to donate some to keep on hand in case they need it. They have some on hand, but more is always better. I let them have it, no questions asked. They do end up needing it after all, because she has lost too much blood and Taven can't give her any of his to start healing her, in case she is too low. We don't want to chance turning her into a vampire.

I sit outside the door, waiting for any kind of news. Duncan is sitting beside me, holding me, as I cry on and off. His soothing tone helps to calm my nerves as he tells me that she is going to be okay. I want to call Cassie, but we don't want to ruin their honeymoon and we know that they would be turning around and coming right back once they hear. I know Liz won't want that either, so I refrain from making the call. Raven finally comes out after three hours.

"We got both bullets out, luckily the one in her back didn't hit any vital organs. We want to wait until her blood supply is back up before Taven gives her his blood. She is on the mend but will need a few days of rest."

"Thank you so much Raven! We are so lucky to have you!" I give him one of my famous bear hugs and he chuckles nervously, looking at Duncan, "Oh, don't be afraid of him. I can hug anybody I want! I'd kiss you too, but I don't want to push it." I laugh and shake my head at the murderous look that Duncan is giving me.

"Well then," he says as he pulls out of my grasp, "you can go in and see her, but don't stay too long, she needs her rest."

"I won't." Smiling and thanking him again as I go through the door.

NINE

DUNCAN

Two days after the shooting, Jill informs Liz that she is able to move back to her own place. Liz is still a little confused as to how she is feeling so much better after being shot. All we can tell her is that she is a fast healer and that we don't understand it either. Just one of those freak things, I guess. She seems to except it and is happy to be going home to her boys.

Taven has three details watching after her for over a week, just to make sure the Hunters aren't watching her house as well. Everything seems to stay quiet during that time and so he pulls all but one of the details off the watch, but I'm pretty sure that he, himself, does a little watching also. I haven't seen much of him lately and with Jax gone too, I pretty much spend all of my time with Jill.

I decide that it is time to do the deed and make her my wife. I figure with everything going on, she can use a distraction, even though that would mean more planning and craziness leading up to it, but I'd suffer through anything for her happiness. I go into town and ring shop. I'm so lost as to what I should pick for her that I'm about to drive myself crazy. It is at that moment that my eyes fall on the most beautiful ring I had ever seen. Not that I pay too much attention to jewelry, but this was definitely an eye catcher.

Sitting on a pedestal was a two-caret, wide band, Princess cut engagement ring. It has five rows of diamonds running down both sides of the band, with an intricate design on both sides of the encased diamond. Such a beautiful piece, but it gives me an idea. I go over to talk to the Jeweler about a special order and leave smiling, excited to see the finish product in a couple of weeks.

As I walk back into the Compound, Jill is in the rec room watching tv and holding Jillian. I had to do a double take, because last I knew Jillian was still with her grandparents.

"Are Jax and Cassie back already? They're not supposed to be back for another three days."

"No, not yet. I just couldn't stand being away from this little girl another day, so they brought her to me for the day."

"Are you sure that was wise? What if the Hunters see them and follow them back to their house?" I ask.

"No worries. I talked to Taven first and he made sure it was safe. Do you honestly think I would put this precious girl or Cassie's parents in harm's way?" She pouts as if I've hurt her feelings.

"Of course, not sweetheart, but I just wanted to be sure." I bend down and kiss each of their foreheads before sitting beside Jill and taking the little tike from her.

"Hey! I wasn't done with my cuddling you ass hat!"

"You better tell your auntie Jill that she needs watch her potty mouth while you are around." I say to Jillian as I lift her over my head and get a giggle out of her.

"Don't make me swear when you are around and I will be good." Jill sticks her tongue out at me and I can't help but lean in and kiss her.

"I love it when you are mad, but here you go, you can have her back. I have to go talk to Taven, is he still here?"

"As far as I know. I haven't seen him leave again. Where do you think he is spending all his time when he is gone?"

"Where do you think? Hm, I am thinking a bet is coming on. I believe I know who will be next in finding their mate." I smile at Jill.

"Technically, he already found her, so the bet wouldn't really work, would it?" She asks.

"Awesome! What are we betting on this time?" Kai comes strolling into the room rubbing his hands together.

Jill answers him. "We think Taven will be the next to find his mate."

Kai bursts out in a fit of laughter. "You think Taven will be next? You will have to remove the stick out of his ass first!"

I smile at Jill and then look over Kai's shoulder. I stop smiling and Kai notices then pales. "Shit, he is standing behind me, isn't he?" He slowly turns and looks over his shoulder.

"Gotcha ass wipe!" I was laughing so hard my gut hurt.

"Not cool dickhead!" Kai scolds.

"That will teach you not to talk about my friends that way." I chuckle again, "So, are you wanting in on the bet or what?"

"Damn straight I do!" He says smugly and then walks out whistling.

"Easy money right there, every time! He never learns." I grin at Jill and then kiss her as I leave in search of Taven.

I find Taven and Kole talking outside of Kole's office. "Hey guys, what's up?"

Taven and Kole look at each other and then back at me, but it's Taven that answers, "The Hunters have been busy at work again. Two more vamps have been found dead, stakes through their hearts. One was taking an early morning run in the park and the other was coming home from work and got jumped on his doorstep. Both civilized vamps."

"How are they finding them?" I ask incredulously.

"I am not sure, but we need to find out what they all had in common and go from there. It's got to be it. Kole is going to compile a list of all known vampires in the area and we are all going to split up and interview them."

"We have got to stop them soon. Their numbers are growing and I think we should start thinking about moving the Compound again. It isn't safe for the women or Jillian."

"You are right, and I have already started searching for a new place." Kole informs me.

"When can you have that list to me by Kole?" Taven asks.

"I should be able to have it to you by tonight. In the meantime, you should contact all the surrounding Compounds and have them do the same. We don't know how far out the Hunters stretch."

"Good thinking, I'm on it. Duncan, do me a favor and go check in on Liz please? Just tell her that you wanted to make sure she is healing okay."

"No problem, I'll go do that now."

I'm about five minutes away from Liz's house when I notice a dark green Lumina following me. It's a few cars behind me, but I am sure it's following, so I take a couple of turns and sure enough, it's there. I speed dial Taven and let him know of my situation and where I am at. With a few other Elite on their way, I decide to pull into a gas station and get gas. The car pulls in towards the back of the parking lot and waits for me. I go inside and pay to buy me more time and then head back out to my SUV. They are there when I pull out again, so I head in a direction that is away from Liz's place.

I get a text letting me know that Cooper and Jayde are a few cars behind the Lumina, so I turn onto a narrow dirt road and drive until I go around a bend and I stop in the middle of the road. Sure enough, here they come around the bend and stop when they see me sitting there. I watch from my rearview mirror as two guys get out of the car and start walking towards me. Their hands are empty, but they are wearing trench coats in the middle of June, so it isn't too hard to figure out that they are carrying.

Just as they get to the back of my vehicle, Cooper pulls up behind their car and just sits there. Then another SUV with Dane and Kai pull up behind cooper. I roll down my window and without sticking my head out, I holler at them, "I highly suggest you throw down all your weapons before you take another step."

"We are not here to hurt you. We have a message from the boss man." They are a couple of young guys, about early twenty's, maybe not even that.

"As I said, throw down all of your weapons. Unless, of course, you don't want to live to see another day. I have four more men behind me that will be on you in a flash and will take your heads if you try anything!"

They not only throw down their weapons, but take their coats off as well to show that they are not carrying anything else. They look like they are about ready to shit themselves. Obviously, they didn't know what they were getting into.

I step out of my vehicle and stand there, arms crossed at my chest and feet spread apart. I wait for the others to walk over and circle the two boys. "So, tell us, what message do you have from the boss man?" My voice drips with sarcasm.

"He wants you to let Jenny go! He knows you have her and he wants her back. Says if you don't release her in the next twenty-four hours, the pretty blonde won't make it out alive next time."

I see Cooper texting and know he is informing Taven to go get Liz and the boys now! "Well, I don't know what your boss man is smoking, but we don't know any Jenny."

"Sure you do," the other kid says, "she's the one that tried kidnapping your girl a few weeks ago." The first kid elbows him in the ribs and tells him to shut up.

"Mika sure knows how to recruit the smart ones, doesn't he?" Kai snickers.

"Shut up vamp, no one was talking to you!" The first kid sneers.

Before the kids knew what was happening, we are on them and have them cuffed and knocked the fuck out, "Cooper, Jayde, you take these losers back to the Compound. Dane, Kai, head straight to Liz's house and I'll be right behind you!" We all scramble back into our vehicles and take off.

By the time we get to Liz's place, Taven is already there. I walk in as Liz is arguing with him that she isn't leaving her home. She is standing there, 5'2" against Taven's almost 7', tapping her foot and poking him in the chest. I can't help the chuckle that slips past my lips. Taven glares daggers at me, so I look away.

"Liz, it isn't safe for you and your kids right now! Why are you being stubborn about this?" I can tell Taven is at the end of his rope with this woman.

"Why should I leave my home to go stay with complete strangers, when I'm not even involved with any of you?" Liz's face is red with rage and she is all but screaming.

I step in, "Liz, unfortunately, because you were at the cottage with us, they assume you are important to us and so they are coming after you. We only want to keep you and your boys safe until we get the bastards. You won't be with complete strangers; Jill is there and Cassie will be back in three days."

"And what about my work? I can't afford to miss any more days!" She screeches.

"We will figure it out, don't worry about that. Just think of it this way, you won't have to pay a sitter for a little while. The boys will stay at the Compound with us while you are at work."

"Oh, so now you assume that I will leave my boys with strangers who have a group of psychos trying to kill them?"

"Again, Jill will be there. She is still on leave from work so they won't be with just strangers. We are only trying to protect you, Liz." I am pleading with her at this point. Man, she is one angry woman! Taven definitely has his hands full with this one!

She throws her hands up in the air, "Fine, I will go for one week, but you better get this mess taken care of!"

"Thank you. We will do our best to resolve this as soon as possible." I assure her. She turns and leaves to go pack their bags.

"God damn that woman is infuriating!" Taven wipes his hand over his face.

"Guess you have your work cut out for you!" I chuckle.

"What the fuck is that supposed to mean?"

Holding my hands in the air, "Forget I said anything." I turn to go outside, but turn back, "Oh, and you are welcome." I walk out the door before Taven can say anything else to me.

JILL

Cooper and Jayde informed me of the situation with Liz when they bring in two young guys. The thought of anything happening to Liz or her boys makes me sick. This is all because of me, all because I went out on a date with a psychopath. He may be dead now, but he created a monster in Mika and now everybody that I love is in danger.

I head down to the interrogation rooms and find Cooper guarding one door and Jayde guarding the other, "You shouldn't have Jillian down here, Jill!" Cooper scolds me.

"Oh whatever. Nothing is going to happen to her with you two brutes around. Now, what is the mind set of these two losers?" I ask.

"This one here did most of the talking and that one over there isn't too bright." Cooper nods at the door Jayde is standing in front of.

Handing the baby to Cooper, I head over to Jayde, "Come inside with me, but I want you to stay by the door. You are only there for intimidation."

"Are you kidding me? Duncan will have my head if he knows that I let you in there! No way!"

"Fine, have it your way!" I bring up my leg and knee him in the balls... hard. He falls to the floor and as I open the door, I hear Cooper laughing his ass off. I close the door and lock it.

I turn and face the prisoner, "So, what's your name cutie?"

"M-My name?" he stutters.

"Yes you. You're the only other one in here." I give him a flirty smile.

"I'm Derrick, and you are?"

"I'm the one that Mika is so hot to trot for."

"Ah, the famous Jill. No wonder he wants you so bad. He never said that you were a fine piece of ass!"

I try not to flinch as bile rises up my throat. I swallow it down and continue, "What all has he said about me?"

"Nothing really, just that you are the reason his best friend is dead and that you chose the vamps over your own kind." He shrugs as if it was nothing.

"Oh, did he now? He never said anything about how he abused me and used me for his own disgusting sexual gratification and then had others come in and do the same?"

Derrick looked confused, "No, he isn't like that! He is a good man who goes to church every Sunday and treats women with respect!"

"Pfft... I would have never taken him for a Catholic."

"He's Lutheran, not Catholic."

"Oh, my bad! Either way, he is a sick sadistic ass hole who will meet his maker in due time! You on the other hand, you can still have time to make amends with the vampires and leave the Hunters. The vamps aren't the bad guys, you guys are, and I would hate to see you lose your life at such a young age because of the piss poor decision you made in following Mika and his group of murderers."

"Vampires are the killers here, not us! We don't drain people of all their blood and kill them."

Neither do the civil vampires. You do realize that they are good and bad vamps, just like there are good and bad people... right? Out of the last few vamps that the Hunters have killed, there was only one bad vamp among them. The others were upstanding citizens who did not deserve to die! The vampires in this building, the Elite, they protect the innocents from both bad vamps and bad people. The Hunters, they have killed more innocents than I can count, so don't argue with me on who the killers are here!"

"You are just saying all this, because you are in love with one! He has you brainwashed!"

"You are an idiot! How can you stand with the Hunters when you know nothing about the vamps? Vampires cannot brainwash people, none of the stories are true. That's why they are called stories ass hat!" I am leaning over the table and in his face, "I highly suggest you tell them anything they want to know or else you won't be leaving here… ever! Oh and before I leave, Jenny isn't here. She told us what we wanted to know and she saw the Hunters for who they really are…killers. We gave her money and she is probably on the other side of the world now living it up. I really hope you enjoy your stay with us!" I smile and walk out.

My smile vanishes the moment I see Duncan standing there as if he wants to murder someone. I go to grab Jillian and Duncan steps in front of her, "I think Cooper better keep her for a few more minutes while we have a little chat."

"Oh, but it's past her nap time and I know how Cassie hates it if she gets off her schedule."

"Then you should have thought about that before you pulled this little stunt!" He picks me up and throws me over his shoulder. Jayde laughs, but it is short lived when Duncan walks by him and my fist reaches out and makes contact with his nuts again.

"God dammit woman!" He cries out.

"Be nice Jill." Duncan warns without turning to see what the commotion is about.

"Put me down vamp!" I kick out, earning me a swat on the ass.

"You should have come with me the first time."

"You don't always come for me the first time." I giggle and then get another swat to the ass.

"You know damn well that I am not talking about that!"

"Well maybe we should be." I pinch his ass.

"There will be plenty of time for that after I blister your ass for pulling that little stunt!"

I just huff and let him carry me down the hall like a caveman wanna-be. What's he going to do, spank me and make me promise that I will never pull a stunt like that again? I am tired of him treating me like a delicate flower. One of these days I will be an Elite and there is nothing he can do about it!

TEN

DUNCAN

When I go down to the interrogation rooms and learn that Jill has locked herself in one of the rooms with one of the prisoners, I am seething mad. I want to break down the damn door and strangle her! How can she put herself in danger like that? I watch from the monitor and even though she does a decent job, she still shouldn't be in there. Good thing it is a regular person and not a vamp or else it could have been a whole lot worse.

My angel can be a little hellcat at times, this being one of them. To think she could try and offer sex to distract me while I'm so mad at her is unbelievable. Not that I don't get aroused by it, the thought of being inside of her always arouses me, but I need to stand firm at times like this.

I plan on carrying her to our room, but think better of it, because she might just get her way if I do, so I bring her into the next closest room, the weight room. I slide her down until her feet are planted on the ground and I take a step back. She looks so cute standing there, her hands on her hips and her nostrils flared, breathing heavily.

"Care to explain what the fuck you were thinking when you went into that interrogation room?" I explode.

"I was 'thinking' that I would have better luck than you bullies! Figured I would try the sweet route and with me being a female, I had a better chance at getting something, anything!" She is yelling at this point, and she looks so damn hot doing it.

"You could have been severely hurt!"

"He is chained to the damn chair, and he isn't a vamp! I can defend myself against a regular person. It would have been different if he was a vamp, I wouldn't have gone in there. At least not without another Elite with me."

"Jill, you need to leave these things to us. We are trained, you are not!"

"Well, when do I get that training? You sure as hell aren't going to do it! You think I'm a delicate female who will hurt myself! News flash big guy, I am tougher than you think and if you keep treating me like this, you will regret it!"

"Oh, I'm sorry if I want to keep the woman I love protected from getting hurt!"

"I understand that, but you need to give me a little space and let me be me. How am I supposed to learn when I'm kept from these situations? I know I can't be a full Elite, but I can be useful in a lot of areas if you would give me the chance! I am not fragile Duncan."

I let out a long sigh. How can I argue with that? She is right, she isn't that fragile, she is one of the toughest women I know, and yet it scares the shit out of me to think of her fighting men or being hurt by anything. I stare at her a long moment before I step up to her and wrap her in my arms.

"It just scares the hell out of me to think of you getting hurt in any way, I am sorry baby."

"Do you not think that it scares the shit out of me every time you are called out on detail? I worry every time that you are going to come back hurt or worse! But I know that this is who you are and it's what you do. I don't want to change you, but it doesn't make it any easier."

I tighten my arms around her. I have never thought about it in that light, and she is right. My job is dangerous, and I now have her to care for and protect. I am not used to having someone who loves and cares for me. Ugh, I hate this predicament, but she is right. I can't change her; I don't want to change her. I'll just have to suck it up and try harder, be more understanding.

"Fine, but never pull a stunt like that again while untrained. You hear me? We will start training in all aspects of the Elite, but just know, you will never go into an interrogation room when there is a vamp in there! Do you understand?"

"Agreed. I know I am not as strong as you guys, but I can and will help when it comes to the regular monsters."

"You are so stubborn, but I'll agree with you on this." I plant a kiss on the top of her head.

"Can we have sex now? I am really turned on, all of a sudden."

I can't help but laugh, "Oh baby, make up sex is the best! You better believe we can have sex now!" I walk over and lock the door. I turn back to see that she already has her shirt off. Her blue lacey bra doesn't leave much to the imagination. I flash over to her before she can remove anything else.

"I do the undressing, remember?"

"Please leave my clothing intact. I get tired of buying new clothes all the time." She chuckles.

"Can't promise. You don't understand what you do to me, Woman! I lose all control with you, baby." I claim her mouth and she opens up for me. I make quick timing in removing the rest of her clothes and my shirt, but she stops me when I reach for the button on my jeans.

"This is my part." She unbuttons them and then slowly starts to unzip the zipper. She is always careful at this, knowing that by now I have a full blown hard on and I always go commando.

She pulls my jeans down and out he pops. Yanking my jeans off the rest of the way, she reaches for me and wraps her hands around my huge girth as she kneels before me. She looks up at me as she licks the precum off the tip of my dick then wraps her mouth around the rest. She acts starved as she continues to suck me off hungrily. Sliding one hand up and down the base of my cock as the other massages my balls. I feel them start to pull up. Her warm mouth feels so fucking good around me.

"You may want to stop right now if you don't want me to come in your mouth. Otherwise, you are going to get a few mouthfuls of my jizz!" This only makes her start sucking me faster and then she uses a finger and lightly rims my ass hole, making me lose my load right then. I start pumping hard into her mouth as she swallows load after load.

Once the last drop is swallowed, I pick her up and carry her to the weight bench where I lay her down and kneel between her luscious thighs. Spreading her legs, I gaze upon her glistening opening. I have never seen such a beautiful pussy such as hers! I look up at her and with a grin, I lower my and begin licking her slick folds. Reaching my hand up, I rub her swollen nub, bringing a moan to Jill's lips and a shudder through her body.

I insert my finger and already feel her walls tightening, ready for climax. My finger pumps more vigorously in her and her pulse quickens while her body quivers.

"Duncan?" She pleads.

I bring my mouth to her sensitive spot and lick, then suck, bringing her release down upon her. She grabs my hair to hold me still as she comes, but I need to taste her sweet nectar. Pulling my finger out, I replace it with my tongue, capturing each drop.

As her body relaxes, I pull away and move up her body, taking her lips with my own, so she can taste her own sweetness. Locking her legs behind my back, I know she is ready for more and with one long thrust, I'm inside of her warmth. Pumping my cock slowly at first, she digs her nails into my ass and quickens the tempo, relaying that she wants more. She wants more? I'll give her more. Picking up both legs, I lift them up high, giving me better access to go deeper and a fantastic view of my dick slamming into her pussy.

"Oh, my fucking God, Duncan! Yes! Just like that, don't stop!" She screams at me. Pretty sure the whole Compound might have heard it. I feel my balls pull up and my cock swell: I know I'm close. Resting one of her legs on my shoulder, I reach down and start playing with her clit. She screams again, only louder, as her climax takes over her body. I shoot my own hot seed into her at the same time, burying myself in deep within her.

We both relax when it's over and I find her lips, kissing her softly. "I think the whole building might have heard you, love." I smile down at her.

"I don't care. It just tells them that you know how to please your woman." She smirks.

Sheer pride comes over me, knowing that I take good care of this special woman and the fact that she has gone through hell and back, but can still take a good pounding from me.

"Hate to do it, baby, but we should get dressed and go back down to interrogation. She pouts at me, and I hate disappointing her, so I tell her that she can come in the room with me.

She perks up real fast, "Really?"

"Yes, really, but you have to get dressed first." I laugh. I don't think I have ever seen her move so fast before. I shake my head and grab my pants.

Taven is just coming out of the room, from questioning the prisoner, when we got there. "Has he talked yet?" I ask.

"Not a fucking word!"

"Damn, I thought for sure we could get him to tell us something!" My frustration is plain to see.

Jill steps in, "Umm, he did say something earlier when I was in there."

"He did? Why didn't you say anything?"

"Well, you went all caveman-like on me and then we got occupied!" She grins at me.

Taven tries to hide the chuckle that slips out, "Wait, what? You interrogated the prisoner? All by yourself? Do you know how dangerous that was?" Taven raises his voice.

Holding up her hand, Jill responds, "Yes, I did and apparently I am the only one who got something out of him, so please save your lecture for another day."

Ignoring Taven's glare, I turn to face Jill, "So what exactly did you learn?"

"I learned that Mika goes to church every week."

"And that is going to help us how?" Taven cocks his brow at her.

Rolling her eyes at him, "Because, we can be waiting for him when he comes out of church and follow him!"

"How do we know which church he goes to? There are quite a few in the area." I state.

She goes to explain how she tricked him into telling her what religion Mika is, "So, we may not know the exact church, but we can cut out all but the Lutheran churches and as far as I know, there is only one in Augusta."

I grab her head, "You, my angel, are a genius, I love you!" I kiss her quickly, wishing that Taven wasn't standing there, so I could thank her properly, but it will have to wait until later.

Taven slaps her on the back, "Good job Earnhardt, but don't do that again until you are trained properly. Do you hear me?"

"Yes, Sir!" she salutes him with a grin.

"Don't ever call me sir again!" He gives Jill a stern look.

"Okay, Sir!" Jill smirks and sticks her tongue out at him.

Taven walks away shaking his head, "Damn women!"

JILL

Duncan takes me to see Liz and the boys after we leave the interrogation room. Derrick seems to have clammed up, so it is no use wasting our time at this point and I am anxious to see my friend and try to reassure her that everything will be okay.

Liz is sitting on her bed, head bowed towards the floor, when I knock on her open door. She looks up at me with troubled eyes. I walk over and sit beside her, putting my arm around her shoulder.

"Hey honey, why are you looking so sad? You are safe here within the Compound." I assure her.

"I'm not so much sad as I am pissed, Jill. My life was perfectly fine until the wedding and now, here I am, needing protection from assholes that I don't even know! How would you feel?"

"I am so sorry that they brought you into this! It's all my fault! If I hadn't gone on that stupid date and given Jason mixed signals, we wouldn't be here!"

"It's not your fault that people are messed in the head! What beef do these people have with you anyway?"

"Let's just say that Jason got himself killed and now his best friend, Mika, is wanting revenge. He blames me for Jason's death and apparently, everyone associated with me?"

"How did he die?" Liz asks.

I hesitate before saying anything. "Jason kidnapped me, because he didn't want me with Duncan. He claimed to be in love with me and thought that in time, I would come to love him too. When I kept resisting his advances, he put Mika in charge of me, to 'help' me see the light. While Mika was in charge, he did despicable things to me and let others do so as well. Duncan and the Elite came and saved me, but not before they took out a few of Jason's men. Duncan also killed Jason that day. Mika was injured as well, but unfortunately, he lived and now he is on a rampage.

They attacked us here at the Compound when most of the Elite were out looking for him and his men. Once Duncan and the rest figured out that they were here attacking, they rushed back here. Duncan was injured and almost died from an arrow that Mika shot at him, but I shot Mika in the shoulder and when that didn't stop him, I shot his dick. Now he is really pissed." I exhale after relaying the story.

Liz bursts into laughter, "You actually shot his dick off?"

"Well, I don't know if I shot it off, would be nice if I did, but yes, I shot him down there." I chuckle.

"Wow. I can't believe you went through all that and didn't tell me!"

"I didn't talk about it for months. Cassie didn't even know what really happened to me during my captivity."

"I'm sorry I have been such a bitch about this whole situation. Especially to Taven. He has been so nice to me."

"He will be fine. Tell me, what do you really think about Taven?" I ask, because I want to know how to proceed in speeding things up between them.

"I don't know. I barely know him, but like I said, he has been really nice to me."

"He is pretty cute too, isn't he?" I grin at her.

"Of course he is, only a blind person would argue with that, but the rest of the Elite are all good looking as well." She laughs.

"Yes, they are, but Taven is Head of the Elite! I think he may have a little crush on you, and believe me, Taven crushes on no one!"

"Really? You think he likes me? Why is he always scowling at me, even when he is being nice?"

"That's just Taven, but I think he is trying to fight his attraction to you."

"I think you are just looking way too into this."

"Maybe, but just keep it in mind. These men treat their women like gold and I think you need one of them in your life!" I wiggle my eyebrows at her.

"I am perfectly fine with not having a man in my life, especially after my last relationship! The only men I need are my boys!"

"Suit yourself, but you are going to miss out on a lot. Especially the insane sex!"

"I'm not objective to one-night stands you know!"

"If you don't want a relationship, then I'm warning you right now to refrain from having a one nighter with an Elite, because you will be ruined for all other men! It's that fucking good!"

"Thanks for the warning." She laughs.

We talk for over an hour before I excuse myself, but not before I assure her once more that her and the boys are safe here. She is nervous about staying here with so many strangers and on top of that, her boys are in awe of the Elite. Liz doesn't want them getting too attached. That is her biggest concern.

Liz's husband passed away when her youngest was just a baby. He was killed by a drunk driver. Since then, she has only been in one other relationship, and he turned out to be a big-time drug dealer. She left him after a year and a half when she found out about his second occupation. She has a heart of gold, and she has had a rough life. I want her to find happiness and I strongly believe that Taven is it, but I won't push her. If it's meant to be then it will be.

Duncan let me ride along with him, Xavier and Cooper as they stake out the church in town, since they are only following to get a location. It still feels good to know that he is at least trying to include me in the work. The rest of the Elite go and stake out other Lutheran churches in the surrounding towns. Kole is back at the Compound keeping an eye on Liz and the boys, along with the security cameras at each of the church locations, in case we miss something.

We look up the times of the Service and get there an hour before, watching and waiting for any sign of Mika. Cars begin filling the parking lot a half hour before the Service is to start, but not once did we see Mika. None of the others had seen him either.

Duncan's phone starts buzzing, and he answers it. He grunts a couple times and then hangs up, "That was Kole. Our guy just pulled up to the back in a tan Chrysler and snuck in the back door. Let's pull around back and wait for him there, since he is trying to be sneaky."

Cooper takes us around back and parks us on the far side of the lot, where we have a good view of the back door and the Chrysler. My heart is beating so hard in anticipation as Xavier gets out and takes a stroll by Mika's car. He squats down and pretends to tie his shoe and then continues on. A few minutes later he is back in the vehicle.

Duncan leans over and whispered in my ear, "You can wake the dead with as loud as your heart is pounding. Take a deep breath and try to calm yourself. There is nothing to be scared of. All Xavier did was put a tracker under his car."

"I'm not scared, I am excited! Hoping we finally catch the bastard, so we can get on with our lives!"

"Well, we don't have much longer to wait. The Service should just about be over."

As if on cue, Mika exits the back door and without even looking around gets into his car and heads out. We stay far enough back so he doesn't see us. Kole calls Duncan to confirm that the tracker is up and running.

"We got him!" Duncan informs us and I can't help but breathe a sigh of relief. Cooper turns us around and we head back to the Compound. I grab Duncan and smash my lips to his and he wraps his arms around me kissing me back and turning it into a passionate one. He breaks away and looks at me, "Thanks to you, angel, we got him."

"I'm not going to celebrate until he is dead, but I'll accept the thanks right now. Although, I believe you owe me a bigger 'thank you' once we are back at the Compound!" I give him a devilish grin.

"I do believe you are right, baby. I will thank you nice and proper." He slams his lips back to mine once more.

"Get a fucking room, will ya?" Cooper scolds as he looks at us in the rearview mirror.

"Stop watching and you will be fine!" Duncan responds back.

I pull away though and snuggle up against Duncan, thinking about the 'thanks' I will be receiving later.

ELEVEN

DUNCAN

We track Mika's car to a few different locations and send a few men out to scope each one. It seems as though he has his men spread out between two locations, with most of the Hunters being at a warehouse about five miles south of town, and a warehouse a mile East of town. A residence is a third location and is found in a gated community. Seems as though Mika has a house that he, himself, lives in and by the surveillance videos, has a family of his own. Interesting! I think it's time that we pay our prisoner, Jenny, a little visit and see if she can spread some light on the situation.

I stop by the kitchen, knowing that Jill is there helping Max cook dinner. I slide my arms around her waist from behind as she is standing at the counter, cutting up some onion, "Hey gorgeous, wanna come with me to go talk to Jenny?"

"Seriously?" She turns to me and her face is a wet mess from cutting up the onion.

"Well, I don't want to take you away from your emotional relationship with that onion." I try and hide my smile.

"Fuck you, smartass! My sense of smell is two-fold since we have bonded and cutting these nasty things suck ass more than they did before! I would be happy to leave the rest for Max."

"Gee, thanks!" Max speaks up.

"Thank you, Max." Jill leans in and kisses him on the cheek, "I owe you one."

"If you give that same attention to the other cheek, we can call it good." He gives me an evil smile as Jill kisses the other cheek as well.

I retaliate, "I am glad you like the feel of my mate's lips on your cheeks. I had the pleasure of having her lips around my huge cock a few hours ago!"

"Duncan!" Jill slaps my chest as Max is frantically wiping at both of his cheeks and gagging.

"You're a dick, Dunc, do you know that?"

"Just thought you would like to know, is all." I walk out laughing as Max flips me off.

Jill catches up to me and I grab her hand, lacing my fingers through hers as we walk down to the cell blocks.

"That wasn't very nice, you know." Jill frowns at me.

"Had to put him in his place and remind him that you are mine. He will think twice before he tries to goad me with you again." I smile down at her and see that she is now grinning herself.

"I love it when you call me yours like that. It makes my lady bits all tingly."

In vamp speed, I have her pinned up against the cement wall, thanking God that Jill is wearing loose, stretchy shorts. Without warning, I kneel before her, sliding the crotch of her shorts and panties aside and shoving my tongue through her entrance. She catches her breath and moans from my attack. Her fingers tangle in my hair, pulling me closer as she grinds her hips against my mouth. In no time at all, I have her spiraling out of control until she is tossed over the edge and coming all over my tongue.

I continue to lap up the nectar until I have gotten every last drop. Once I put her clothes back into place, I stand as I steady her shaky legs. Wiping my mouth, I then press a kiss to her forehead, grab her hand again and continue down to the cells. I quickly glance down at her and she has a smile plastered to her face, which in turn, puts a smile on my face.

I unlock Jenny's cell door and step in with Jill. Jenny has one of the luxury cells with a full-size bed, tv and a screen to give her privacy for her bathroom needs. Jenny is laying on her bed reading a fashion magazine and doesn't even acknowledge our presence. Jill walks over and grabs the magazine out of Jenny's hand and tosses it at the bottom of the bed.

"Sorry to intrude, Jenny, but we have a few things to discuss. Please sit up, I will not ask you again." I really dislike this woman and would like nothing more than to leave her to rot in here for what she tried to do with Jill, but then my softer side recognizes her as a female, and I have just a little regret at keeping her locked up.

"I have nothing to say to you, vamp!" She sneers at me.

"Well then, maybe you and I can have a little chat?" Jill moves to stand in Jenny's line of vision.

"Nope. I believe I don't."

"Fine, then you sit and listen to what we have to say!" Jill remarks and looks at me to continue.

"It has come to our attention, Jenny, that Mika has a family. I guess I didn't realize that you like fucking married men, but hey, to each their own. It does show what kind of person you are though. One who has no morals and no respect for anyone." I stare at her and examine her response to what I just told her. She truly looks surprised when I mention that Mika is married. "By your reaction, you seem shocked by my words."

"What kind of lies are you telling me? Mika isn't married, he was going to marry me!"

"Well, if he did marry you, he would be committing bigamy." I say matter-of-factly.

"All lies! I am not buying what you are trying to sell me and I'm not telling you a God damn thing about Mika!"

I pull my phone out and bring up the saved video that I stored on my phone exactly for this reason. I step in front of her and press play. The sound on the video is amazing. You can see Mika's wife walk him out to his car and give him a kiss goodbye, calling him honey and telling him that she will see him after work. You can also make out both their wedding bands.

"He is not coming for you, if that is what you are waiting for. If anything, he is probably glad that you are not around anymore." I feel bad for the lie, but we need her to talk.

"I was planning on breaking it off with him anyway." She shrugs, but I can see the deep hurt in her eyes.

Jill sits on the bed beside her and takes her hand, "Jenny, you are just another victim of Mika's. He doesn't deserve your loyalty. What he does deserve is to be locked away, never to hurt another female again!"

Tears are now rolling down Jenny's cheeks and she wouldn't say anymore. Laying back down and turning her back to us, she remains silent, and I know we are done for now. I motion to Jill that it is time to leave and with one last look towards the crying woman on the bed, we walk out, locking the cell behind us.

We stop by Taven's office to report our conversation with Jenny and head back to the kitchen to see if Max still needs help. Dinner is actually just getting done, so we grab our plates and take our seats at the long table. Kole comes strolling in and grins when he sees the two of us.

"What's that shit eating grin for?" I ask.

Filling his plate up, Kole takes a seat across from me, ignoring my question, but asks one of his own. "How long have we worked together, Duncan?"

"Too long it seems like on some days, why?"

"Do you know how all of our security cameras work?"

"Uh, yeah. That's a dumb question!"

"Then please, for the love of God, turn the cameras off when you decide to have sex or you want to please your mate anywhere other than your room! I am tired of looking at the screen and seeing shit that I shouldn't be seeing!"

I start to shake with laughter until I see Jill turning beet red with embarrassment, covering her face with her hands. I try to reassure her, "Oh, love, no need to be embarrassed. I know where the cameras are at, and I keep you hidden from them at all times."

"He does do a pretty good job at hiding you, believe me! I would rather look up at the screen to see a naked woman than to see Dunc's bare ass!" Kole snickers.

"That's supposed to make me feel better? Why didn't you tell me that there are cameras all over?"

"Angel, it's a Compound. Of course, there are cameras all over, I thought you knew that."

"Don't you angel me, warrior! You should have known that it would embarrass me!"

I look over at Kole who is trying to cover his smirk, "Thanks asshole! You could have brought this up in private!" I lecture him.

"Don't you dare put this on Kole! Just for this little stunt, you warrior, are cut the fuck off!" She scrapes her chair back and walks out, leaving me sitting there stunned and Kole shaking with laughter.

I look at Kole and stare daggers at him! Shit! I am in the doghouse now and I haven't the slightest idea on how to get out of this one! I throw my fork down on my plate and scrape my own chair back, "Just fucking great! Thanks for that, now you can clean up both our plates and I storm out.

I figure I would let Jill cool off a bit before I try talking to her, so I go and spend an hour in the weight room, blowing off my own steam and trying to come up with a really good apology. By the time I finish going through all of my sets and reps, I assume enough time has passed, so I decide to head back to our room and try to talk to her.

I walk into our room, but Jill isn't there and something else seems amiss. I look around and then go into the bathroom. All of Jill's belongings are gone. I'm really nervous now. I leave our room and head towards her old room. I try the knob, but it's locked. Bingo! My heart slows a little back to normal, at least she didn't leave the Compound.

I knock on her door, but get no answer, "Baby, let me in so we can talk."

"I am not ready to talk to you yet!" She yells through the door.

"You didn't have to leave our room over this little incident."

"You think this is little? Then you are more of a pig than I thought! If you can't understand my point of view on the matter then, there is nothing to talk about! To your last statement, when I said you are cut the fuck off, I meant from everything!"

"Oh, baby. I am so sorry. What do I have to do to prove that to you!"

"That is for you to figure out Duncan McPherson! Now, I am done talking to your inconsiderate ass!"

And she is. I can't get another word out of her. Man, this is bad, really bad! I turn and go back to my room to lick my wounds. How the fuck do I get myself out of this one? In all honesty, I had forgotten about the cameras, and I am glad that Kole covered my lie when I said that I made sure she was covered at all times. I will definitely, remember in the future, if I ever get the chance again!

JILL

I can't believe the nerve of him! He knew all along that each room had a camera and yet he still fucked me and ate me in front of them! Do I regret having those times with him? No, but the embarrassment is still there, knowing that Kole can see what we are doing! It is going to take Duncan a hell of a lot of groveling to be able to get back between these thighs! And just to make him suffer more, I'm going to tease the shit out of him in the process! I love the guy with every fiber of my being, but he needs to be taught a good, hard lesson!

The next morning, I go down to breakfast wearing a new set of workout clothes for training. It consists of a sports bra that plumps up the girls and the tiniest pair of spandex shorts that just barely covers my ass cheeks. I bought them for when we have our private training sessions, but today I will start training with everyone else, my decision.

"Morning everyone!" I say cheerfully as I walk into the kitchen. I get a hello back, but then all eyes are glued on me, including Duncan's. His mouth hangs open for a second and then he shuts it and glares all around the room.

"Don't you guys need to hurry and eat, so you can get to training?" Everyone looks down at their plates and refuses to look at me for the duration of the meal. Duncan shoots daggers at me every chance he gets. Finally, he stands, "You ready for your training?" as he looks me over.

Without looking at him, I reply, "I will start training with the rest of the group today, thank you very much."

"Like hell you will be!" He roars.

Every chair in the room scrapes and the occupants file out the door as fast as they can. I glare up at Duncan, "Was that necessary?"

"Is this necessary?" He moves his hand up and down towards my body.

"What? They are called workout clothes for a reason!"

"Yeah, if you are working out to be a stripper!"

I roll my eyes at him and move to clear my plate, but he steps in front of me. I look up at him and act as if I am bored of the conversation.

"Jill, I understand that you are pissed at me, but you go too far with this! I don't want every guy in this Compound staring at MY woman like she is a piece of meat!"

I whip my head back up at him, "Oh, but you can let them watch you fuck me and eat me out?" I am seething mad.

"I didn't realize that the video plays on the screen constantly. I assumed that they only check it if something happens!"

"Oh, did you now? I am sure you have been here long enough to know better than that! Try another excuse buddy!" I try to walk around him, but he blocks my path yet again, "Let me through Duncan."

"Not until you promise me that you will go change into a different outfit."

"I bought this outfit to work out in and that is exactly what I am going to do!"

"Over my dead body!" He picks me up and throws me over his shoulder.

"What the fuck are you doing? Put me down right now, ass hat!"

He ignores me and continues down the hall towards our rooms. He opens my bedroom door and walks in, not putting me down until he is by my dresser. Yanking my drawers open, he finds the one that holds my workout clothes and grabs a new set. He slams the drawer closed and then finally, he puts me down, putting the new set in my arms. He walks over to the bedroom door, closing it and stands there with his arms crossed over his chest and his legs spread apart.

"Oh no you don't! You don't get to see me undress! You lost that perk when you pulled your little stunt!"

"You are my mate, Jill. I can see you naked whenever I want."

"Is that so?" I stomp over to the bathroom and slam the door closed, locking it behind me. Take that Mr. Big Bad Warrior! I change quickly and exit the bathroom with a big ass smug grin on my face. I walk right past him and out the door, but he catches my arm and pulls me into his embrace. It feels so good to be here because I missed him holding me last night; I melt just a little. Then I harden myself back up and try to pull away, "Let me go!"

"Tell me that you didn't miss my arms around you last night, angel. Tell me that you slept like a baby and didn't miss me at all!"

I can't lie to him, so I remain quiet. The truth is, I barely got a wink of sleep. I spent most of the night wondering if he was asleep or if he was missing me as much as I was missing him, but I can't tell him that. He hasn't learned his lesson yet.

I feel his lips on my forehead, "I love you, Jill, and nothing will ever change that. You can be mad at me all you want during the day, but please put the anger aside when night falls. I can't spend another night without you in my arms."

I blink back the tears that want to fall and then step back when his hold loosens. Without looking at him, I walk away in a hurry, before my damn bursts. Damn him and his loving words! I have to be a heartless bitch if I didn't let them affect me. They did affect me, almost to the point of forgiving him right then and there!

I walk into the training room, and I hear the word bet before they all notice I am here, and their mouths shut tight. I roll my eyes at them and cross my arms. "So, guys, anyone want to share what you all are betting on?" I cock a brow.

"What are you talking about, a bet? There is no betting going on here." Kai answers quickly.

"Okay, fine. I want to make a bet of my own... who wants in?" I know at least one would answer and he doesn't disappoint.

"You can put me in every time! So, what's the bet?" Kai asks rubbing his hands together and grinning.

"I bet you a hundred bucks that you were just betting on how long it would be before Duncan and I made up!"

His smile fades away and his eyes widen, "Ah shit! You tricked me... you are evil!"

"You are the one that took the bet, dumbass. Now, pay up!" I smile sweetly at him as he pulls two fifties out of his wallet and slaps them in my hand.

"Thanks for having my back guys! Don't trust this one, she's a sneak!" He glares back at me, and I can't help but to giggle.

"Okay, fun is over! Let's get started." Xavier claps his hands together. "Jill, I want you to work with Cooper on kicks and then move to Dane for punching. Everyone else, you know what to do, so get to it."

Duncan walks in ten minutes later and starts sparring with Xavier. I can't help glancing his way and each time it costs me and I end up on my back. Cooper scolds me every time for not concentrating, which in turn makes me more determined. By the time I move to Dane, I have forgotten all about Duncan being in the room and I throw my punches like a savage. I throw in kicks here and there, surprising Dane every time. At the end of the session, I'm so sore and in need of a hot bath. Duncan tries stopping me once, but I hold up my hand and continue on. My heart is breaking by doing so, but my mind is drained. Maybe tomorrow....

TWELVE

DUNCAN

It's been three days since Jill has talked to me or laid in my bed, but it feels like a lifetime, and I am beginning to wonder if I will ever hold her again. I am at a loss as to how she wants me to make amends when I have never had a woman in my life before, so I have never needed to. Jax and Cassie got home last night from their honeymoon, and I was so thankful because I thought Cassie would be able to help me out with this, but nothing she says to Jill works either.

I have to get out of the Compound. It is so hard seeing my angel every day and not being able to hold her or even kiss her goodnight or morning. I've decided to stay in a hotel not far from here. I still want to be close in case I am needed, but just far enough away where I am not tortured by the hurtful looks from her. Taven and Jax are the only two that know where I am at, and they both have promised not to tell a soul and to make sure that Jill stays safe.

I can't bring myself to actually leave Augusta, okay, I am only 2 miles away from the Compound, but it is still far enough. I occupy my time by doing detail on the two warehouses that Mika's men are at. It doesn't add up. Why two warehouses when all the men would fit into one? What are they hiding? I think about these questions constantly. That's it, I need to find out! I'll probably catch hell for it, but it wouldn't be the first time that I have pulled a stunt like this, and it certainly won't be the last.

I figure I will start with the closest warehouse on the east end first and then make my way south. I plan on going at dusk, so I have plenty of time to collect everything and plan. Once dusk arrives, I head out, only taking about fifteen minutes to get there. I park right on the outskirts of town and run the rest of the way. When I arrive, I find a tall chain linked fence with barbed wire at the top. Not sure if it's electrical, I throw a rock at it and I see that luck is on my side. I take out a pair of wire cutters and start cutting through the links until I can fit through. Staying low, I make my way towards the building hiding in as many shadows as I can.

I only see two guards right now, one at the front doors and one on the roof, but I assume there is one at each of the three doors. I continue on, watching for motion sensors and security cameras, which I spot at each corner of the building. I pull out my silencer that shoots paint darts, silently thanking Kole for making them, and I shoot the first camera on my side. I will leave the others, so they don't get suspicious when more than one goes black. Watching the guard on the roof make his way to the other side and out of my line of vision, I flash over to the guard at the door and quickly put him in a choke hold until he is rendered unconscious.

This all seems too easy, but I move forward, taking extra precaution. Pulling the code box off the wall to expose the wires, I quickly snip them, earning me access to the inside. I open the door a crack and peer in, but the lights are off. I slip in and plaster myself to the wall as I make my way to the other door that opens up into the warehouse. I peek in and find darkness again, so I sneak in. Thanks to my vampire senses, I don't need light to see the hundreds of crates stacked up throughout the room. I quickly go to the first set of crates and open it up. I find nonperishable food items. What the hell? Why would they need guards to secure food? I continue down the rows until I finally come to larger crates. I open one up and just as I suspected, weapons. Crates upon wooden crates of guns, crossbows, knives, grenades, dynamite and even wooden stakes. I chuckle at this last one.

Not wanting to waste any more time and still wanting to check out the other warehouse, I sneak back outside and to the fence line without being seen. Within a few minutes, I am back in my SUV and making my way south.

I'm squatting in the shadows, trying to figure out a way in, because unlike the other warehouse, this one has more guards, more cameras, and it has motion sensors. The fence is the same as the last, but do I really want to chance going in when I have no backup? I can't, I just can't. It's not just me anymore, I have a mate that depends on me, even if she is being stubborn at the moment. I decide to head back to my SUV, but before I take another step in that direction, I feel a pinch on the side of my neck. I lift my hand to the area and pull out some sort of dart that is imbedded deep within. As I examine it, everything starts to blur, and I am falling to the ground. My last thought is that the sons of bitches just tranquilized me!

I wake up with a pounding headache and in chains, hanging from the ceiling. My arms stretched above my head, my feet in chains and barely touching the floor. I'm honestly surprised that I am even alive, as much as they hate vampire's. They must be planning something if they are keeping me alive. Dammit Duncan, you really got yourself into a situation this time!

I look around my surroundings and notice that there are big metal cages, about forty of them, lined up against one of the walls, all with bunk beds in them. I start to count them, just to be sure, when I realize that there are people, more specifically... women, doubled up in ten of the cages. What the fuck are these sick fucks about? All I can do is stare, but then my senses kick in and I can smell them. Oh my God, un-fucking-believable! How the hell did they figure it out? Every woman being held captive has type O blood! They have started collecting women that could possibly mate with a vampire. I am feeling sick to my stomach at the thought of what these poor women are enduring, because I can guess that they are being treated like traitors even though they know nothing of what and why they are being held.

I see movement in my peripheral view and turn to see a guy with a limp and what looks to be a prosthetic arm walking towards me. Mika! It brings me joy that he wasn't able to save the arm that I took from him and the fact that my woman gave him a limp by shooting his dick, brings me even more joy! I glare at him as he comes to stand right in front of me.

"Ah, Duncan, isn't it? You don't know how happy you have made me by coming to my warehouse! Not sure how you found us, but here you are, and with no back up. We took the liberty of searching you for any tracking devices and my men are out, as we speak, searching for your vehicle."

"How in the hell were you able to tranquilize me? That stuff should have burned up quick in my system!"

Mika chuckles, "A double dose of elephant tranquiller is what it took. You were only out for ten minutes, but it was enough to get you in here and in the chains. You are our first test subject, actually. I think I will up it to a triple dose though."

"Why the women in the cages? I thought you were all about protecting the innocents, that is not protection!"

"On the contrary, we are protecting them from becoming victims of you vamps. We are also ruining them for any possible vampire mate."

Just as he is telling me this, one of his men goes in and grabs a woman from one of the cages and drags her over to a bed in the corner of the warehouse that I hadn't seen. Chaining her up, he proceeds to rape her right in front of everyone. The worst part is that other men are lining up to do the same. These sick fucks are going to pull a train on the poor woman!

"The best part is that they keep my men satisfied!" Mika says with a sadistic smile.

I hear the woman screaming for help and it looks as if the men enjoy hearing her screams. I start pulling at my chains, trying to free myself so I can help her, but as strong as I am, I cannot break them.

"You are wasting your time vamp, you can't break those chains, no matter how strong you are! They are made of Chromium, the hardest metal around. Although, it's amusing watching you struggle." He chuckles.

"You are a sick fuck! I should have killed you when I took that arm of yours!"

"Come Duncan, how fun would that have been? Granted, I was pissed when you took it, but I'm happy to be alive, so I can have my revenge. I am especially looking forward to torturing your bitch once I get my hands on her! She will pay dearly for what she took from me!"

Even though I am seething at his threat against Jill, I can't help but smile, knowing that my angel took his manhood from him. Thinking of Jill brings a thought to my head. Our bond! I can contact her and have reinforcements here within the hour! I try calling to her, but nothing. 'Come on, baby, hear me! I need help!'. I continue to call out to her, but with no luck.

I hear Mika talking again, "The things I am going to do to that little slut of yours is going to make her wish for death! I should have fucked her the first time, then maybe she wouldn't have gone to you!"

I can't stand listening to him talk about my mate like that, "What are you going to do to her when you have no dick to use? You're not even considered a man anymore!" I sneer.

This pisses Mika off and he picks up a chain with what looks like spikes on the end of it and brings his arm back. Pain slices through me as he whips it across my chest, but I don't make a sound. He gives me four more lashes before dropping it to the floor.

"Even though you will heal fast, the pain it inflicts with hold me over until I can kill you!"

"What are you waiting for?" I ask and spit in his face.

Wiping his face with his sleeve, he laughs. "I want you to witness the vile things that we will do to your precious mate before your demise. Knowing that you are too helpless to save her!"

Mika walks away and I drop my head, still hearing the cries of the woman being used over and over. I continue to call out to Jill, praying that she opens her mind up and hears me.

JILL

I find out through Cassie that Duncan has left the Compound and is staying away, but she doesn't know where he is at. Jax and Taven are the only two that know, but aren't saying anything. I feel abandoned, like he doesn't care to work things out with me, but to be truthful, I wasn't giving him much of a chance. He has tried talking to me, but I keep ignoring him. Does he not realize what this separation is doing to me also? I cry myself to sleep every night missing my warrior.

Just when I decide to try and talk to him, I find out that he is gone. I head to Taven's office to demand that he tell me where Duncan is, so I can go to him, and I will not leave until he tells me his location. I hear quiet whispers as I near his door and knock. All talking stops as I hear Taven's voice telling me to enter. Jax is in the room with him, and I am getting a strange vibe.

"I'm glad that both of you are here. I need you to tell me where Duncan is. I want to talk to him." I look at both of them sternly.

They exchange looks with each other, but do not say anything, which irritates the hell out of me.

"Listen, I am sure that he told you not to give away his location, but I need him back, I miss him!" I feel my lips tremble and my eyes tear up, so I look away.

Jax is the first to speak, "You are right. He asked us not to say anything, but...", he doesn't go on and the worried look on his face sends alarm bells going off in my head.

"But what, Jax?"

"We haven't been able to reach him since yesterday and it's not like him to not communicate. Honestly, it feels like the whole Jax situation all over again." Taven says glumly.

"But that doesn't mean anything is wrong." Jax quickly adds in," "He was pretty messed up when he made the decision to leave. He was hurting, so maybe he is just needing some time."

"How do we know for sure though? Like you said, this isn't like him!"

"Has he tried contacting you at all?" Taven asks me.

"I haven't had any missed calls in over a week."

"No. What Taven means is, has he tried contacting you through your bond?" Jax explains.

"Through our bond?" I'm confused for a moment, but then the light turns on about what he is talking about, "Oh! I had forgotten all about that. We haven't communicated like that since we bonded. I don't even know how!"

Jax grabs my hands and leads me to a chair, "Here, sit down and I will tell you how to do it. I sit and look up at him, waiting, "Now, you need to concentrate on him. Open your mind and just call to him in your head."

I close my eyes and think of my handsome vampire warrior. His smile, his touch, the way he looks at me so lovingly. I call his name, 'Duncan, can you hear me?'... nothing. I call out again. This time I hear a soft groan, 'Duncan, it's me, Jill. Can you hear me?'

'Angel? Is it really you?' He answers but it sounds as if it hurts him to talk, as if he is straining to get the words out.

'Oh my God Duncan, what is wrong? Are you okay?' I start to panic a little.

'I'm okay... for now... need... blood... soon!'

'What's wrong? Why do you need blood and why do you sound like you are hurt?'

I hear Jax trying to talk to me, "Jill, are talking to him?" I hold my hand up and nod my head yes.

'Lost... too... much... blood. Send... back... up... now!' I can barely make out what he is saying, and I am now terrified.

'Send back up? Where do you need back up?' I get no response, 'Duncan, baby, stay with me! Where do I need to send back up?'

'Almost...... out of...... strength. South...... warehouse............ Mika....' And then there is nothing else. I didn't realize that I was crying and screaming his name until I feel hands on me, shaking me.

"Jill, what's going on? Why does he need back up?" Taven is shouting at me, trying to get me to answer him.

"Duncan needs blood, soon! He is hurt, but I don't know why! He said to send back up south and then he mentioned a warehouse, but the last thing he said was Mika's name!"

"Fuck, that son of a bitch!" Jax slams his fist down on Taven's desk.

"I don't know what he is doing there, but he sounds so weak, and he said he is almost out of strength! We need to get to him now!" I am screaming frantically.

"We will suit up right away and get there, but we are outnumbered, and I have to call in reinforcements. Jax, you go get the men ready and I will have Kole send out the S.O.S to the other Compounds!" Taven commands.

"I am going with you!" I inform them.

"No, you're not, Jill. This may be a trap to get you to come and help him." Before I can argue, Taven continues, "I need you here, because I am taking all of my available men except for Kole, so it will only be the two of you here protecting this Compound!"

"But I need to know that he is going to make it! I need to see for myself!"

"We will be wearing our body cameras and earpieces, so you can see everything that we are seeing. I need you to stay here! Please, do this for Duncan!" Taven is pleading with me, and his last words get to me.

"Fine, but I am going to Raven right now and having him take my blood. Do not leave until you have what you need for Duncan!"

"Okay, hurry and go now!"

I take off running through the Compound and meet Raven coming out of the medical ward. "You need to take my blood to Duncan. Hurry, there is no time to spare!" As much as I want him to take more, I can only give a pint of blood, but it is better than nothing. It makes me feel as if I am contributing to his rescue even though I cannot be there. Raven grabs a few more pints of blood from stock, just in case and is off.

Still sitting in the chair, I close my eyes and try to reach out for Duncan, 'Hey Baby, can you hear me? Your brothers are coming for you, so please hold on. Hold on for me! I can't lose you, baby, you are my world! We need more time, fight for me warrior!' Tears streaming down my cheeks. I feel someone take my hand and I look up. My best friend is here for me, Cassie, she will be my rock.

'I… hear… you… angel. I'm… trying. I… love… you. You… are… my… heart…' I cry harder at his words.

'I love you Duncan and I am so sorry for how I have been acting. I will never forgive myself! Come home to me!' That is the last I hear from him. I jump up out of the chair and drag Cassie out the door with me.

"Where are we going, Jill?"

"To Kole's office. I need to be there. I need to see everything that is going on!"

"I don't understand how Mika has Duncan. How and where did he get captured?" Cassie is rambling the whole way.

"Only Duncan can answer that, but he is so weak, Case, I don't know if he is going to make it!"

Cassie pulls on my hand to stop me, "Don't think like that, Jill! Never think like that! He loves you and has a reason to fight. YOU are going to help him fight, to come home! Just keep thinking positive, okay?" I shake my head yes and fresh tears fall as Cassie pulls me into her embrace, "The two of you have come too far to lose each other. He will be fine, honey, I promise!"

"Thank you for coming home when you did. I wouldn't have been able to get through any of this without my best friend!"

"Yeah, well, I'm still kind of pissed that you didn't call me when Liz got shot!"

"Please, I can't get into that again right now." I go on, "We have got to take Mika out! This will never end if we don't... ugh!"

"I agree one hundred percent with you, but let's worry about getting your man home first, okay?" She smiles at me, and I try to smile back, but it is a lost cause.

It's been two hours since I first made contact with Duncan and the men are finally ready to go in. Needing to wait on other Compounds to send in back up is what took the longest, because they were between one to two hours away. There are now about forty-five Elite ready to break down the walls of the warehouse. They are all waiting on Kole's signal, but he is still trying to break into Mika's security system, so he can have eyes on the inside.

The moment he breaks through, the three of us gasp at what we are seeing on the screen. Lots of cages with bunk beds filled one wall. Looking closely, there are women inside some of them. Kole relays what he is seeing to the men who are waiting to storm in. He keeps moving the camera around the warehouse, giving them locations of men, doors and windows, but then I see something strange.

"Wait! Go back." I urge him and he swings the camera back a little bit and then stops when he sees what I am seeing. I cry out, "Duncan!", as I see him hanging from his arms which are in chains, hanging from the ceiling. His head is hanging down. On the floor, under his chained feet, is a puddle of blood. Lots of blood!

'Duncan, the men are about to storm in! I see you, baby! Can you look up at the camera? Can you make any kind of movement to let us know that you hear me?' I plead with him while Kole is talking to the men.

The tiniest of movement is seen when he tries to put weight on his feet but ends up slipping on his own blood. My heart leaps when I see him move and I know that he will be okay.

Next thing I know, all hell breaks loose as the Elite come crashing in through windows and doors. Mika's men are grabbing their weapons, a lot of them don't make it to their weapon before they are taken out. The order was to take out everyone and by golly, that's exactly what they are doing! Call me sadistic, but I watch the scene unfold with a big smile plastered on my face.

THIRTEEN

DUNCAN

As I hang here in chains, bleeding to death, my body no longer able to heal, because I can't get any blood in my system, I wonder how the fuck I am going to get out of this fucked up situation. Mika beat me with chains for a good half hour, until he got called away. I am slowly healing, but the more blood I lose, the weaker I get.

I am weak and can barely move. Not sure how much longer I can hold out, but I know I have to try. Then I hear an angel, my angel, calling out to me through our bond and I literally want to cry. I am so happy to hear her voice! It's hard to communicate and I have to drag out each word to make sure she hears it, but I do get it out, and she tells me that my brothers are coming for me and to hold on.

At last, Jill tells me that the guys are here and then I hear a commotion and everyone scrambling around. Gunshots are fired, screams are heard and then I hear my name and footsteps running towards me. I look out my one good eye, the other swollen closed from getting punched too many times. Raven and Xavier are at my side trying to pick the locks.

I shake my head, "No, free... the... women... first."

"Sorry buddy, but you are in worse shape than they are." Raven is trying to get me to drink blood, but my lips are cut open and swollen like my eye and it's hard to drink anything, "You need to drink this bag. Jill will be pissed if you waste the blood she made me take from her so you could have it!"

The picture I got in my head from that statement tickles me, because I know how much Jill likes her blood drawn. The fact that she did this for me makes me double my efforts and drink it down. Mm, it tastes like her. I have missed her so much! I finally drink it all down and hold off drinking more until they have me out of the chains. I fall into both of their arms, because I have no strength to hold myself up and next thing I know, I am cradled between the two of them and being carried out the door. A van is at the entrance with a stretcher, and I am laid down on it, straps going around me to hold me in. Both Raven and Xavier lift the stretcher up and into the van.

"Raven, you and Ryder go with Duncan and get him back to the Compound as fast as you can. I am going to stay here and help clean house." I hear Xavier give the order and I am trying to think of who this Ryder person is that is coming with us, but my brain is foggy.

I grab Xavier's arm before he moves away, "Save the women... they were raped... and brutalized... by these... men."

"Don't worry, Dunc. I will bring them all back to the Compound with us. You just worry about yourself, buddy." He looks to Raven next, "Call Dr. Howard and tell her you will be needing her assistance."

"Will do!" Raven replies and then we are off. "Ryder, I don't care how many traffic laws you have to break, just get us home fast!"

There is that name again, Ryder. How do I know that name? I pass out before I can think on it anymore.

I wake up to find something warm snuggling up to my side and I breath in deeply, smelling the sweet scent of wildflowers. I don't need to look to know that my mate is the one laying with me. The stubborn woman is probably going against doctor's orders by being in my bed. I try to talk, but my mouth is too dry, but Jill feels my movement and lifts her head to look at me.

"Oh my God, Duncan, you are awake!" Tears flood her eyes, "How do you feel?"

"Water," It's all I can whisper. She brings a straw to my lips, and I suck it down. The cool liquid feels so good on my dry throat.

"Don't drink too fast, baby."

I let the straw slip from my lips and look up at her, "Kiss me." I say a little louder this time. That is all I want to do right now, is to feel her lips against mine.

"Your lips aren't completely healed yet, I can't." Her eyebrows crinkle together.

"Don't care. I need… to feel them."

She brings her head down slowly, and taking care not to push down too hard, grazes her lips with mine for a feather light kiss. I close my eyes and revel in the feel of having her lips on mine again. I try to lift my arm to embrace her, but they feel heavy and sore.

"Don't try to move too much, baby. You still have a lot of healing to do. You haven't had much blood. I have been laying with you, hoping you would wake up and feed. Here, take what you need." She moves her hair to the other side and leans in, so her neck is against my mouth.

I hesitate, because I don't feel right taking her blood this way. It only feels right when I am making love to her.

"Please Duncan, just take it. You need it to heal!" She pleads with me.

Her scent is calling out to me, and her pulse quickens. I lick her vein and slowly sink my fangs into her. Ah… sweet paradise. I hear her moan with each pull and can smell her arousal. What I wouldn't give to be able be inside of her right now.

Just as I am retracting my fangs, we are rudely interrupted by Jax, "Whoa there, big guy, none of that until you are healed!" He jokes because of the raging hard on I am sporting right now. I flip him off the best I could.

"Glad to see you're awake and trying to get laid already." Jax snickers

"Leave him alone Jax, he just woke up." Jill scolds him on my behalf.

"This is the best time to give him shit! He can't retaliate." He winks at me and smiles.

"Fuck off asshole..." I croak out.

"Just messing with you, buddy. You gave us quite a scare, even worse than last time! Were you on a suicide mission or what?" Jax's worried look makes me change the smartass comment I had for him.

"No. I was just scoping the place out, but they must have seen me, because when I turned to leave, they shot a tranquilizer dot at me. Gave me a double dose of elephant tranquilizers. Put me out for ten whole minutes." I take another drink of the water Jill offers, "Thanks, baby." I smile at her.

"Well, fair warning, Taven is not too happy with you."

"I figured as much. It was a dumb move, but I was going crazy sitting in that hotel room."

Jill turns her head the other way, knowing I was there because of her, "Hey, look at me angel. This is not your fault! I was just trying to give you space. I thought that my presence wasn't helping, so I ran out. I am to blame for everything."

"We can talk about this later, Duncan. Just concentrate on getting better."

"You are to blame for one thing," Kai states as he and the rest of the Elite come strolling through the door, "This little stunt you pulled cost me fifty bucks! You couldn't wait another week, could you? That's a hundred and fifty that I have lost in the last week!"

"Is it now? Where did the other hundred go?" I asked a little confused.

"To the little sneaky hustler you call your mate! Swindled it right out from under my nose!"

"Hey, it's not my fault you have a gambling problem. Maybe you should hear what the bet is first before you place it!" Jill smiles sweetly at him. She proceeds to tell me what the bet entailed, and I burst out laughing and then start coughing and groaning from the pain it causes.

"Look what you are doing Kai! Be good or you can get your happy ass out of this room!" Jill scolds him.

Raven walks in, "You all should be letting him rest."

"Yes, exactly and I need you men to pull out all the spare cots and air mattresses that you can find and set them up in the gym for the women." Taven says as he walks through the door. All the guys start filing out again, saying their goodbyes.

"Jill, I am pretty sure I told you to stay off his bed." Raven cocks a brow at her.

"She stays right where she is at." I respond and Jill sticks her tongue out at Raven, making him roll his eyes at us.

"Fine! How are you feeling? Did you feed when you woke up?" Raven is looking down at his clipboard as he asks me these questions.

"Just really sore, like I got beat up with spiked chains and yes, my sexy nurse here, gave me my feeding." I give Jill a devilish smile.

"Jill, can you move for just a moment? I want to examine his chest and see if it's healing." Jill hops off and Raven brings my covers down to reveal the bandages covering my torso and chest. Being careful not to hurt me, he slowly peels the bandages away and I hear Jill gasp. I look over at her and she has her hand covering her mouth.

"Am I that grotesque?" I wink at her.

"Baby, why haven't you healed? And no, it still looks better than your ugly mug."

"There's my girl! I will heal once I get more blood into my system, but I'll probably have a few scars from this one I'm afraid. No worries though, they will just add to the appeal."

"Damn, shit is getting deep in here! Better remember to wear my boots next time…huh?" Raven jokes.

Finally, when we are alone again, Jill hops back up and snuggles me again. Now, that I have had fresh blood, I am able to wrap my arms around her. I press a kiss to her forehead and flinch at my sore lips, "I love you, baby. I want you to know how deeply sorry I am about the camera situation. To be completely honest, yes, I knew they were there, but when I am with you like that, I forget everything, nothing else matters but you and me. I promise to try harder next time."

"Don't! So, Kole got a few free peep shows, so what? I shouldn't have taken it as far as I did. I guess I was really more embarrassed than anything and I took it out on you. I was miserable sleeping by myself every night. I blame myself for everything." She kisses my chest and rubs her hand up and down my side.

"Darlin, as much as I would love to be inside of you right now, I honestly don't think I have the strength and big guy down there doesn't realize it." I chuckle.

"Why Mr. McPherson, you are the most randy guy I have ever met in my life!" She smirks at me.

"When I have a delectable piece of ass rubbing me up and down, then yes, I do get a little randy."

"A little?" She cocks a brow at my arousal.

"Do me a favor? Bring those lips over here now." I demand and as always, she concedes.

JILL

The next morning while Duncan is still sleeping, I go down to the gym to see if any of the women need help with anything. Taven explained to them that it would be in their best interest to stay under protected custody until the Elite makes sure all involved are caught. Unfortunately, Mika was not at the warehouse anymore by the time the Elite showed up, so he had gotten away yet again. A few others ran off as well, but the death count was fifty-two. What they did with all those bodies, I don't even want to know, but I am glad that a big percentage of them have been destroyed.

Although Taven strongly recommends that the women stay put, he does allow them to leave if they really need to, it is their choice. All but five women have left, and we are now in the process of moving them to actual rooms. We have three rooms available so four will have to double up and one will get her own. There is one woman which has not spoken to anyone yet and is very edgy when any of the men are around. I fear the worst has happened to her. Dr. Howard examined them all last night, but this one wouldn't let anyone touch her.

I walk over and sit on the cot across from her. Looking at her closely, she looks to be only about nineteen, maybe twenty years of age. She is a pretty little thing with an athletic body, thick, blonde, wavy hair and light blue eyes. There is a bruise on the right side of her cheek and bruising around her wrists. I frown at the thoughts going through my head, thoughts of Ir time and another girl who was held captive by the same people. I shake it off and look back at the woman.

"Hello, my name is Jill. What's yours?" I ask in the softest voice possible, but she remains quiet. "Do you remember the man that they had chained up at the warehouse?" This time she slowly shakes her head yes, "He is my husband. His name is Duncan. He is wanting to make sure you were doing okay, so I told him I would find out for him. He is in the medical ward healing from the beatings."

Just as I am about to give up, she speaks, "I am glad he is healing. I was worried he wouldn't make it. He tried breaking free to help me, but of course he was in chains, and no one can break through chains, but I am grateful that he at least tried."

"That's my Duncan, always to the rescue. I just wish he would keep his self out of trouble." I giggle. She gives me a small smile, "What is your name?"

"Alexandria Murphy, but my friends call me Alex."

"Such a pretty name. Do you live in Augusta?"

"I am originally from New Hampshire, but I went to school at UMA and was in the MLT Program. I just graduated. I was actually out celebrating when I was taken." A sad expression comes over her face.

"You know, I was kidnapped a little under a year ago and held captive for a few months before Duncan and Jax found me. Mika was my warden, so I can probably guess and relate to what you went through a little bit. I am so sorry that this happened to you. Are you sure you don't want to be checked by Dr. Howard"

"Not yet, I can't."

"It's okay, take your time, hon. Hey, you wanna know something funny?"

She just looks at me and so I continue, "Mika is dickless. Well, I don't know if he lost the whole thing, but I shot him right where it counts and now, he can't use it!"

Alex's eyes widened and then she bursts out laughing, "You didn't. Did you really?"

"I did, right after he shot my husband in the back with a crossbow. My husband is the one that took Mika's arm the day he found me. It really pisses me off that he keeps slipping through our fingers, but we are getting closer. No worries, we will get him."

"I'm scared, Jill. Scared to go back to my life."

"You can stay here as long as you need to, okay?"

"Thank you! I don't know how to ever repay all of you."

"Don't worry about that. Just concentrate on putting yourself back together. It will take time, but you can do it, I promise. Now, how about I help you get settled into your own room?"

"Sounds good. What do they use this room for anyway? It looks like a gym."

"It's exactly what it is. This is where we train. We also have a weight room and a sparring room where we practice with weapons."

"You are an Elite too?" She looks surprised.

"Well, I'm in training anyway. I train with the men every day. I am the only woman among all these fine ass men! Don't tell my hubby that I said that." I wink at her, "I started training after my own incident. I wanted to be able to protect myself and I fell in love with the lifestyle, so I continue to do it. It's helped me overcome my fear after my ordeal. You are more than welcome to join whenever you want."

"Maybe I will, but I need time to myself first. Thank you again for everything."

"Pfft... enough with the thank yous. Let's get you settled in."

Once I have Alex settled in, I stop in the kitchen to grab some breakfast for Duncan and head to the medical ward. He is sitting up when I walk in, and he graces me with his sexy smile, "Well good morning handsome! I brought you some food to get in that belly of yours." I set the tray down on the table beside the bed and he grabs my arm to pull me up on the bed.

"I only need one thing right now." He says before claiming my lips with his. God, I have missed his passionate kisses; I open up for him.

After a moment, I pull away slowly, "You know, we really need to talk about your caveman-like tendencies." I chuckle.

"Oh, admit it, you love the caveman in me."

"Maybe, but not when you are supposed to be healing. Now, first things first. I want you to feed before you eat your breakfast."

"Only if you bite me too."

"It kind of defeats the purpose if I feed from you while you are taking my blood to heal. We will hold off until Raven gives us the green light and he won't give the green light if you are not healing properly, so eat up!" I offer him my neck, but he shakes his head no, "What do you mean no?"

"I'll feed, but I want to pick the spot." He wiggles his eyebrows at me.

"You are incorrigible!" I laugh but get up off the bed and walk to the door to lock it, "How do I turn off the camera?"

Flashing me a smile, "There should be a button under the camera."

I drag the chair over to stand on and switch the button to off. Walking back to the bed, "Now, where were we? Oh yes, you were about to feed."

"Straddle me, baby."

"I don't want to hurt you!"

"The only thing you are going to hurt are my feelings if you don't straddle me now."

I carefully swing my leg over and straddle him. I have barely touched him, and he is already hard as a rock! He kisses me tenderly and then starts to make his way down my neck. I feel his fingers rub against my sensitive spot through my shorts.

"I need you to take these off for me."

"Duncan! I can't do that! What if we get caught?"

"You locked the door, didn't you?"

"Yes but.."

"No buts, do it now before I rip them off you." I pull my shorts and panties off and his hand is back playing in my already wet folds.

"Mm, already wet for me." He pulls my shirt over my head and licks me through my lacey bra. His hand picks up tempo and his mouth moves to my other tit, causing a moan to slip out of my mouth. He pulls my bra down and latches onto a nipple. I am soaked at this point, and he has a finger thrusting in and out. I throw my head back with another moan and that's when I feel his fangs sink into me.

Heat starts to build, and I tingle all over with each pull he takes. Next thing I know, he is sliding me onto his cock, and I gasp, "You are not supposed to be doing this!" I hear him chuckle as he picks up speed. My body is on fire as he pulls from my breast and slams into me over and over at the same time. I'm there and I'm taking him with me. He thrusts one last time, seeding himself deep in my pussy while he gives me his load. I cry out, "Yes, Duncan! Oh, my God, yes!" He retracts his fangs and smiles at me as my body continues to quiver while I come down. He takes my mouth again in a tender kiss.

"I've missed you so much!" He says and hugs me to him.

"I've missed you too, I'm sorry."

"Stop apologizing, baby. It's done and over with and we will never allow it to happen again, agreed?"

"Agreed, I love you, Duncan."

A few minutes later, I pull away from him and get dressed. I give him his breakfast and we chit chat while we eat. I am so glad that we have this chance once more. Yes, we will have our fights, but never again will I ever go to bed without my warrior!

FOURTEEN

DUNCAN

The morning after my incident, Jill and I have a nice long chat about the woman that had been raped while I was there. I have yet to see the gal that Jill talks to, but it sounds like the one that I had witnessed being used and violated. Jill has done good using me as an excuse to get the woman to talk to her, even if it is a fib. I do want to know how she is doing; I just haven't voiced it yet.

I'm making it a point to go and visit her before I am completely healed, so she won't ask questions about my quick recovery. Raven is against it, but I promise to stay in the damn wheelchair the whole time. I feel like an invalid having Jill push me down the hallway, but it looks better this way while playing a beaten-up guy. Besides, I think it makes Jill feel better being able to take care of me.

We meet Xavier coming down the hall as we near Alex's room. I haven't had a chance to talk to him since he helped me out of the building, so I stop him as he is passing, "Hey buddy! Thank you for all that you did for me, I owe you one."

"I only acted like any one of us would have when a brother is in trouble. No thanks needed. Glad to see you healing nicely." He smiles.

"Still, thank you. You….", I don't finish what I'm about to say, because at that moment I get a whiff of fresh blood, "Do you guys smell that?" I ask Jill and Xavier.

They both sniff the air, "Yeah, I do." Xavier replies.

"Is that blood?" Jill asks looking confused.

"Yes, it is, and it smells like it's coming from Alex's room!"

Xavier is quick as he throws Alex's door open. Her room is empty, but the bathroom door is ajar, and the light is on. I tell Jill to go check on Alex, in case she isn't decent. I doubt Alex would appreciate a man barging in on her if she is naked.

Jill hurries to the bathroom door and knocks, "Alex, it's Jill. Can I come in?" No response, so Jill opens the door. Her scream vibrates through the room and both Xavier and I jump into action. I knock the wheelchair over jumping out of it. The sight before us as we enter is terrifying. Alex must have decided that she could not deal with the gang raping and thought to take the easy route. She lays before us in a tub full of water, blood running from both wrists.

Xavier rushes over to her and checks for a pulse, "It's faint, but she is fading fast! We need to make a decision now!" He looks to us for the answer.

Jill has grabbed a towel and is now holding them to Alex's wrists trying to stop the blood flow. She looks at me, pleading with her eyes.

"The question is, would she want this?" I look at Jill since she is the only one who has held a conversation with the woman.

"I honestly don't know! She just graduated college and was looking forward to her future when all this happened! I don't think she could deal with what happened to her, but at the same time, she is so young and has so much potential! If you are asking me if we should change her, then I vote yes!" Her thoughts are my own, so I agree.

Without wasting anymore time, Xavier bites into his wrist and then holds it against Alex's lips. It seems like hours waiting for her to start responding, but it is only a moment later when we see her start swallowing. She continues to drink for a couple minutes before she stops. Jill bandages up her wrists and Xavier throws a towel over her as he picks her up to carry her over to the bed.

"Jill, can you go grab Taven and Raven and bring them here?" Xavier asks.

"Yes, of course!" She replies and leaves, running in search of them.

I look over at my brother, "Is this your first turn?" I ask because of the concern I see etched on his face.

"I tried once before, but it didn't take. That's why I want the others here, in case we need to do more."

I squeeze Xavier's shoulder, "It will be okay. You have done all you can do for now. We just have to let your blood take its course and hope for the best." I look solemnly at Alex laying lifeless in the bed. Her coloring is looking better, so that's a good sign.

Taven is the first to arrive with Jill and Raven rushing in a moment later, "What the fuck happened?" Taven inquires.

"We don't know! We were talking outside her door and smelled the blood. We found her in the bathtub, wrists sliced open." I respond.

"She still had a weak pulse, so we all made an executive decision. I am not sorry for doing it. She is young and has her whole life a head of her. I am not going to let that asshole take it away!" Xavier defends his actions with such emotion, that I wonder if he only did it because of the life he lost the last time.

Raven is sitting beside Alex checking her vitals. He lifts her eyelids to look at her pupils and then looks up at all of us, "I think she is going to be fine. Her vitals are a little low, but they are getting stronger. I'm going to run and grab some pain meds to make her a little more comfortable, but someone will need to stay with her and give her another dose every half hour for the next two hours. I will know more when she wakes up."

"I'll stay." Xavier volunteers, "I am responsible for her, since I am the one that changed her."

"Okay then," Raven stands, "Text me if there are any changes."

"Same here." Taven requests.

"I will."

"Would you like any company? I can stay too." Jill offers.

Xavier smiles at Jill, "No, that's okay. Go tend to your mate... and get him back into that wheelchair!" He winks at me as he finishes his sentence, so I flip him off.

We all leave the room, leaving Xavier with his patient. Man, I wouldn't want to be in his shoes when she wakes up and learns that she is now a vampire! He can take it though. He is the best man for the job, but it's going to be a long road for him, trying to train a newly made vamp. Especially one that has been through what she went through, but she will live and will eventually get her life back together. She seems like a strong woman, just like my angel. I smile as I glance up at my mate.

"What's that smile for?" she asks.

"Just thinking of how strong you are and how far you have come since your own ordeal. I am one lucky son of a bitch, having you as my mate and spending eternity with. Wouldn't want anyone else."

"Well, you are stuck with me regardless." She smiles back at me and winks.

"Can we stop off at our room? I need to grab something."

"Sure." She wheels me into our room and walks around me, "What do you need, I'll grab it."

I flash to the door and close it softly and then flash to her as she is turning around to face me. I pull her into my arms and grab her ass, squeezing it as I ground my arousal against her. "Oh, I think I can grab it just fine on my own!"

"You, warrior, are a little sneak!" Jill giggles.

"No, I am just in need for some serious one on one attention from my sexy nurse!" I give her my best devilish grin.

"Oh? What exactly is it that you need?"

"I am feeling a little out of breath, maybe a little mouth to mouth to help with my oxygen levels?"

"I don't think it works that way, but I can give it a try." She reaches up and takes my lips with her own. Still grabbing her ass, I lift her up and she locks her ankles behind my back. She breaks away from my lips long enough to tell me that I need to get back into bed. I oblige and sit down on the edge of the bed and laying back, keeping her straddled atop.

She sits up, "You seem to be doing much better with your breathing. Is there anything else that I can do for you?" Her flirtatious smile makes me even harder.

"Actually, I am cold. All the way down to my bones," I look down towards where our crotches meet, "I think I need some skin-on-skin body heat to help warm me up." I wiggle my brows at her.

"I think I better ask for a pay raise for going above and beyond in helping my patients." She grabs the bottom of her shirt and lifts it over her head. She's wearing a plain white cotton bra underneath and that goes next.

My hands go straight for the silky globes and massage them, squeezing her nipples as I do so. I drag one finger down her flat torso and stop at the top of the workout shorts that she is wearing, "Let me help you with these." I say as I let my claw out and drag it down, ripping the material as I go.

She blows out air, "I really liked these shorts you know!"

"I'll buy you ten pairs." My claw retracts once I have torn all that was needed, but I keep my finger at her heated core, feeling the dampness within her folds, "Ah, seems like this nurse is all hot for her patient! That's against the rules, you should be punished." I grab hold of her torn shorts and rip them away completely, but as I bring my hand back, I slap her ass and she gasps, "Now, how about warming me up!"

She swiftly removes my shirt when I lift my arms up and then comes up on her knees so she can pull down my sweats, just enough for my cock to pop out, "I think I had better warm up the most important part first." She says as she wraps the base of my cock with her hand and slides down my body.

"Oh nurse, my face is pretty cold. Can I use your muff to keep warm while you are down there?"

My words make her chuckle, but she swings her body around and settles her pussy over my mouth. I am in fucking heaven as I begin lapping up her wetness. She licks the precum off the tip before sinking her warm mouth down onto my cock. My stomach clenches as she slides almost all the way down, swirling her tongue as she goes. Fuck! This feels so good. It's been so long since I've felt her mouth around me.

I start fucking her with my tongue as I rub at her sensitive nub. I reach with the other hand and rim her back door, running my finger through her juices and then back up to enter her bud. She moans and it vibrates my cock, making me jerk. We both start grinding our hips against each other's mouths as the fire builds between us. She pumps the base of my cock vigorously as her mouth moves up and down to the same tempo. I'm thrusting into her ass and pussy with the same rhythm, if not harder and faster. I feel her body tighten as it gets ready to explode, so I pump my hips harder into her mouth, so we can come together. Just a few more thrusts and we are there, shooting out over the edge. I grind my hips, so my cock is at the back of her throat, and I let myself go as her vagina soaks my mouth with her cum. Her swallowing motions are keeping me going and I groan at the sensation of it.

Her mouth slides off my cock once she has swallowed the last drop and turns herself around, slipping my still hard shaft into her wet sheath. She begins to move up and down, while licking her own nectar from around my mouth. Now that is fucking hot! A woman who loves to taste herself, fuck! I turn, flipping her to her back. I hitch my arm under one of her legs and bring it up higher, opening her up so I can reach her very core. I keep my pace slow and steady, circling my hips as I thrust in and out. I feel the need to take it slow, to make slow, sensual love to this breathtaking woman. My own body quivers as I move inside of her, and her walls suction my cock.

She arches her back and I dip my head capturing her nipple with my mouth, swirling my tongue around it and then sucking. She's moaning my name, begging me for her release, but I keep my pace and move to the other nipple, "God Duncan, I can't take anymore, please!"

I release her nipple, "What? You don't like that?" I tease.

"Yes! Very much, but I need to come. It feels so good!"

"Bite me first and I will put an end to the torture." My voice is just above a whisper.

"I can't. You're not healed completely yet." Her eyes are closed, and she arches her body again.

I nip at her nipple, causing her to suck in a quick breath, "I need to feel our bond, baby. I've missed it. Please do this for me and I will make you come so hard. You want that, don't you?" I look into her glazed eyes as she nods her head yes. I lean down lower while keeping tempo, "Go ahead and sink those gorgeous fangs into me, love. Now!"

I feel the pinch and then complete ecstasy washes over me and I sink my own into her neck. I can't help but to thrust into her harder as she pulls my very essence into her. I reach my climax first, causing hers to crash over her at the same time. My favorite part is coming together. She retracts her fangs, but I keep mine in, taking a few more pulls and tearing yet another orgasm from her. Finally, I pull out of her neck, but not her pussy and I roll to my side behind her, pulling her up against me. We fall asleep with her wrapped in my arms just like we always do.

JILL

I wake up to Duncan's phone buzzing like crazy, so I answer it. It's Xavier letting us know that Alex is waking up. I thank him and hang up. Duncan is already moving inside of me, and I lay back down, enjoying the feel of his cock. I start grinding my ass against him, "You like that don't you?" He whispers in my ear.

"Very much so, but that was Xavier. Alex is waking up." I am breathlessly trying to convey the message.

"Well, then I guess we better make this a quick one. Are you ready for it, baby?"

"Give me all that you've got, warrior."

I asked for it! He lifts my leg and bends me forward for better access and he just starts ramming the fuck out of me from behind! I am trying to muffle my screams with the bedding as he slams me over and over, "You want more? I can give you so much more." He states.

"YES! I want more. I want your vampire to fuck me!" I beg.

"Fuck, I love you and this god damn pussy of yours! Hold on tight, baby, here we go!" He warns and lets loose, taking me in vamp speed. In no time at all, we are both screaming as we are tossed over the edge, "FUCK ME, BABY! Hell yes! That's it, come on my dick, it feels so good!"

"OH... Oh... Oh... Fuck Duncan! I can feel you filling me up! Oh, My Fucking God!" I scream, no longer muffling my cries.

We crash down together and lay spent for a moment, "I didn't hurt you, did I angel?" He swipes a strand of hair that falls over my eye and hooks it behind my ear.

"No. As always, you did everything just right."

"Mm... you are my everything. Do you know that? Stay right here, I'll get you a cloth to clean up." He kisses my temple and pulls away. He grabs a wet cloth from the bathroom and returns to the bed, "Lay still, baby. Let me do it." He spreads my legs and runs the cloth over my folds and then cleans the entrance to my pussy. He finishes by cleaning my inner thighs and then heads back to the bathroom and cleans himself off before throwing it into the hamper.

We get to Alex's room about fifteen minutes after the call, "Well, it's about time." Xavier scolds us, but smirks afterwards.

"Sorry, we were kind of in the middle of something." Duncan explains.

"Uh yeah, I know. I heard you." He gives a full belly laugh, "I think the whole Compound heard you!"

"Oh, my God, how embarrassing!" I mumble and cover my face.

"No need to be embarrassed, it's perfectly normal. I'd be very disappointed in my boy here if I didn't hear it!" Xavier shakes with laughter.

I just shake it off and turn my attention to Alex's empty bed, "Wait. Where is she?"

"She needed the restroom." He nods towards the door.

"How is she doing?" I whisper.

"She's kind of groggy right now. Doesn't remember much of anything. I was hoping you would get here soon so we can explain together. Raven is supposed to be on his way also."

Just then, the bathroom door opens, and Alex comes walking out rubbing her eyes, "Wow, I am a popular girl today! To what do I owe this pleasure?" She almost seems normal. Maybe in her transition, she forgot about her ordeal. This ought to be fun.

"We just wanted to see how you were feeling is all." I say nonchalantly.

"Oh, well I am feeling a little tired and my head feels foggy. How long have I been out for?"

"Only a couple of hours. Do you remember anything from earlier?" It was Xavier that spoke up and asked.

"What do you mean? Of course, I do. Why do you ask?"

"What do you remember from earlier?" Again, it's Xavier who asks.

"I woke up and had breakfast. I remember my muscles were kind of tight so I decided to soak in a hot bath. I thought maybe I would go and check out the training session when I was done and see if it was something I'd be interested in. Then I was waking up in my bed."

I spoke up before Xavier could ask another question, "So, you remember everything that has happened this past week? Am I correct?"

"Unfortunately, yes. What's with all the questions? You are kind of freaking me out!"

"We don't really know how to tell you this without just coming right out with it, but we found you in the bathtub unconscious. You had slit your wrists, Alex." I probably could have worded it better, but I just wanted to get it out there.

Alex looks around at all of us and then bows her head, "I thought I had dreamed it." But then her head pops up and she looks at her unbandaged wrists, "Is this some kind of joke? Why isn't there a mark on either of my wrists then, if I slit them?" She holds them up to show us.

"Nice one!" Duncan says as he looks at Xavier, who shrugs it off, "Why don't you do the honors of explaining this one to her."

Xavier's eyes bulge out and I know that he isn't comfortable being the one to tell her, "I will explain it, don't worry." I let him off the hook.

"Someone better start explaining something soon!" Wow, I'm thinking the vamp in her is starting to come out already! This is not her usual attitude.

"Did Mika or any of his men tell you why you and the other women were taken?" I figured I would start with this.

"They would ramble on about vampire's and mates and other rubbish. I don't know the real reason or the method to their madness."

"You are right about one part… they are mad… among other things, but they weren't lying about the vampire part." I had to stop her from interrupting me by holding up my hand. "Please let me explain everything first, okay?"

She nods her head and I continue, "The vampire's they were talking about, are not the ones that are in all the stories you hear, but Mika and his followers believe them to be and that is why they became Hunters. You see, there are humans out there that have a little something extra in their DNA, which makes them a little different. They are stronger, faster, their senses are magnified tenfold and they do need blood to survive, BUT they don't go around killing people by draining their blood. They still need to eat regular food and sleep. They heal faster and they can heal others… to an extent. These types of humans are not to be feared. Actually, there are quite a few who spend their life protecting both innocent vamps and regular people. Just like there are murders out there and other bad people, a few vamps do take up that lifestyle as well, so those are the ones that need to be hunted and destroyed. Mika and his group, they are monsters who need to be stopped."

I am not sure how to take the expression on her face. It's a mixture of both fear and awe. "Are you okay? I know it's a lot to take in, but you need to know about this. We keep the vampires a secret, because nobody understands and they fear the unknown and, also by what they read."

"So, you are telling me that vampires are real, but not killers?"

"Yes, that is what I am telling you." Then I really get confused, because her face lights up in a huge smile.

"Are they all hot as well? You know, like in all the vampire romance books?" She is giddy by this revelation, apparently. I decide to let the cat out of the bag.

"Well, you have seen the Elite, haven't you?" I ask.

"You mean to tell me that they are even more hotter than the Elite?" She is almost screeching with excitement.

"No, you don't understand," I chuckle and look at the guys who are smiling, "The Elite ARE vampires!"

"Oh, my God, Shut the fuck up!"

FIFTEEN

DUNCAN

Giving Alex the low-down on vampires is not as bad as I had expected. Jill does a great job explaining what we are and what we are not, but there is still a lot to explain, which we will leave up to Xavier to do, since he is her maker. As good of a job that Jill does on the first part, I can tell that she is struggling on the next step, telling Alex that she is now one of us. I decide that I will take it from where she leaves off.

Grabbing Jill's hand in mine and squeezing, I use our bond quickly, 'Love, I can take it from here. You did a great job, but you don't have to be the one to tell her that she is now a vampire. I'll do it.'

'Thank you. I just can't find the right words.' I squeeze her hand again.

"Alex, you understand why we can't tell people about us, right?" I want to know if she truly understands why.

"Yes, I understand, and I promise not to tell anyone. Not that anyone would believe me anyway."

"Good. Now, this is a little difficult to tell you and we are not sure how you are going to take it, but here it goes. We did find you in the bathtub with your wrists slit. Luckily, we found you in time and you still had a faint heartbeat. Xavier gave you his blood. If we would have gotten there any later, you would be dead."

She turns to Xavier and smiles, "Thank you for what you did, I don't know how I will ever be able to repay you."

"There is no need. I did what we thought would be best for you." Xavier responds with a smile.

"Of course, saving me would be best for me, silly!" She giggles.

"Alex," I get her attention back, "The only way that we were able to save you was to give you blood. Because you were just about drained of your own blood and on the brink of death, by giving you vampire's blood, you are now one of us."

"So, I am now considered family, right? That's what you are saying?" Damn her blonde is really showing through her brain, I think to myself.

"Yes, you are part of our family, and you are now also a vampire." I just have to put it out there, because she is not catching on very quickly.

"I am a… vampire?" She looks as if she has just been told that she is dying. I feel bad but ripping the band aid off is always the best way, I think.

"Yes, you are one of us now."

"But I don't feel any different." Her lip trembles a little bit.

"It can take up to twenty-four hours for the change to be complete, but your senses will most likely be magnified by morning, so don't be alarmed." I try to reassure her.

Jill jumps in and grabs her hand when it looks like Alex is about to break down, "This is not a bad thing, Alex. Just think of all the possibilities you now have and that you didn't have before! You can do whatever you want and not be afraid. You can take on any attacker, you have an eternity to live your life. Once you find your destined mate, you can have a family with kids and all!"

"But I have to drink blood from people. I don't know if I can do that." Her voice cracks.

"No Alex, you don't have to. The first time it does have to come from a human or an animal, it has to be fresh, but after that, you can drink from blood bags. You can drink from me your first time, since I am your maker." Xavier explained to her.

"Trust me, Alex. I could not stand the sight of blood before I met Duncan, and now, I love drinking his blood!" Jill smiles at me lovingly.

"You're a vamp too?"

"Oh no, but I am his destined mate. I have to drink his blood to keep the bond between us."

"You have fangs too?"

Jill gives an embarrassed giggle, "Yes. I need them so when we are intimate, I can drink from him to keep the bond."

I cut in to save her, "Our mates take on some of our traits once we are fully bonded. Jill's senses are also heightened, but not as much as ours. We can also remain in contact with each other with our thoughts. That is how I was able to send for help. They had no idea where I was until Jill and I spoke through our bond."

"Wow, that is pretty neat, I guess."

Raven and Taven walk in finally. Those fuckers could have come a little sooner and helped out! They probably did it on purpose.

"I assume they told you what happened?" Taven asks Alex. Yep, that's exactly what they did, pussies!

"I am sure you have a lot of questions, but right now it's best that you feed and get some rest. We will bring you some dinner when you are hungry." Raven informs her.

Jill and I slip out as Alex is being examined, "My God, I never want to go through that again!" I smile at Jill as I lace my fingers through hers.

"I totally agree with you! All this talk about food and now I am hungry." As if on cue, her stomach growls loudly.

"Geesh… we better get food in that belly of yours then!" I pick her up and flash us to the kitchen. Max is just pulling garlic bread out of the oven for the lasagna that he made, when we walk in.

"Why is it you two are always the first ones in the kitchen at mealtime?" He laughs and shakes his head.

"Hello, you do know who I am mated to, right?" I ask him, but really just teasing Jill.

"And what is that supposed to mean?" She stands there with her hands on her hips.

"Baby, you know that you are a human timer when it comes to food! You always know when it's done. If food is involved, then you are there." I chuckle, "You're lucky you have me to work it all off you!" I wink.

"I really hate it when you are right!" She reaches up and plants a kiss on my cheek.

It's been a full week since the warehouse incident, and everything is back to normal. Well almost. We now have an audience during our training sessions, and I mean all of our training sessions. Whether we are in the gym working on our fighting techniques, in the weight room lifting or sparring with the weapons, the four women that stayed when Alex stayed are always there, watching and giggling behind their hands.

During this afternoon's session, Jill and I are closest to them while we are working on her punches and kicks. I can hear them plain as day and so can Jill. They keep referring to my bare chest and ass. I can't keep the smile off my face every time Jill hears their comments. She gets so mad; I have to keep reminding her to concentrate. When one of them comments on my "package", that is it. Jill throws off her punching gloves and walks up to the woman who made the comment, startling her.

"If you make one more comment about any of MY husband's body parts, I'm going to use you as my punching bag! Do you understand me?"

The woman stands up, not wanting to seem like a pussy in front of all the men. She stands two inches taller than Jill, but my girl doesn't back down. The woman has the audacity to look down her nose at my mate, "Well, maybe if he wasn't so damn hot and half undressed, we wouldn't be making comments! He is too much of a man for you honey. Why don't you send him over here to where the real women can take care of him!"

Oh no, she did not just say that to Jill! Every Elite stops what they were doing, and I already hear the bets going around the room. I turn towards them and mouth my bet. Of course, my bet is on my little hell cat.

"Do you want to say that one more time? And I would honestly rethink your words before opening your mouth!" Jill warns.

"Oh, you poor thing. I see you are deaf as well." She continues in a much louder voice the second time, "I said, he is too much of a man for you. Why don't you send him over here where the real...." That's all Jill allows her to get out before she gives her a right hook right in the jaw and sends the woman flying to the side. The room erupts in laughter. Well, all except for the women, who pick the one up off the floor and starts walking her out.

Jill yells as they leave, "I suggest you all stay out when we are in training! You may get hurt!" More laughter echoes through the gym.

"Thank you for defending my honor, baby!" I tease her.

"If you weren't so damned hot, I wouldn't have to!" She smiles smugly.

"You do realize that it was an unfair fight? We all knew she didn't stand a chance against you, Darlin." This coming from Kai.

"Yeah, well I gave her a chance to back down. It's her own damn fault! And don't think I didn't hear all of you placing your bets either! That goes for you too, buddy!" She points to me. "You all are lucky that you all placed it on me!" She smiles as she slaps Kai in the chest, "I knew you would finally warm up to me!"

"Hell, that wasn't me warming up to you. That was me not wanting to get my ass kicked by you!" He winks at her, and she just shakes her head.

I pull her to the side, "Do you realize that you called me your husband?"

"You are my husband, aren't you? We are mates."

"Well yes, but I didn't think you would consider me your actual husband until we got married."

"I still want the ceremony, but you are my husband in every sense of the word." She beams at me, and I can't help but to claim her lips right then.

"Get a fucking room already!" Cooper shouts.

"Doesn't matter with those two. We can still hear them even when they are in their own room!" Jayde jokes. Once again, the room fills with laughter.

"We really need to put soundproof padding up in our room." I whisper to Jill.

"Nah, I'm really starting to like annoying them with all of our lovemaking. They are just jealous." She grins and walks out the door.

JILL

I'm just stepping out of the shower when there is a knock at our door. "Jill, you in there?" It is Cassie.

"Bitch, get your ass in here!" I call out to her, and she comes in.

"I hear that I missed some excitement in the gym today?" She cocks her eyebrow at me as she sits on the bed.

"In my defense, I took as much as I could take, and I still gave her a chance to keep her mouth shut."

"Dammit! I was hoping it wasn't true, I can't believe I missed it!"

"Well, if you would get your fat ass to training once in a while, you wouldn't have missed it!"

"I am definitely going to have to get my ass in gear in about five months! I will need to work off all my weight!" She gives me a sideways glance.

It takes me a second to catch on, "Get the fuck out of here! Seriously?"

"Yep, just took the test an hour ago. You are the first to know, so don't say anything please!"

"We have been best friends for most of our lives! You know I'm not a chatty Kathy when it comes to us! I'm hurt that you would even think that!"

"I know, but I mean Jax doesn't even know yet and I didn't want you seeing him before I do and congratulating him."

"Oh, my God, you mean I really am the first to know!" I am all excited now. I was hurt that I wasn't the first to know about her pregnancy with Jillian, but I understood, "I am so happy for you, Bitch!" I bring her in for a bear hug.

Duncan comes walking in, "Am I missing something here?"

I let Cassie go, "No, can't best friends hug?" I wink at her and she rolls her eyes at me.

"I need to go find that husband of mine. Just thought I would pop in and say high to Mike Tyson over here." Pointing her thumb at me.

Duncan laughs, "She was something else, I tell you!"

"I don't doubt it! I will see you guys later." Cassie leaves and Duncan comes over and wraps me in his arms.

"Have I told you lately how much I love you?" He nuzzles my neck.

"Yes, but you can tell me again."

"Such a greedy Hell Cat you are!"

"But I'm all yours! I do feel the need to tell you something though." I frown up at him.

"Uh oh, that doesn't sound good."

"It's bad, really bad!"

"Okay, lay it on me!"

"You, my dear husband, are in need of a shower!"

Duncan throws his head back and laughs, "You are such a smartass! Care to take another one with me?"

"I would love to, but I want to spend some time with Jillian. I have barely seen her this past week!"

"Okay, your loss, babe." He winks at me and heads for the shower. I walk over to the dresser to grab some clothes and I see my birth control sitting on top. Shit! When was the last time I took my pill? I pick it up and count the days. FUCK! I haven't taken them this whole week! Then I think, would it really be so bad having a little Duncan running around? I smile to myself as I pull my clothes out and get dressed.

I run into Liz as I'm coming out of my room, "Hey girlie! I am so sorry I haven't spent much time with you. It's been nothing but chaos around here! How are you and the boys doing?

"Oh, I understand and no worries. I have had Cassie and Taven keeping me company and the boys are doing good. Mimicking all the moves that the Elite do, you know, idols and everything." She laughs.

"Taven huh?"

"Is that the only thing you picked up out of everything I just said?"

I chuckle, "No, I heard you, but I am happy to hear that the two of you are getting along."

"He is different from the other men I have been around. It's kind of nice."

"I hate to say it, but I told you so!" Grinning at her, I elbow her in the side.

"Hey, watch it! I'm not one of those hussies that you can knock around!"

"Jesus, will I not live that down?"

"Not any time too soon, Tyson!"

"Stop calling me that! I didn't bite off her ear for Christ's sake… at least not yet." I smile smugly.

"Okay, I'll give you that! Where are you headed?"

"Looking for my adorable little niece. You haven't seen her, have you?"

"Actually, I have. She is in the rec room… with the women." The expression on Liz's face is comical, like she is ready to get slapped.

"It's all good. As long as the bitch doesn't open her mouth! Wanna come with?"

"Hell, yeah I do!"

I find Jillian right where Liz said I would. Without making eye contact with any of the women, I walk in and start talking to Jillian, "Well, there is my little cutie pie! I have been looking all over for you!"

I look at the woman I hit earlier, and she has a bruise on the right side of her jaw, "Can I please have my niece?"

Apparently, this bitch didn't learn her lesson, because she hugs Jillian to her tightly, "Sorry, but she was left in my care, and I take my job very seriously. You will have to wait."

"Are you seriously going to keep my niece from me? Do you want another ass whooping?"

"You wouldn't touch me with her in my arms!"

"You are right, but you will have to let go of her sometime."

One of the other women speaks up, "Shelly, just give her the baby. She has more right to her than you do."

"Hell no! Her daddy asked me to watch her for a bit and I am keeping her until his fine ass comes back! That right there was some mouth-watering eye candy, if I do say so myself!"

"I am guessing you are looking to get a matching bruise on the other side of that jaw, aren't you?" Cassie comes walking into the room, "Time for some education if you are going to be staying here. Number one, never talk about mine or Jill's husband in that regard ever again! Number two, when my daughter's aunt wants to take her, you give her to her. Last, but not least, I don't want to hear you talk about any of the Elite like they are a piece of meat! You are under their protection, so I highly suggest you treat them with the upmost respect! If I have to ever repeat myself to you, you will find my size ten shoved so far up your ass, it will need to be surgically removed! Do you comprehend what I am saying?"

"Yeah, whatever. Take the brat, I don't even like kids!"

I dive for Cassie, knowing she is pregnant, and stop her from going after Shelly, "Liz, grab Jillian please." Shelly hands the baby off to Liz and I take that second to remind Cassie about her pregnancy, which calms her down.

"What a bunch of hoodlums these men have married! It's such a waste." She stands up and pretends to smooth down a wrinkle or two,

"I don't know how they allow women like you to be mothers, such bad examples!"

That was the last straw! I push Cassie back and back hand the bitch. I stun her for a moment, but now she is coming at me with her claws out. I grab her arm and duck around, twisting it up behind her back, making her go to her knees, "How about you apologize to my best friend about those remarks you just made."

"Fuck you, I don't need to apologize to anyone! If anything, it will be you apologizing to me once I talk to the head Elite and tell him how I have been treated!"

Cassie, Liz, and I all laugh at her statement, "Yep, I would like to see that happen!" I shove her away, causing her to fall on her face, "Get the hell out of here before I change my mind and just beat your ass! Do me a favor, make yourself scarce for the duration of your stay!"

Shelly runs out and goes straight in the direction of Taven's office. I look at the other women, "Are you ladies actually friends with that bitch?" They all shake their head no.

The woman with the red hair responds, "We just try to keep the peace with her, so we don't have to deal with her. She can't really get you into trouble, can she? We can talk to him if need be."

"Thanks, I will be fine. She did the damage to herself." I point up to the camera in the corner of the room, "It's video and audio." I smile and walk out, taking Jillian from Liz on my way.

Well, that takes care of that skank. She will be gone by morning!

SIXTEEN

DUNCAN

All hell breaks loose the following morning when Taven calls us all in for a meeting. Everyone is here except for our four guests and Liz and the boys. I can guess what it is about, but what I want to know is why he is wasting our time over this woman who does nothing, but cause problems?

"Now that we are all here, I want us first to officially welcome Alex, not only to the family, but also to the Elite. She will begin her training tomorrow." We all welcome her into our little clan.

"It's about time we get a female in the building that is easy on the eyes!" Kai winks at Alex.

"What? Are Cassie and I chopped liver or what?" Jill smacks him in the back of the head.

"No, but we don't want to get our asses handed to us from gawking at the two of you!" He defends himself. Jax and I smile at each other.

"Okay, that's enough. We are getting off track here." Taven raises his voice above the snickers, "It's been brought to my attention that one of our guests, which is under our protection, has been attacked multiple times in one day. Jill, what do you have to say for yourself?"

Dear Lord, he did not just call Jill out on being the instigator. Shit! This is not going to be pretty. It sounds like he is taking the woman's side over one of our own and I am not okay with that, even if it wasn't my mate, it still wouldn't be okay. Looking around the room, I can tell the rest of the men feel the same way.

"What do I have to say for myself? Nothing at all, but I do have something to say for the rest of the people in here. That woman has been nothing but a chauvinistic pig all week! We have had to deal with her being at all the training sessions, gawking, drooling and making rude comments all week! You know it's bad when all these single men in here are annoyed with her remarks! I kept my mouth shut, even when she was talking about Duncan's chest and ass, but I drew the line when she started talking about his dick! I gave her a warning and gave her a chance to walk out, and the stupid bitch continued!" She takes in a breath after her rant, but she isn't finished.

"The second time, she wouldn't hand Jillian over to me, because she was waiting for Cassie's husband's "fine ass" to come back, but that wasn't the icing. She had the audacity to tell Cassie that she was a horrible mother and that she should not be allowed to raise kids! Are you going to let this woman talk about us like this? Are you telling us that we have to take it?"

"That is not the story that she told me, Jill." Taven informs her.

"Wait a minute." I spoke up, "Have you not watched any video from these incidents? You called us in here so you can lecture my mate because she stuck up for us?" I am furious with him right now.

"No, I haven't watched any videos, because I am a busy man, but Shelly was very upset and crying. She seemed sincere."

"You know my wife, Taven. Does it sound like her to "attack" a woman over nothing?" I demand an answer.

"You are right, and Jill, I am sorry. I should have looked into it further. I have a busy day ahead of me and wanted to get this meeting over with. I will talk to her again, but she is demanding an apology."

"The only thing she will be getting from me is my foot up her ass if she crosses my path again!" My mate states furiously.

"This kind of puts me in a predicament. Her father is the County Attorney, and she may have him press charges."

"Let them press charges, I'll press my own sexual harassment charges against her!" I warn him. All the guys in the room mumble in agreement.

"Fine! I'll see what I can do, but in the meantime, please steer clear of her." He looks at Jill.

"I am okay with that, but she better keep her nasty mouth closed when I am around."

Taven rolls his eyes, "You all are dismissed. Oh Alex?"

"Yes?" she answers nervously.

"Please don't be a pain in my ass like these two are!" He points to both Jill and Cassie, and they smile at each other.

"Yes Sir!" All of us guys break out laughing at her response knowing that he hates being called Sir by others, and Taven's tick in his jaw starts throbbing.

I throw my arm around Jill's shoulders as we walk out, "You sure are going to make life interesting, aren't you?" I plant a kiss on top of her head.

"Would you want it any other way?" She looks up at me.

"Nope, you are perfect in every way, Baby!"

I look at my phone and see that I have a voicemail, so I go in and check the message. A smile brightens my face and I hang up. Seeing Jax coming down the hall from his suite of rooms, I stop him, "Hey, have you seen Jill at all?"

"Actually, yeah, she's in with Cassie."

"Awesome! Do me a favor and keep her occupied, I have to run out really quick!"

"Will do, Buddy, but be quick. I am a horrible liar."

"Should only be twenty minutes tops." I am informing him of this as I jog towards the front door.

I pull up into a parking spot outside of my destination and I just sit here. I don't know why I am so nervous. I already know Jill is going to say yes and I have been dying to see the ring that they designed for her.

With that being said, I wipe my sweaty palms on my jeans, step out of my SUV, and walk up to the door to the jewelry store. The bell above the door jingles as I enter, and I am welcome by a smiling jewelry clerk.

"Oh, good Duncan, you got my message!" She walks over and shakes my hand, "I have been waiting for you to come in and see what a beautiful job they did designing the engagement ring. I know she will absolutely love it!" The lady steps behind the counter and disappears into a back room while I wait at the counter. She returns less than a moment later with a ring box in her hand. She removes the case from its box and opens it up, setting it down on the counter.

I sit here a second, staring at it, before I take the ring out and examine it. I turn it around in my fingers and bring it up for a closer look. I want to make sure they get every detail correct. It is beyond gorgeous, just like Jill! I smile and place it back into its case, "Thank you very much, it is beyond perfect! Do I owe you anything more?"

"I am so glad you love it. It is definitely one of a kind! You paid for everything already, so you are good to go! Hope to see you again and congratulations!" She smiles at me as I leave.

Now, the next part is to figure out how I'm going to propose. I have to think of something soon, because I can't wait much longer to give her the ring.

I find Jax in the weapons room sharpening his knives, "Jill is still with Cassie, baby planning, if that's what you're wondering." He smiles up at me.

"Another one all ready? Congratulations man!" I beam at him.

"So, when are you and your better half going to have one?" He inquires.

I blow out a breath, "I honestly don't know. I know she wants kids, but she is still on birth control. I thought for sure that as potent as we are, the birth control wouldn't hold up, but I was wrong. It's all good though, we can live with spoiling yours for a while longer and still get to keep our privacy." I tease him, "But hey, I have a surprise of my own." I say as I pull the box out of my pocket and open it for him to see.

He whistles at the sight of it, "Whoa man, you really went all out! I can't believe my big brother is finally going to do it, congratulations!" He slaps me on the back.

"Well, she has to say yes first."

"Come on Dunc, she already refers to you as her husband! Why wouldn't she say yes?"

"You're right, I guess I am just a little nervous."

"So, when are you going to pop the question?"

"I am hoping tonight sometime. I can't wait any longer." I give a nervous chuckle.

"Stop being so nervous… and act normal or else she is going to know something is up!"

"Yeah well, thanks for the chat. I'll catch you later." I squeeze his shoulder on my way out.

I am on my way to go see Jill and Cassie, when I see Shelly coming down the same hall. I try to avoid her as she is passing, but with no such luck, "Well hello Duncan, fancy meeting you in this deserted hallway." She winks at me and stops right in my path.

"Don't even start Shelly. I am not in the mood for you!" I glare at her.

"That's too bad. Come find me when you get tired of the riff raff." She grabs my ass as she walks around me, and I whip around on her.

"Don't you ever talk about my wife that way again, if you know what's good for you! And another thing, you lay a finger on me one more time and you will lose the whole hand!" I spin back around and stomp away, leaving her with her mouth hanging open.

JILL

I have been visiting with Cassie, Jillian, and Liz for most of the morning and afternoon, getting in some much-needed time with them. I assume

Duncan has been busy with the guys since I haven't heard from him, but that's okay. He can use some time with his brothers as well.

I can't believe how much Jillian has grown! She is only eight months old and already has a head full of hair and most of her teeth have already come in. She listens well for her age, more like a two-year old. Not that toddlers listen well at that age, but you get the gist. I am starting to wonder if Dr. Howard really knows what she is talking about when she says that vamp babies grow just like regular babies, because Jillian's growth isn't normal.

My sister and I have been estranged most of our lives and never talk, but I do remember how her two kids grew after they were born, and it was not as fast as this! I am not saying it's a bad thing, but I don't know if Jillian will ever be able to attend a regular school, growing as fast as she is. I voice my concern to Cassie while Liz is checking on the two boys, and she is in agreement with me.

"I guess you will have to start having your own brood so we can open an in-home vamp school for all of them." She jokes. I giggle nervously at her comment, and she looks at me with concern, "Hey, what's wrong?"

"Remember yesterday, when you stopped by? After you left, I went to my dresser to grab my clothes and saw my pills sitting on top. I haven't taken them all week."

"Oh wow! You never forget those, but hey, that doesn't mean anything. They could still be in your system." She tries to reassure me.

"I thought the same thing, until I woke this morning feeling a little nauseous. On top of that, for the last ten minutes, I have been getting little stabbing pains in my gut."

"Oh My God, Jill! You are pregnant!" She loudly whispers.

"Shh! I don't know for sure, and I don't want to get Duncan's hopes up."

"Well, get in my bathroom and use the other test that came in my box. It's in the medicine cabinet. GO!"

I hurry into the bathroom, find the test and tear the package open. It takes me a little bit to actually be able to pee, but I finally get the job done. The instructions say to wait five mins, but the results are shown after one minute. Two lines... positive! I slide down the bathroom wall, not knowing whether to be happy or sad. Of course, I love Duncan and I want to give him children, but on the other hand, am I ready yet? Well, it doesn't matter, because we are having a baby now, so I better make the most of it! I throw the stick in the trash and walk back out to the room. Liz is back and is sitting on the bed with Cassie.

Cassie looks up at me and must be reading my face, because she smiles from ear to ear. Liz looks at the two of us, confused, "What am I missing?"

I walk over to the doorway, look up and down the hall to make sure no one is within earshot and then close the door and lean up against it, facing them both, "I'm pregnant."

"Eek! We are having babies together!" Cassie grabs my hands and starts bouncing up and down.

"I am so happy for you, Jill!" Liz says as she hugs me. They are both all excited, jumping up and down, and I'm over here like, what the fuck... I'm pregnant?

There is a knock at the door and they both go quiet as I put my finger to my mouth. Cassie opens the door to find Duncan on the other side. Shit! Did he hear the conversation, I wonder?

"I am looking for a little short woman, feisty as hell, has a mouth like a sailor, but is the most beautiful woman you have ever seen. Have you seen her?" My heart melts at his description of me.

"Awe, I want a man that describes me like that!" Liz says as she holds her hand to her chest.

"As a matter of fact, yes. She is here and I hope you have come to take her off our hands." Cassie teases.

Duncan walks into the room grinning, "What was all the commotion about when I knocked?"

Cassie quickly answers, "Jax and I are expecting again!"

"Ah yes, he just told me a few minutes ago, congratulations!" He kisses Cassie's forehead, "Sorry, I just had a run-in with your favorite person. It was not pleasant." He walks over to me, "Are you almost ready to go?"

"Yes. You ran into skanky Shelly?" I ask.

"I did, but I really don't want to get into it right now." He plants a kiss on the top of my head.

"Okay. I think I want to take a soak in the tub before dinner, if you don't mind." I look up at him.

"I don't mind, as long as I get to wash that delectable back of yours." I hear a sigh coming from Liz.

"Hey Liz, how is Taven?" I wink at her and wave goodbye as I walk out with Duncan's hand on my back.

I sit on the bed as Duncan starts the bath for me. I am so glad I have him in my life! Who would have thought that I would be sitting here, mated to a smoking hot vampire and carrying his child? Sure the hell not me! It's weird what life throws at you sometimes, but that's my life, full of weird stuff!

Duncan comes over to me and holds out his hand for me to take, "Your bath awaits, my Lady." I chuckle as he walks me into the bathroom. Standing behind me, he lifts my shirt slowly as I hold my arms up. Once it's off, he slides a bra strap down and places tender kisses on my shoulder, "So silky..." he murmurs. He shows the same attention to the other shoulder before unclasping my bra and sliding it all the way off, letting it fall to the floor. Sliding his hands around and to the front, he gently massages both breasts while kissing my neck and I feel a stirring down below. He inhales, "Ah, I think I better stop molesting you before you don't get your soak. The smell of your desire is too tempting." He removes his hands from my breasts and unbuttons my jean shorts, sliding them all the way down. He then kneels behind me and removes my panties as he places little kisses across each of my ass cheeks.

He undresses quickly and then he is here, lifting me up, stepping into the tub and then sliding down, placing me between his legs. We barely fit in the tub together, but we make it work. As I lean against his chest, he begins to wash my front with the loofah, lathering me up with the smell of lavender. I moan because it feels so good to just sit back and relax. The pains in my stomach are still there, but nothing I can't handle. I plan on giving what the baby needs after my bath, so I deal with the discomfort for a bit longer.

"What is it that you want most in this world." Duncan whispers into my ear. It takes me a moment to register the question.

I sigh, "This. These moments right here, for the rest of our lives." My eyes are closed, relishing in the quiet moment with the man that I love. I feel his lips on my neck and I open my eyes to look back at him, but he is holding something in front of me. It takes my eyes a moment to adjust before they widen with surprise at the most gorgeous ring that I have ever seen! I whip my head to the side to look at him and see him smiling at me with all the love in his eyes.

"Will you do me the greatest honor by marrying me?" I watch as so many emotions dance in his eyes while waiting for my response. I look back at the ring as he takes it out of its case and slides it on my finger, "I had it designed especially for you. Do you see the designs on the sides? That is my family's crest. Once you say yes, it will forever be your crest as well. I take pride in it, as I do you and no one else is worthy enough to wear it but you."

Tears roll down my cheeks at his words. I have never heard more of a romantic proposal than his, "Yes..." I croak out. I clear my throat and try again. "Yes, Duncan. I will marry you and I will be honored to wear your family crest upon my finger for eternity." I turn my head towards him, and he claims my lips in a slow, passionate kiss. A moment later I break the kiss, "I love you so much Duncan McPherson... you are my life."

"I never thought I would ever find my mate, and then fate brought you into my life and it has never been the same since. I love you, Jill, my angel." He kisses the tip of my nose and then I turn my head back forward and stare at the ring.

"It really is the most beautiful ring I have ever seen! Thank you for this." A grin forms on my lips, "I am so glad your child has two parents who love each other so much!"

"Yes, our children will know the love that we have for each other and they will never feel unloved themselves." I don't think he is catching on to what I am trying to tell him. I roll my eyes and smile.

I grab his hand and place it on my stomach, hoping he understands, so I wait. I feel his head snap up and the pressure of his hand on my stomach, "Are you telling me what I think you are telling me?" The excitement in his voice warms my heart and I shake my head yes. "Oh, my God, baby, I can't believe it! I thought you were on the pill?"

"I was, but with everything that happened with you and since then, I have forgotten to take it. I noticed yesterday and said screw it. Wouldn't had done any good to start them again since the deed was already done, but I didn't find out until today."

"You are not upset?"

"No, of course not. I mean, I was a little nervous, but I love you and I know you will make a wonderful father, so no, I'm not upset." I smile back at him, "I do need something from you, though."

"Anything you want, love, name it!"

"I want your blood, so these pains can go away!" I chuckle.

His eyes widen, "The baby's hungry? Why didn't you tell me sooner?"

"They have only been minor pains and I planned on taking advantage of you after our bath. I would have gotten the blood needed then."

"You weren't going to tell me about our baby?" He looks very hurt.

"Yes, I was, but wanted to do it in a special way, but then you went and pulled the most romantic proposal ever and I felt I needed to give you back something in return."

Grabbing my hips, he lifts me up and has me turn around and straddle him, bringing my head down to his neck, he tells me to drink. I sink my fangs into him and roll my eyes. His blood is heaven on my taste buds. The pains have stopped now as well. "Fuck baby, that feels so good!" I feel his cock at my entrance a half a second before he thrusts into me and then his own fangs sink into me, making me lose all train of thought.

Water sloshing out over the floor, I'm riding his cock so fast and hard, that in no time at all we both hit our climax and tumble over. We both retract our fangs and sigh, as we just sit here in the aftermath of the very hot quickie. Not wanting him to pull out, but knowing it must be done, I lift myself off him and stand up. He wraps me in a towel, then carries me to the bed where he holds me in his embrace until I fall asleep.

SEVENTEEN

DUNCAN

The last week and a half has flown by and I have been on cloud nine the whole time, thinking about our upcoming wedding and of course, the baby. Dr. Howard will be coming tomorrow to examine Jill and to do an ultrasound. I feel like a kid on Christmas Eve, waiting for Santa Claus to come and I am driving Jill nuts. We tell the guys at our weekly mandatory meeting this morning that both Jill and Cassie are pregnant, and the room explodes in shouts and laughter, congratulations going all the way around. Taven informs Jill afterwards that her training will be limited for now, but that she did not need to quit altogether. That was her biggest fear at the moment, so when she hears that she isn't being pulled all the way out, she is relieved.

"Well, it's a good thing that we bought that land on the outskirt of town and construction will begin in a few weeks." Kole interjects, "Looks like we will be adding some housing units on the property as well. Can't have all these kids running around all the time, we uncles won't get any work done, because we will be too busy playing!" Everyone joins in on his laughter.

"Unless, of course, you guys plan on moving into your own place." Taven asks, kind of looking worried.

"Don't worry," Jill responds, "we don't plan on going anywhere. Although may I suggest making all the suites inside the Compound soundproof for future mates?"

"Definitely!" comes everyone's reply.

As everyone else leaves, Jill and I are the last to head out. Jill stops at the doorway and turns back towards Taven, "You might want to have a third housing unit built for yourself."

He looks confused, "Why is that?"

"Well, for you, Liz and the boys of course!" She winks at him and hurries out the door before he can even respond.

"Can't you control that woman of yours just a little bit?" Taven growls at me.

I chuckle, "What for? She makes everything more interesting!" I wink at him as well and walk out as Taven shakes his head and grins. See, we couldn't move away. He would miss us way too much!

Taven catches up to me, before I round the next corner, "Hey, I meant to ask you something. What do you think we should do with Jenny? We can't possibly keep her locked up the rest of her life."

"If I had my way we would, but I suppose you are right. What are you thinking?"

"I think when Mika is taken care of once and for all, we should set her free. I think by then, she will have learned her lesson."

"I am okay with that, and I am sure Jill will be too. She will just want to move on with her life once it's over."

He slaps me on the back, "I figured you would be okay with it, but I just needed to check."

At that moment we hear voices, loud voices and one of them is Jill's, warning someone to stay away from her. We head towards the kitchen, where the voices are coming from and as we near, Jill speaks, "Shelly, I have nothing to say to you except to stay away from me and my husband. I am done going rounds with you. You are not worth it!"

"What? Do you think you can attack me twice and get away with it? Not a fat chance!"

"I admit that I might have gone overboard, but you deserved it! I could beat your ass right now, but like I said, you are not worth it!"

Taven and I walk through the door and see that Jill is standing up against the refrigerator and Shelly is in front of her, with her back to us. Before we can say anything, Shelly grabs her by the hair and throws Jill, who is taken completely unaware, to the floor and kicks her in the stomach with her pointed boot, "JILL!" I yell and flash to her, throwing Shelly out of the way before she can do anymore damage.

Jill rolls into a fetal position as she howls in pain, "Baby, talk to me! Where is the pain?" All she can do is cry out as I try to move her.

"That's what the bitch gets for attacking me! You don't mess with me!" I turn to look at Shelly, who is being restrained by Taven.

"If my wife loses our baby because of your little tantrum, there will be no place that you can hide that I will not find you!" I growl at her, feeling my vampire trying to come out.

"Duncan! Try and control yourself! See to Jill." Taven looks at me in warning, which means my eyes must have flashed. I look back at Shelly and see a horrified look on her face. I turn back to Jill and lift her up even though it gives her pain. I start running to the medical ward and practically collide with Kaid and Dane.

"What happened to Jill?" Dane frantically asks.

"That fucking bitch Shelly kicked her in the stomach! Call Dr. Howard for me now and bring her to the medical ward when she gets here!" I take off again, Jill now crying softly in my arms.

I get to medical and burst into the room, laying Jill down on the first bed I come to. Raven comes out of his office to investigate the noise and then flashes over when he sees me placing Jill on the bed, "What happened?"

I proceed to tell him the events of the altercation and when I finish, I grab Raven's arm, "Please help her! She cannot lose this baby!" As if on cue, Jill howls with more pain.

"I need you to undress her and put her in a gown." Raven instructs, "I assume that Dr, Howard has been contacted?"

"Yea, Dane is taking care of it."

"Good. Put the gown on her and then I will check her over." Raven walks away, closing us behind a curtain.

"I am so sorry, baby, but I need to get your clothes off. Let me know if it's too much and I will stop, okay?" I watch to see if she has even heard me, but then she nods her head yes. I carefully pull her shirt up and take one arm out at a time before pulling it up over her head. I then undo the button and zipper on her shorts and very slowly pull them down. I choke on a sob as I see her shorts full of blood. I turn away so she doesn't see my face as I try to collect myself. I throw her shorts in the garbage can and quickly remove her underwear and do the same with those. Lastly, I remove her bra and slip the gown on her. I call out to Raven as I pull the blankets up over her.

Raven walks in and I quickly looked down at the garbage can, his eyes following mine. He understands, "Jill, can you rate the pain that you are having between one and ten?"

"A fucking twenty!" she cries out, "Please make it stop!"

"I am going to give you a little something for the pain and the good Doc should be here shortly. This medicine will most likely make you tired, don't fight it, your body needs to rest." I see Jill nod.

"What if she drinks my blood? Will it help at all?" I ask trying to offer any help as possible.

"It may, but until we know what kind of damage we are looking at, I would rather hold off until Doc arrives." I shake my head, not liking his response, but I agree. I don't want to do any more damage.

Jill is out within five minutes after Raven gives her the meds and Doc arrives shortly after. "Thank God you are here, Doc! Please help her!" I point to the garbage can, "Does that mean…?" I can't finish my sentence.

She grabs my arm, "Not necessarily. Let's do an ultrasound first and when she wakes up, I will check her vaginally. I will need you to stay calm for me though, okay?" I shake my head yes and let her set up the ultrasound machine.

I sit beside Jill, holding her hand and petting her hair while she sleeps as I wait patiently for Doc to start. Finally, after what seems like forever, she squeezes some kind of gel onto Jill's stomach and uses a wand-looking thing to rub it in. I don't understand what I am looking at, so I watch Doc's face instead. I see her eyebrows crinkle, but then a slip of a smile appears before it disappears, "What is it? What do you see?" I am tired of waiting.

"Well, it does seem to appear that she is having a miscarriage, I am so sorry." I hang my head and feel tears spring to my eyes, "The other two babies look to be perfectly fine though." I snap my head up to see her smiling at me.

"Did you say two babies? We are having twins?" My voice cracks with emotion.

"Yes, you are having twins. Would have been triplets, but the third one must have taken on all the impact. Again, I am sorry. Would you like to hear the heartbeats?"

"Of course!" I say with a little too much enthusiasm. She hits a button and then clear as day, there they are, two heartbeats, in sync with each other.

"Unfortunately, it's too soon to tell the sex, but we should be able to tell in about five more weeks. Looks like these little tikes will be here in time for Christmas this year!" Doc is beaming at me and I can't help hugging her when I stand up.

"Thank you, Doc! Will you be sticking around until Jill wakes up?"

"Yes. I want to examine her before I leave and make sure her pain is gone. I will go visit the other soon-to-be-parents until she wakes up. Text me as soon as she does."

"I definitely will. Thank you again!"

I sit back down and watch Jill sleep. As much as it hurts knowing that we lost a child, I am thankful to still have the other two. Man, we are having twins! That means double of everything! I smile as I place my hand over her stomach and lay my head down to rest my eyelids.

JILL

I wake up feeling really sore and groggy. I feel something holding my hand down and look over to see Duncan sitting in a chair, holding my hand and asleep with his head on my bed. It all comes back to me now and I want to cry. Yes, once I found out that I was expecting, I was happy, but my heart breaks for Duncan, knowing how bad he wanted this child. As much pain that I was in, I know that it didn't survive the vicious attack from Shelly. I reach over and run my fingers through his hair, stirring him awake. He looks at me with sadness in his eyes, "Hey baby, how long have I been out?"

He sits up and looks at the clock, "Almost three hours. How are you feeling? Any pain?" Concern is etched on his face.

"No pain, just really sore and groggy. Has Dr. Howard been here?"

"Yeah, she did an ultrasound, but wanted to wait until you woke before doing the exam. I am supposed to text her when you wake." He pulls his phone out to text, but I put my hand over his.

"Before you text her, please tell me what happened. As much pain that I was in, it could not have been good."

"Oh sweetheart, I am so sorry. It wasn't good, you had a miscarriage." I nod my head in acknowledgement as tears roll down my face, "Wait baby, I am not done. We still have two healthy buns in that oven of yours! You were pregnant with triplets. Unfortunately, the third one took the hit and didn't make it, but we still have two. We are having twins!"

"T-Twins?" I am trying to let my brain catch up to everything that he is saying, "So, I miscarried, but I'm still pregnant? With twins?"

"Yes, angel, we are still having babies!" He kisses me on the lips, and I throw my hands around his neck as tears flow. I am not sure if I am crying because I am happy that I am still pregnant or because I am sad for the baby that I lost but being in Duncan's arms gives me comfort.

I pull away and wipe my tears, "I am sorry, I am usually stronger than this. You can text the doctor now."

"Jill, we just lost a baby. You have every right to cry and show emotion, don't ever apologize for it! I cried myself earlier."

"You did?"

"Of course. Our baby died because of that bitch and just because we still have two more babies, doesn't lessen that sense of loss. I would think you heartless if you didn't cry over it." He hugs me tightly and I feel his shoulders shudder as he lets his emotions out. We sit holding each other, crying for the loss of our child.

"I want to know if it was a boy or a girl, Duncan. I want us to give them a name. Do you think that is possible?"

"I honestly don't know. That is something we will have to ask Doc. Why don't I text her now, so she can come look you over and she can answer all our questions. Besides, I am sure you want to hear the heartbeats of our children that are still with us. It helped put my mind at ease… a little."

"Yes, I would like that very much." He sends the text off to the doctor and then turns his phone to silent, so we won't be disturbed, "Will you lay with me in bed?" I ask as I scoot over to make room.

"Only if it doesn't make you uncomfortable, but I want to wait until after the Doc checks you."

"Okay." We sit in silence for a little while, but it's too much, I have to occupy the time. "Duncan? How did Triplets come into play? I know I don't have any multiple births on my side of the family."

"I don't know about triplets, but my father was a twin. It must be every other generation or something, I'm really not sure."

"Are you telling me that we may have more than one set of twins?"

"Possibly. Would that be a bad thing?"

"Well, no, but I am hoping that they are spread out over many years." I can't help but chuckle at the thought of having twins with every pregnancy. Then out of the blue, I think of my parents, "I don't ever want our kids to be estranged like my sister and I or like me and my parents. I want a home full of love. Promise me that we will always be close to our kids."

"Oh, baby. That, I can and will promise you all of that. You never talked about your family before, so I thought that something either happened to them or there was bad blood."

"There is bad blood between me and my sister, always has been and I don't know why. As for my parents, they live in California now and I talk to them, maybe once or twice a year. They don't talk to either one of us, because they don't want to get in the middle of it. As long as I can remember, my sister has hated me, and I don't know why. Cassie and her family have been my family all these years. Now I have you and our children. That is all I need."

"You also have the Elite." He smirks, "More family than you thought possible, huh?"

"Oh God, how could I have forgotten about them? Yes, I have the Elite… all those brothers!" I laugh and it actually feels good.

Dr. Howard comes in to examine me and I ask her about finding out the sex of the fetus. "Well, I can take it to the lab and see if we can find out for you, but I can't promise you anything, I am sorry."

"That is all I ask, thank you." It calms me knowing that she will at least try, "So, can I see my babies now and hear their heartbeats?"

Doc smiles, "You sure can!" Once I see for myself that the twins are doing good and hear their strong heartbeats, I feel so much better. Even though I am still feeling the loss of the third, I can only thank the good Lord for saving the other two. The doctor gives us our ultrasound pictures and tells us to call if there are any problems, otherwise she will see us next month.

"I will let you know if I get any results back, Jill. Take care and rest for a few days."

"I will, thank you Dr. Howard."

I am able to go back to our own room the next day and when I step through the door, I am taken aback by all the flowers, cards and chocolates that are placed throughout the room from everyone in the Compound. As big and bad as the Elite make themselves out to be, they are a bunch of softies at heart. Before I can even settle back in, they are all filing in wanting to make sure I don't need anything. Duncan hasn't told them yet that we are still expecting, so when we tell them that Duncan seems to shoot more than one smoking bullet and that we are still having twins, our room explodes. Everyone is slapping him on the back and hugging me. They stay for about ten minutes and then leave me to get some rest after I thank each one for what they bought me.

Taven lingers behind and once everyone is gone, he shuts the door and sits down, "Jill, I can't tell you how sorry I am at what Shelly did. It is my fault, I should have taken care of it after the first situation, but I was more worried about her father causing trouble for us. I want you to know that she has been in her room since the incident and a guard stands outside of her door so she can't leave. I called her father and explained everything, and he is pretty understanding. Seems she has been causing trouble her whole life and he sends his deepest condolences. He will be sending a car for her tomorrow, and she is leaving."

"I don't blame you, Taven. You were only trying to help protect her and like you said, you have enough on your plate as it is."

"It's no excuse, Jill. If there is anything that I can do for you, please let me know." He stands up to leave, but I stop him.

"Actually, there is one thing you can do for me."

"Anything, you name it."

"Take Liz out on a date." I smile smugly at him, and he just stares at me dumbfounded.

"Take Liz out? Are you serious? That's what you want me to do for you?"

"Yep. That's it." He looks at Duncan and then back at me and starts laughing.

"It's good to have you back Earnhardt!" He turns and walks out.

I love giving these guys shit, but I am dead serious about getting those two together. Men are so stubborn, it irritates me! Duncan, now he is different. He chased me around when I was playing hard to get.

"You really won't let that go, will you? You are dead set on hooking them up."

"I am and you had better start helping if you care anything for your brother. We both know that they are destined mates. Sometimes it takes a little push to open someone's eyes."

"Hm… and what do I get out of it?"

"Besides for self-gratification? Anything you want, once I am up and about again, that is."

"You drive a hard bargain, angel."

"And that, warrior, is one of the things that you love about me! Now, why don't you come over here and hold me for a while? Unless, of course, you need to be somewhere else."

"The only place I need to be is right here with you, love." He climbs in beside me and pulls my back up against his chest. My head rests on his arm and his other arm lays protectively around me and our babies. No one can get to us as long my warrior is here. I close my eyes and drift off to sleep.

EIGHTEEN

DUNCAN

It's been two months since the raid on the Hunter's warehouse where I, along with twenty possible vampire mates, were being held prisoner. Although the Elite took out the majority of the Hunters, a few, including Mika, got away and we have been hearing reports that he is recruiting more. Mika has been in hiding the whole time, having his minions doing all the dirty work. We watch his residence daily, but there has been no sign of him coming or going.

Taven calls me to his office this morning and as I enter, another familiar face is sitting down in front of Taven's desk. I know he is one of the newer recruits that came on board during Jill, Jax, and Cassie's capture, but I can never remember the names of all five of them.

"Ah… Duncan, there you are. Have a seat please." Taven instructs me, "I called you and Ryder in here today to go over a new training tactic for the new recruits." That is why I knew the name of the driver of the cargo van when I was being transported back, sounded familiar. I should probably learn all their names if they are going to officially be part of the Elite in a few short weeks, "I am assigning all five recruits to five of my best Elites for the duration of their training and I have chosen you to be Ryder's mentor. He will follow you on all of your details, train with you, eat with you, pretty much shadow you in every aspect."

"With all due respect, Taven... I don't think Jill would appreciate him hanging around in "every" aspect." I joke.

"Why do you have to be such a smartass all the time, Dunc?" Taven shakes his head and chuckles then turns to Ryder, "He is a damn good Elite, and you will learn a lot from him, but do not pick up his bad habits! Between Duncan and his mate, I get enough headaches."

Ryder snickers, "Don't worry boss, I get myself into enough trouble on my own, without needing to pick up his bad habits."

"Oh great! Maybe I should assign you to Xavier instead."

"Nah, he will be fine with me." I assure him, but then look at Ryder, "Just don't think you will be sharing my bed, my mate isn't into threesomes." He grins at my joke.

"Can't you be serious for once, Duncan?" Taven scolds me.

"There is no fun in that, now is there?"

"Anyway. I want you to take him down with you to go talk to Jenny again. Try and get any kind of information you can from her on other locations that Mika may be at. Let her know of our plans to release her once he is in custody. Maybe that will entice her enough to talk."

"I don't know, she has been adamant every other time we have tried."

"Yes but, that was when she didn't know that she would be released. This may work."

"I will try anything if it helps. I will report back to you when we are done." I turn to Ryder, "Ready to go?"

"Yes Sir." I stop him right there, "If this relationship is going to work out, never call me Sir again. It's either Duncan or Dunc, got it?"

"Yes, Si... Duncan!"

"Good, let's go then."

We reach Jenny's cell, unlock the door, and open it. To my dismay, Jenny is curled up in the corner of her bed, thin as a rail, hair looking like a rat's nest even though we have supply her with all her toiletries, and big dark circles under her eyes. She looks like a shell of the woman that Jill and I saw only weeks ago. There is a stench in the room that I can't quite put into words, but it burns my sense of smell like no other.

Ryder and I look at each other and then back at Jenny, who has yet to look at us. I walk over, so I am in her line of vision, but she just stares right through me, "Jenny, are you feeling okay? You look terrible."

Ryder nudges me with his elbow, and behind his hand, he says to me, "Dude, you never tell a woman that she looks terrible! Do you have a death wish?"

"Well, when she does this to herself then I am going to be truthful and voice my opinion," not caring if she hears me. Turning back to the woman, "Jenny, why are you doing this to yourself?"

"Um, Duncan?" I look down and find Ryder on his hands and knees, holding the bedspread up and looking under the bed. "I think I found the source of the stench." I kneel down beside him and look under the bed. There, underneath, are at least two weeks' worth of untouched food trays. I have to cover my nose, because smelling it that close makes me gag and want to lose the contents of this morning's breakfast.

I straighten myself up and pull out my cuffs, "What are you doing?" Ryder asks quizzically.

"She is not going to starve herself on our watch, so if she wants to be stubborn and not eat the food that we provide, then she will be restrained in the medical ward with a feeding tube." I inform him.

As I reach for Jenny, she starts screaming and lashing out. Without being told by me, Ryder quickly grabs and holds her so I can cuff her. She refuses to budge, so I lift her up and place her over my shoulder to carry her up. She screams the whole way, bringing others out of different rooms to see what the commotion is. Once we reach medical, Ryder enters ahead to retrieve Raven for his help.

"What is going on, Dunc?" Raven asks.

"She is starving herself in her cell, so she needs to be restrained here and be fed by a tube."

"I don't understand how nobody noticed that she wasn't eating!" Raven is very disturbed by this.

"Those are my thoughts as well and I will find out the answer to it, but in the meantime, let's get some nutrients into her and hopefully by tomorrow, I can get her to talk. We don't want to hold her prisoner forever, but if she doesn't tell us what we want, then we will have no choice." I hope she is hearing what I am saying. Maybe it will persuade her to give Mika up.

It takes all three of us to get her strapped to the bed and Raven ends up sedating her to get the tube in, so she won't hurt herself. I thank Raven, and then Ryder, and I take our leave to go in search of Taven.

We find Taven in the kitchen, sitting with Liz and the boys, while they eat, "Hey, buddy. Can we have a quick word with you? It won't take long." I look at Liz, "I apologize for the interruption. We will only be a moment."

"Oh, it's okay. No need to apologize." She smiles at me. I watch as Taven squeezes her shoulder as he strolls past. My mouth twitches, trying not to smile.

The three of us step out into the hallway and Taven is the first to speak, "So, what do you have for me?"

"We have no new information on Mika's whereabouts. We had to take Jenny to medical and restrain her. She has been starving herself." I report to him.

"How the fuck did that happen?" He roars.

"I would like to know the same thing! There is at least two weeks of uneaten food under her bed. Who has been taking the meals to her?"

"Max is in charge of taking the meals down, but whoever is on duty, watching the cells, are supposed to return them when their shift is over. I have had the new recruits on guard duty down there." He informs me and we both look at Ryder.

"Hey, don't look at me!" He holds his hands up in defense, "I have only had guard duty down there twice in the last two weeks and nobody said a word about bringing any trays back to the kitchen!"

"Ugh, seriously! Can nobody follow orders around here?" Taven throws his hands in the air.

"Hey, don't worry about it, Tav. I'll take care of it. Just go back to visiting with Liz and relax for a bit." I urge him "I'll come find you later."

"Thanks Dunc. I should be in my office most of the day." He turns to go back into the kitchen, but stops and turns back towards me, "By the way, I need you, Jill, Jax, and Cassie to go over to the building site and choose the spot where you would like your housing unit built."

"Great, we will. Thank you for doing this for us."

"Don't mention it. We are stronger when we are together and besides, I really don't know how much more the rest of us can take, hearing you all go at it all the time!" He chuckles and disappears into the kitchen.

"Just means that we know how to keep our women happy." I mumble to myself and then look over at a smirking Ryder, "You will do well with your future mate to take pointers." I chuckle.

"Believe me, I know how to please women. I am a younger generation than you and Jax. I could probably give you a few pointers, there buddy!" His statement gets a laugh out of me, and I decide right then that Ryder is an okay guy in my book.

First things first, we needed to get Jenny cleaned up and get the stench off her, so I go to find my lovely bride-to-be and find her in the Rec room with Cassie and Liz looking through bridal magazines, "Well, this right here looks like trouble!" I kid, looking at the three of them. I bend and steal a quick kiss from Jill, before glancing at Liz, "I hope I didn't spoil your time with Taven."

"Oh, no, he needed to get back to his office anyway, so I came here to help the girls." She smiles.

"I wouldn't call us trouble," Cassie pipes up, "more like adventurous. It's not our fault when trouble finds us. We attract the good and the bad, but never with intention."

"If that explanation makes you feel better, then by all means, keep telling it." I smile at her. "I don't mean to bother you women, but I need a huge favor." I go on and tell them about Jenny's issue, "Could you please go and clean her up? Give her a bed bath while she is sedated and a good head wash?"

"Of course, whatever you need, babe." Jill squeezes my hand.

"You ladies are awesome, thank you! Oh, and before I forget, come find Jax and I when you are through. Taven wants us to go over this afternoon and pick out a spot for our homes." Jill and Cassie both squeal with excitement right before Jill throws herself into my arms and smashes her lips to mine. I love seeing my mate happy again. It is my mission and pleasure to always put a smile on her face and keep her happy for eternity.

JILL

Cassie and I make our way over to the medical ward to go bathe Jenny while she is sedated, but when we arrive, she is already awake and stares daggers at us when we come near. "Jenny, Cassie and I are here to help you clean up a little. I am sure you will feel so much better once you are clean."

She just sneers at us, "Are you going to let us help you or will we need to sedate you again? It will be a lot easier for all of us if you cooperate." I convey to her.

"Why can't you just leave me be and let me die?" Jenny glares at us, "Oh, I see. You like seeing me suffer, don't you?"

"Jenny," Cassie sighs, "we don't like keeping you here like this! We have tried getting you to cooperate with us so we can set you free, but you are stubborn! Even knowing that Mika has lied to you and has a family, you still insist on protecting him! We don't understand."

"Apparently, you know nothing about being loyal to the ones you love!" She gives us a disgusted look.

"Oh, make no mistake, we know loyalty! We also know the difference between the good and the bad, which, apparently, you do not!" I raise my voice. I just can't fathom how she can justify Mika's actions and allow herself to believe that he loves her. Who can care for someone like him knowing what type of person he is. It nauseates me.

We don't have time to just sit and go rounds with this woman and so I go find Raven, so he can sedate her again. Once she is out, we thoroughly clean her body and hair and dress her in a clean gown.

"Cassie, can't Jax just get the information that we need from her, so we can be done with it?" I glance at her.

"I am sure he can, but you know as well as I do that he hates doing it."

"I am sure that you can get him to change his mind." I grin at her and wiggle my brows so she gets my drift.

"Jill! I will not use my charms to make my man do something that he is against doing! Even if it would be fun doing it, I just can't, I am sorry."

"I know, and I am sorry for even asking you. I just hate knowing that monster is out there hurting innocents." I frown as I look at the floor.

I feel arms around me, "I know you are, honey, but we will get him, and he will pay for all of his crimes," she reassures me, "Now, how about we go find those gorgeous men of ours and go pick out our land?"

That puts a smile back on my face and I smile at her, "Yes, lets! I can't wait until we have our own space!" Just then my phone buzzes with a text notification. I read the text and roll my eyes, "Really? They couldn't pick a better time?"

"What's up? Who is it?" Cassie has a concerned look on her face as she asks.

"My parents." I hesitate, "They texted me to tell me that they will be coming to visit in about a month!"

"Oh wow! What is the occasion?"

"I haven't the slightest idea, but whatever it is, it won't be pretty when they get here and find me knocked up and unmarried!"

"God, I didn't even think about that! They are going to throw a fit!"

"Well, let them! I am an adult and it's not like they care enough to know how I am doing on a daily basis, so whatever."

"That's a good way to handle it, but I know you Jill. You are going to stress about their visit every day until they come, and that is not good for the babies. Or the rest of us, I might add." She snickers as she elbows me.

"Ugh, you are right. I'll figure something out, but right now, I want to put the thought aside and enjoy the task ahead."

Putting her arm around my shoulder, "That's my bitch! Now let's go find our men!"

An hour later, we are driving down a road, hidden by forest on both sides. The road is about a mile long and then opens up to the most beautiful land that I have ever seen! Acres upon acres of open field, hidden deep within the forest. To the right, a huge structure, at least a half mile long and almost just as wide is being constructed. The metal beams are up, outlining all three above level floors. Looking closely, the cement has already been poured and set for the lower level, all the separate rooms outlined with the beams as well. It doesn't take a Rocket Scientist to know that this is the new Compound.

As we continue on, we see signs in different areas that are close to the Compound, labeling what they are going to be. The medical building will be right beside the Compound and then the Armory, which will hold the gym for training, the weight room, and a room for sparring. I see another sign which reads pool and playground. I can't believe that Taven thought about the children! That right there warms my heart.

Duncan stops the SUV and asks one of the construction workers where the housing units will be built. The friendly worker directs us towards the back of the Compound where there is a beautiful lake. Taven wants the houses to go up around the small lake and I am not going to argue with that. Every morning we will wake up to a beautiful view! Of course, Cassie and I pick land right beside each other. We had that planned before we even got here, but the land that we pick is quite a way from the Compound. We want to be far enough away to make it feel like the guys aren't at work all the time, but close enough that it doesn't take long for them to get there if needed. Not that it really matters with their speed, but they humor us women with our way of thinking.

Taven had informed us that all the units would have four bedrooms, each with their own bathrooms, a kitchen, dining room, living room, a family room in the basement and a bathroom on each floor. The layouts will be the same as all the others, but we are more than welcome to add or change something, as long as the extra comes out of the warrior's own pocket. Which we do add a few extras to the house, like an oversized jacuzzi tub in the master bath and an extra room so we can have our own gym/exercise room.

Later on, Cassie tells me that her and Jax added a connecting room to the master bedroom for their own little pleasures. Thankfully, she doesn't go into detail. Being best friends for most of our lives, I know all about her twisted little fantasies. I am happy that she is able to find someone that is just as twisted as she is when it comes to sex. I like the kinky shit, but she goes beyond kinky, almost, but not quite sadistic.

When we get back to the Compound, I head to our room to try and get a little nap in. On my way, I see Alex and stop her to ask how she is adjusting to her new life.

She smiles at me, "It's going really well! Xavier has been great with teaching me the ins and outs of everything and helping me to control my cravings and vampire senses. I don't know what I would ever do without him, and he is so easy on the eyes!" She has a dreamy-eyed look upon her face, and it worries me.

"Alex, you do realize that he is your maker? You can't have a relationship with him."

"What do you mean?"

I look around and then take her hand, dragging her into my room, "I am not surprised that Xavier hasn't explained this to you yet, since he is all about his work, but the Elite do not form relationships with anyone unless they are destined mates."

"But I have the right blood for it?" She looks at me confused.

"First of all, you "used" to have the blood for it, but now you are a vampire and unless you secure the bond before turning, you cannot mate with another vampire and just because you have type O, doesn't mean that you are a destined mate to just any vampire. Second, you now have your own mate out there somewhere. You need to mate with a regular person if you want to be able to have kids." I explain this to her, but I don't know if she is really taking it all in.

"Well, what if I decide that I don't want kids? I can then be with whoever I want."

"Alex, these men here, mainly the original members of the Elite, have waited centuries to be able to have a family. They are not going to throw it all away just for a roll in the hay with someone that can't give them what they need." I probably should have used other words, because I could see the irritation on her face when I had finish.

"I am not just a roll in the hay and quite frankly, it is none of your business who I hook up with!"

"I am sorry Alex; I didn't mean it to come out that way. I am just wanting to explain how it all works, so you don't get hurt by rejection."

"Well, I'll have you know that I never get rejected, but like I said, it isn't any of your business anyway!" With that being said, she spins and leaves my room, slamming the door behind her.

Oh boy! Things are going to get really interesting around here with Alex, I think to myself. I will have to talk to Duncan about this, so we can take it to Xavier. He needs to make her aware that their relationship is strictly platonic. Unless of course, he wants to tap that and then it's all on him! Maybe I will just stay out of it. Yeah right! Since when have I ever kept my nose out of any one's business when it comes to their happiness, I snort to myself. I pull my shorts off and climb into bed, thinking of a way on how I am going to bring this to Xavier's attention.

Nineteen

DUNCAN

I enter mine and Jill's room to see that she is sound asleep. I don't want to wake her, but I can't help climbing into bed beside her and wrapping her in my arms. She snuggles closer to me and then sighs in her sleep. Smiling, I kiss the top of her head and close my eyes, but Jill must have woken up, because I feel a warm hand cupping my cock, "Mm, just what I am needing." She whispers softly. Her fingers are unbuttoning my jeans and then the zipper slides down. She slips her hand inside and begins to massage me, making my member swell.

"Baby, don't stop." I say softly as I start moving my hips, pumping myself within her soft hand. She dips beneath the blankets and moves south, until I feel her tongue lick my tip. My stomach clenches as I suck in my breath, "Fuck Sweetheart!" I hear a giggle before my cock is engulfed in the sweet warmth of her mouth. She works her hand, sliding it up and down the base while her mouth keeps in sync sucking and licking the rest. I slowly pump my hips, involuntarily. Her other hand massages my balls, rolling them around and then squeezing. I can feel them tightening with her touch, causing me to pump a little faster. The head of my cock hits the back of her throat with each thrust, and I know I am going to blow at any moment. I entangle my fingers through her hair and move her head up and down at a quicker pace, not enough to hurt her, but enough to give a little more friction. I jerk as hot seed bursts out of me and hits the back of her throat as she swallows continuously until I am done.

I close my eyes and sigh, but then I feel movement and open my eyes back up to see her up and bending over to pick up her shorts. I am up in a flash, shoving her against the wall. My still hard cock poking her in the back as I press myself into her, "Where the fuck do you think you're going?"

"I'm hungry, I was going to the kitchen."

"What, my cum wasn't enough, do I need to give you more?"

"Oh baby, it was more than enough, but you know how I am when it comes to food." She grins.

"You should know better than to try and leave this room without me getting you off, especially when you just gave me one hell of a blow job!"

"I did it because I wanted to, not because I wanted you to return the favor."

"Fuck that, you know better!" I grab her arms and pin them above her head with one of my hands, before ripping off her cotton panties. I then lift her shirt, stopping once it's up over her eyes. I unclasp her bra in front and let her girls out, so they rub against the rough wall, "I am going to fuck you right here and I am not going to stop until I feel you have been fucked thoroughly. Do you understand me?"

"Yes, but you don't have to, babe. You can return the favor tonight."

"You better believe I will be giving it to you tonight as well, but I want that sweet pussy now!" With that being said, I bring my hand between her thighs and feel a bit of dampness. "Well that won't do. I want your pussy soaked as I slide my cock into you." I whisper in her ear. I reach around and squeeze her sensitive nub and roll it around in my fingers. I hear her whimper as I continue my assault, dipping a finger in every so often until I feel that she is wet enough. I place my cock at her opening, slide my hand up and place it over her little baby bump, "Hold on children, I'm going to take mommy for a wild ride and it's going to get bumpy!" I plunge myself into her, thrusting in and out with everything I got. I grab her leg and lift it up to the side, so I have better access and can go deeper. She is moaning with each thrust as her pussy gets slammed and her nipples rub against the wall.

"Sounds like someone likes it." I nip her ear when she mewls and take her faster yet, "I love fucking your tight pussy! I want you to come for me now." As if she is waiting for my permission, she lets go and spasms wrack her body until she is done. As she stands there panting, I pull out and use my dick to rub her juice through her ass crack, lubing it up for my invasion.

"I don't know if I can't take more right now." She says out of breath.

"Oh, you're going to take more, baby. You're going to take a hell of a lot more! I am far from done with you." I kiss her cheek and push the head of my dick into her waiting bud. She is so tight back here, it's like fucking a virgin every time. I thrust inch by inch until my whole dick is deep inside her ass. Letting her leg go, I go back to playing with her clit, "How does that feel? Do you still want me to stop?"

"Please don't stop… take me…take me now!" She urges me and I lose it, slamming into her ass as I extend my fangs and sink into her neck. She screams in ecstasy, "Fuck yes! Oh my God… faster Duncan! Oh… Oh… Argh!" Her walls tighten around my cock, making it difficult to move within her ass, so I rub her clit more vigorously and I continue to drink from her. Her climax continues as it rips my own from me and I am filling her ass with my cum. I release her neck and her orgasm begins to calm.

I pull out of her ass and spin her around, so her back is against the wall. Letting her arms go, I kneel before her, spreading her thighs and begin to lick the folds of her pussy. I need to taste her! Her own cum is running down her inner thighs and I lap it up, first one thigh and then the other. When I am all done cleaning her with my tongue, I pick her up and carry her to our bed, but instead of laying her down, I sit down and keep her on my lap. "You need to feed, Angel, and then you need rest. I will go grab some food for you and bring it back here, now feed."

Without hesitation, she bites into my neck, and I feel my arousal stirring. I do not have the willpower to be good and I lay her down as she drinks, "I am sorry baby, but I need to come once more into your pussy." In one thrust I am seeded deep within. She pulls harder, it's too much! My vampire comes out as I pound into her over and over, showing her no mercy. "FUCK! That's it, take it!" I roar as my liquid fire explodes from my cock and floods her, "God damn, baby. You sure can take a pounding!" I am grunting as it continues to pour out of me until she retracts her fangs. I pump into her a couple more times and then I lay down over her, keeping my weight on my elbows. I take her lips and tell her how much I love her through my kiss.

Rolling off her a moment later, I pull up my pants. She is already fast asleep again as I reach the door, and with a smile, I open the door and walk out. I think to myself that I probably shouldn't have taken her like that, but damn, she brings it out in me and deep down I think she really likes it, but she is too shy to ask for it that way. I do know one thing, if she didn't like it, she would definitely tell me.

I go to the kitchen to see if dinner is done, but Max says it will be another twenty minutes yet, so I decide to find Ryder and go over a few things. On my way to the gym, I walk by the medical ward and then back track. There is Ryder sitting beside Jenny's bed as she sleeps. What the fuck is he doing? I open the door and he looks up, his face flushes, but he gets up and comes over to the door. I motion out to the hallway with a nod of my head, and he steps out.

"What are you doing sitting in there with her?" I question.

"What? Is it against the rules or something?" He responds with another question.

"Well, no, but it's a little weird."

"I went to find you, but you were... a little busy, so I came here to see if she was awake and figured I would sit a while and see if she wakes up."

I ignore his comment about me being busy, knowing that he must have come looking for me at my room and heard me and Jill, "Are you sure that's all it is?"

"Of course, what else would it be?"

"Whatever you say, buddy. I just wanted to go over a few things with you about what to expect out on detail and whatnot. Do you have a few minutes?"

"Yes, I have been bored. It is you that has been busy for almost an hour." He snickers.

"Yeah, well like I said earlier, I keep my woman happy." I grin. We head back to the kitchen to go over the items that I thought was most important about detail.

When Max informs me that supper is done, I wrap things up with Ryder, but before he leaves, he looks at me, "Duncan, did you know that Jenny has type O blood?"

"What do you mean? She does?"

"Yes. I didn't smell it on her before. I think it is because of the stench, but now that she is clean, I can smell it."

"Hmm, that's interesting. I wonder if Mika knew what her blood type was?" This is something I will have to discuss with Taven, "How old are you Ryder?"

"I was turned at age twenty-five, but I just turned forty…why?"

"I was just wondering, because it usually takes a long time to figure out the scent of type O. Hell, I still have issues with scenting them out. You did good kid!"

"It is nothing. I really didn't know the scent until we brought all those women here from the warehouse."

"Well, it's good that you know now. Maybe one of these days you can find yourself a woman."

"Are you crazy? I'm not looking for a mate just yet! I still have a lot of oats to sow." He smiles at me.

"Believe me, you don't have a choice once you meet. You're a goner whether you like it or not."

"Bet me!" He says as he walks out the door.

I shake my head and look at Max, "Can you believe that kid? Who doesn't want to find their mate?"

"I didn't at that age and if you really think about it, did you?" he chuckles.

"I guess you are right. What I don't understand, is why after waiting for so long are they just now starting to pop out of the woodwork?"

"That, I do not have an answer to, but I sure can't wait for mine to pop out. I am so ready to settle down."

"Jill is the best thing that has ever happened to me. I will have a family by Christmas, and I can't ask for anything better than that. Well, except for getting a plate of food for an expectant mother of twins, which she wanted earlier until I distracted her. She should be waking up any time now and I don't want to go back empty handed!" I joke.

"Hell, I wouldn't want to deal with a hungry Jill period, never mind a pregnant one!" Max responds and hands me a tray of food.

"Thanks buddy, I'll see you later." I walk out and down the hallway to our room.

JILL

I wake up to the sound of our bedroom door closing. I can tell that I didn't sleep too long by the stream of sunlight coming in through the bedroom window. I look over and see Duncan carrying a tray of food and sit up quick. I am starving! I was hungry before our sex session, but now I'm famished.

"Good evening beautiful, hope you are hungry." He gives me his charming smile, knowing very well that I would be starving.

"Well, when you are deprived food to be used as a sex slave, you would be hungry too!" I wink at him.

"You know you love being my sex slave as do I being yours, love!" He kisses my forehead and then lifts the lid off my plate.

"Mm, country fried steak! One of my favorites; I knew Max loved me."

"Hey now, I don't want to hear that kind of bullshit come out of your mouth again!" he teases.

"If you cook for me the way Max does, I will never mention it again."

"You have a point there, I guess."

We eat in silence for a while, and I think back on the events of the day. Remembering the text from my parents, I turn towards Duncan. "I haven't had the chance to talk to you today, but I got a text message from my parents this morning."

"Oh really? What did mom and good ole dad have to say?"

"Um, they are coming for a visit next month."

"Seriously? Maybe that's a good thing. Maybe they want to work on their relationship with you." I could tell that he isn't even buying the words that are coming out of his own mouth.

"I doubt it. As always, they will come, find every bad thing in my life and bitch at me about it."

"Won't they be happy that they have grandkids on the way?"

"Possibly, but then they will bitch at me for getting knocked up before I am married." I look down at my plate and now, I don't feel so hungry anymore.

"Hey," Duncan grabs my chin and makes me look at him, "don't let this stress you out. We will figure out something."

"Maybe they will just think I put on a few pounds. Then I would be able to handle my mom calling me lazy and that I need a diet and a gym membership."

"Fuck that! I will not hide our children from them, and I'll be damn if I let them say anything negative to or about you!"

"Then they will start in on how I found a rude dead-beat dad to be my baby daddy." I couldn't help but laugh.

"I got it then. We will just plan the wedding for when they are here!"

"Are you crazy? That is only a month away? I can't possibly plan a wedding that soon! Even if I could, every place is booked for months!"

"So, if we can figure out a place to have it in a month's time, you will agree to marry me while your parents are here?" He gives me a quizzical look.

"I suppose, but it will be non-stop planning until then. I don't want a big, frumpy dress, so I should be able to find something by then."

"The dress is the last thing you have to worry about. I know people and that's all you need to know!" He leans over and gives me a kiss before walking out the door without finishing his supper.

What is his deal? It doesn't matter, because I have checked everywhere and every place is booked until November and even then, there are only a few dates open. I will just have to find a way to avoid my parents as much as possible while they are here.

After taking a shower so no one can smell all the sex on me, I go in search of someone, anyone, because I am bored. I don't know how, with as many bodies under this roof, that I can be bored, but I am. As I near the rec room, I hear voices and laughter which draws me to the doorway. The room is full of people, but Kai is the first to see me standing there.

"I see you have decided to journey out of your little sex den!" He teases.

I blush, "Shut the fuck up Kai before I stick my foot up your ass!"

"Meow! Put your claws away tiger, I was just fucking with you!" He laughs. I hiss at him and act as if I'm going to claw him, "Dude," he looks at Duncan, "tame your hell cat why don't you!"

"Nah, I love her claws." He says as he winks at me, making me grin.

"What's everyone doing in here? Having a party without me?" I pout.

"Actually," Cassie comes from around the couch and stands in front of me, "we are planning your wedding!"

"You are doing what?"

"Planning your wedding. Duncan came to me with the idea of having it when your parents are in town, and I totally agree with him.

I know your parents Jill, and no matter what you plan to say or do, we both know that they will find fault in all of it, and we can't have you stressed out!"

"Did you find a place that has a cancellation?"

"Nope." Duncan replies, "Taven here, suggests that we have it out at the new Compound, on the lake." He pats Taven on the back.

"Oh! That would be a gorgeous place to have it. Thank you!" I really am in love with the idea, and I start to get my hopes up, but then I remember that the ministers are booked as well, "What about the minister?"

"What do I look like, chopped liver?" Cassie pretends to be hurt, "I'm not a minister, but did you forget that I am Ordained? Sheesh… Jill! You were there that night when I married that guy and chic at the bar!" Cassie laughs as she turns to everyone else, "These two people absolutely hated each other, and they were always picking fights with each other. One night, it was so bad, we got the two of them so drunk that they agreed to marry each other for shits and giggles. Let me just say, I had to stay hidden for months afterwards, because they were so pissed when their marriage license came in the mail!" The whole room erupted in laughter at her story.

"Oh my God, how did I forget about that! She is right, for two months she only left the house to go to work and would have to hide at work when one of them would come in looking for her!" My gut hurts from laughing so hard.

"See, so problem solved bitch!" Cassie puts her arm around my shoulder.

"But you are supposed to be my Matron of Honor."

"Oh, it's okay. I would much rather be the one to marry you to his sorry ass!" She winks at Duncan, "Liz can be your Maid of Honor and Alex, Paige, Carrie, and Ally can be your Bridesmaids."

"Who are Paige, Carrie and Ally?" I ask confused.

"Oh, my God, do you mean to tell me that we have had three women living at the Compound and you don't know their names?"

"Oh... them. Oops, sorry. I haven't really had much time to hang out with them or get to know them. I guess I had better rectify that, huh?"

"Or, you can just have Liz in the wedding so none of us other guys get suckered into wearing a monkey suit!" Kai pipes in.

"Kai, can you zip it until we ask for your opinion?" Xavier scolds him.

"Hey, I was watching out for your back, brother. I know I won't be part of the wedding party, but you will be! See if I ever try helping you out again!"

Ignoring the bickering going on between Kai and Xavier, I look at the others, "Wow, you really have found a way to pull this off, haven't you?"

"We know how stressed you have been, and we just wanted to help relieve you of some of it. I hope you don't mind." Taven replies.

"I don't mind at all. Thank you all so much, I love you guys! Well, most of you anyway." I joke as I look at Kai.

"You know you love me, Earnhardt!" He grins.

"Keep telling yourself that, kid!" I slap him in the chest.

"Who are you calling a kid? I am way older than you are!"

"Maybe physically."

"Whatever." He gives up and walks away. Happens every time he argues with me. I do love the guy like a kid brother. He is definitely fun to pick on like one.

I look around the room and see Alex sitting by Xavier, hanging on every word that comes out of his mouth. I pull Duncan out of the room and down the hallway. Once I know we are out of ear shot, I begin to voice my concern, "Can you talk to Xavier about Alex?"

"What about Alex?"

"Have you not noticed how she follows him everywhere and hangs on his every word? She has developed the wrong kind of feelings for him, Duncan. I have tried talking to her about it, but she doesn't care about the whole mate thing. She fancy's herself in love with him!"

"Good Lord! That's just what we need, a fledgling with a crush on her maker! Ugh, I will talk to him about it. Hopefully, he can put a stop to it before it gets out of hand."

"Thank you, babe." I put my arms up and around his neck while crushing my body to his. "You do realize that our wedding will be the perfect avenue to push Taven and Liz together, right?"

"Are you trying to seduce me into helping with your evil schemes?" He asks me seductively.

"There is nothing evil about this scheme, but yes, yes, I am. Is it working?"

"Oh baby, you know I would help either way, but I love this way so much better, so it may take a little more coaxing on your end."

"I think I can handle that. The question is… can you?" I remove myself from him and step away. I leave him standing there, fully aroused.

TWENTY

DUNCAN

During our training the next day, Jill is working on her punches and uppercuts with me as her partner. I must say, she is getting stronger every day and her technique is practically flawless. The only thing she doesn't have is the strength of a vampire, but I would place my bet on Jill against any regular person in a heartbeat. I love watching her train, when she gets all hot sweaty, her body glistens. Before the baby bump, her abs were well defined, and they will be again. Not that I would have an issue if they don't go back to being defined. I think once a woman has a child, there is nothing sexier than the battle scars that she carries because of it.

"Okay, let's take a short break and get some water into you, angel. Can't be having you pass out from dehydration now, can we?" I grin at her as I pass her a bottled water. We sit down and watch over the rest of the Elite training. My boy Ryder is getting the best of Jagger, another new recruit and then Phoenix and Axel are up against each other. I spot Stone working with Alex and continue to watch them. Xavier walks into the room and I see Alex deliberately fuck up on her uppercut.

"Oh Xavier," Alex calls out to him, "Could you show me what I am doing wrong? I just can't seem to get it right!" she pouts. Stone makes a face at the lie she just told Xavier.

I watch as Xavier stands behind Alex and grabs underneath her forearms, causing him to be plush up against her back side. He starts swinging her arms in uppercut motions for a few minutes until she "gets the hang of it" and then steps back.

"Are you watching what I am watching?" Jill asks me.

"If you are watching the shit that Alex is pulling and not the sweaty half-naked men in here, then yes, I am." I give her a sideways grin.

"You are such a jealous ass hat, you know that?" she kids.

"I am not jealous; I know I take care of my woman and I'm the best looking one in here! Nothing to be jealous about there."

"Conceded much?"

"Nope, just confident." I stand up and plant a kiss on the top of her head, "Continue to rest. I'm going to go talk to Xavier quick, okay?"

"Yes Sir!"

"You will be punished for that later, brat!"

"Oh, I'm counting on it!" Damn that devilish grin of hers gets me aroused every time!

I walk up to Xavier and slap him on the shoulder, "Hey man, can I talk to you outside for a moment?"

"Yeah sure." He turns back to Alex, "Just like that, Alex, you got it. Keep it up and I will be right back." She gives him her biggest smile.

He follows me out the door and into the weight room, where I close the door, "This seems serious. What's up?"

"How is everything going with Alex? I mean, how is she coming along with the change and new lifestyle."

"Not too bad. I mean, she is really shy, so it's taking longer for her and the whole blood drinking thing, but I think she will come around soon enough."

"What do you mean it's taking longer? How is she drinking it?"

"Well, she can't bring herself to drink out of the bags yet and she feels bad for the animals, so she won't touch them."

"How is she getting her blood then?" I am pretty sure I know the answer, but I want to hear him say it.

"She is still drinking from me. I know, I know, I need to wean her off soon, but I can't be mean. I still feel sorry for her."

"Dude, she is playing your ass hard core!"

"What are you talking about?"

"Jill was talking to Alex the other day and it seems that your little protégé has a crush on you!"

"Get out of here, she does not! I'm like her big brother."

"All I am telling you, is that when Jill tried explaining the whole mate thing to her, she got upset and told Jill to mind her own business. She also went on to say that she didn't want kids anyway, so there was no point in waiting for her own mate."

"That doesn't sound like the sweet Alex that I know. She always speaks highly of Jill."

"I sure hope you are not calling my mate a liar, because you know damn well that she is far from one! We barely even know Alex! I mean, it's understandable that she may have a crush on you, since you saved her life and all, but she is kind of taking it a little far. First with pretending to be too shy to drink from bags, then her conversation with Jill, and now, you should have seen her before you walked in! She was throwing pretty good uppercuts, but the second you walk in, she fucks up on purpose and asks for your help. Dude, even Stone noticed it. Don't believe me, talk to him."

"First of all, I am not calling Jill a liar, I am just shocked that she would act that way towards Jill. Second, I have noticed little things about her, but I just assumed it was nothing. I guess I better keep my eyes open from now on. Thank you for coming to me with this."

"No problem at all. Just let her down gently, Casanova, she's fragile." I tease.

"It's about time you come to see me as being the better of the two of us!"

"Oh my God, did you just make a joke?"

"Hell no, I am being dead serious!" He punches me in the arm and then walks out.

I head back myself and find Jill exactly where I left her and still resting. What's wrong with this picture? She never listens to what I tell her to do? I sit back down beside her and glance at her.

"Are you feeling okay?"

"Of course, why do you ask?"

"Because you actually listened to me for once and rested, that's why."

"I have come to realize that this fat belly of mine will not allow me to keep going like I used to."

"Never call yourself fat, angel! Besides, you barely have a bump."

"You would say that. But thank you, I love you more for saying it! Now tell me, how did it go with Xavier?"

"It went pretty well. He is going to keep his eyes open. Did you know that she was still feeding from him?"

"What? Why has he let it go on this long?"

"He felt sorry for her. He assumed she was too shy to drink from the bags and she told him that she couldn't possibly drink from animals. Oh, and he could hardly believe that she talked to you the way she did, because she speaks highly of you all the time."

"Ah, I see what she is doing there. She is playing the nice person in case I did say something. She is trying to discredit me. I hope he doesn't buy it."

"No worries there, he knows that you are not a liar. Well, we have done our part in this. Let him do his part now."

"Okay, but if I see something sneaky, I won't hesitate to call her out on it."

"Oh, I know you won't, babe, I know you won't." I snicker, earning me a slap to the chest.

Jax came searching for me an hour later to inform me that he made an appointment for the two of us, as well as Taven, Xavier and Cooper, for our tuxedo fittings this afternoon. "Also, Cassie wanted me to tell you that she got a hold of that gal you had her call about making a dress for Jill and she will be here tomorrow to get her measurements, along with the other women."

"Awesome, thank you for helping out in all this. You know, maybe we should just buy our tuxedos, seeing as how we are all starting to meet out mates."

"I think you are right." He laughs. "I will see you out front in two hours."

I turn to continue on, but I only make it five steps when a hand reaches out and yanks me into the hall closet. I know right away who it is, because I'd know that floral scent anywhere. "Mm, hanging out in hall closets never did anything for me, but with you here, I think I can stay in here all day!"

Jill giggles, "I need you, warrior! I didn't think Jax would ever shut up!"

"Baby, I talked to him for two minutes."

"Yes, two minutes too long! The babies are starving!"

"Oh God, are you in much pain?"

"No, not yet. I swear I am needing your blood a lot sooner that Cassie needs Jax's. Guess it's a twin thing."

I pick her up and she wraps her legs around my waist. Wait a minute. Since when does Jill wear skirts? My hand slips underneath and I find she has gone commando! I grunt in extreme pleasure and undo my jeans, letting my cock spring out. A second later, Jill's fangs sink into me as my cock sinks into her. I let her feed a bit first before I bite her as I fuck her against the wall. We are both crazy with need and know it has to be a quickie, so I give one more hard pull at her neck, and she erupts with me following soon after. She finally releases my neck and purrs. She seriously purrs after I just fucked her against a wall in the hall closet!

This woman in my arms is definitely my soulmate. She doesn't care where we are at, as long as I take her with everything I've got, and there are no cameras. I learned my lesson quick with that one!

A few moments later, we are exiting the closet when we hear Kole behind us, "Are you fucking serious? You two better sanitize everything in that closet!" Jill and I both laugh our asses off.

Jill turns to Kole, "If I didn't know any better, I'd say you enjoy it! First watching us on video and now following us to catch us in the act; shame on you Kole!"

"There is something seriously wrong with you; you are not right, Jill!"

"I would say the same about you too." She grins. Giving me a quick kiss and a "Love you baby", she skips down the hall and turns the next corner.

"Dude, the hall closet, really?" Kole has a grin on his face when I turn to him.

"Hey, she attacked me!"

"Oh? Are you calling rape?"

"Hell no, she can rape me any time she wants!"

"Man, there is something wrong with both of you! The worst part is that even Jax and Cassie are not as bad as the two of you!"

"Well then, I guess Jax isn't doing something right."

"I can't wait to move to the new place." He laughs and walks away leaving me standing there grinning from ear to ear.

JILL

I have been walking around with a smile on my face for last next thirty minutes. The whole hallway closet incident was a snap decision on my part. An overwhelming need for release and the hunger mixed together must have fried my brain, but I have to admit, I liked it a lot. I think I surprised Duncan with the little interlude as well. I may just have to start working it into a daily thing that I do.

I find myself sitting in the rec room flipping through the channels when I hear giggling and female voices coming down the hall. I turn towards the door and see Paige, Carrie, and Ally walk in. They come up short when they see me watching them. I don't know if it is the whole incident with Shelly, but they seem a little on edge in my presence every time we are in the same room. I would like to rectify that. Everyone else in the Compound seems to like them, but I haven't given them a chance.

"Hey ladies, what's new?" They look at me and then each other as if trying to figure out if it is a trick question, "Come here and sit with me." I request as I pat the cushion beside me.

I wait for them to settle in before I speak again, "I know I haven't really tried putting in much effort to get to know you girls since you have been here and for that, I am sorry. The whole thing with Shelly had nothing to do with you and I don't want you thinking that I am holding a grudge or anything."

I see relief flood their faces as I finish, and I feel bad for making them think otherwise, "Now that we have that out of the way, I need to know who is who, with you three. I mean, I know names, but not which one it belongs to." I giggle nervously.

The girl with dishwater blonde hair and blue eyes, offers me her hand first, "I am Paige." She is a pretty girl in a quiet way, with a quiet voice. I look to the next one who has dark brown hair and brown eyes, a very pretty girl and more outgoing compared to Paige.

"I'm Carrie. Nice to officially meet you!" She gives me a warm smile.

"Same here." I chuckle. I turn to the last and recognize her to be the one who spoke up when Shelly wouldn't give me Jillian, "And you must be Ally?" Light brown hair, pulled back in a bun, dressed in capri yoga pants and a college t-shirt, her blue eyes sparkle as she gives me her hand to shake.

"The one and only!" she smiles.

"It is nice to meet all of you and again, I am sorry for not getting this out of the way sooner."

"It's all good. You have been going through a lot lately, we understand." Carrie responds.

"So, tell me all about yourselves. Where are you from?"

We spend the next couple of hours chatting it up in the rec room and I find that I really do enjoy their company and like them a lot. I bring up my wedding and ask if they will do me the honor of being my Bridesmaids. They all screech at once, scaring the shit out me, before apologizing for their outburst. They accept after they finally settle down and so I inform them that the fitting for their measurements will be tomorrow. I thank them and then excuse myself.

The guys are not back yet from their own fittings, so I mosey on over to the kitchen to see what is on the menu for supper tonight and offer Max some help. I feel sorry for the guy, having to feed the whole Compound. He loves to cook, though, so he never complains.

"Hey handsome!" I greet him as I walk into the room.

He gives me his sexy smile that Duncan hates, "Well, hello gorgeous! What brings you to my neck of the woods? Oh, right… never mind." He chuckles to himself, "Sorry, food isn't ready yet."

"Ha, ha, ha! Actually, I was going to see if you wanted any company and maybe a little help?"

"Well, the chili is already cooking, but if you would like to get the cornbread ready and stick that in the oven, that would be great!"

"Sure. I think I can handle that."

Max walks into the pantry just as Alex comes strolling in. She looks around and then her eyes land on me, "Is Max around?"

"Oh, he is grabbing something. What's up, can I help you?"

"You sure can. You can learn to mind your own fucking business and stop telling lies about me! I am taken aback for a moment, but then she continues before I can say anything, "You went and said something to Xavier about me, didn't you?"

"I most certainly have not said anything to Xavier about you!" It isn't a lie. I talked to Duncan, and he is the one that went to Xavier.

"It's not a coincidence that he just happened to come tell me that our relationship is strictly platonic not too long after our talk! How dumb do you think I am?"

"Alex, I am sorry, but you have it wrong. I did not say anything to Xavier and before you go around accusing people, you need to get your facts straight!" Oh man, she has me pissed! "I tried telling you how the whole mating thing works. You can't make any of them settle down with you. Their future mates mean more to them than just settling with anybody."

"You can stick the whole mate bullshit up your ass! I don't believe in it for a minute." She lowers her voice just a little, "I will get Xavier into my bed, you can count on it!" She spins and stomps out of the room, never seeing Max standing in the doorway to the pantry.

"Wow! That is a different side to Alex that I have never seen! I don't think I like it very much!" Max stands there in complete surprise by what he just witnessed.

"You and me both! I knew about her crush, but I think she has now taken it to a whole other level!"

"Does Xavier know about all this?"

"Duncan talked to him this morning about her crush. I am assuming that he had a little chat with her before he left. I am thinking we better keep an eye on that one."

"More than one eye, I'd say! I'll talk to him too and warn him of her intentions."

"Good idea. I think he is going to need to watch his back with that one. I am also thinking that Taven should be informed as well."

"What do I need to be informed about?" Taven inquires as he walks through the door.

I stick the cornbread into the oven and walk over to the door to make sure no one is near. I shut the door and sit down at the table, motioning for Taven to do so as well. Max goes into Alex's outburst first and then I finish with everything that had led up to it.

Taven throws up his hands, "Why me? Why do I have to have all this craziness inside my Compound? No offense Jill, but life was so much quieter before the females entered it." He snickers.

"We make life interesting for you… admit it!" I tease. It finally hits me that Taven is here, which means Duncan is home, "Sorry boys, I need to go find my warrior, it's feeding time." I hop up and am just opening the door when Taven calls out to me.

"Oh Jill, one more thing before you go." I look back at him and wait for him to finish, "No more screwing in the closets please."

"Hey, I can't help the hormones! They make me do it!" I smile and run out the door in search of my warrior.

TWENTY-ONE

DUNCAN

Jill comes running up to me and jumps into my arms as soon as she sees me. If it wasn't for my fast reflexes, I probably would have dropped her on her ass. I laugh, "Happy to see me, angel?"

"I am always happy to see you, warrior, but right now you need to feed me!" She whispers the last part into my ear in case there are others around.

"Nothing like making me feel wanted or anything." I pretend to be hurt.

"How about I make a deal with you? You feed me, and I will make sure that you feel very wanted right afterwards!" She traces my lips with her finger as she tries to seduce me. Okay, there is no "trying" about it. She does seduce me, which is why I don't waste any time hurrying to our room.

Before I can even set her down, she is lifting my shirt up and I quickly lift my arms for her, so she can pull it off. I let her push me down on the bed as she climbs on top and straddles my thighs. She begins by circling my belly button with her tongue while she twists my nipples between her fingers. Working her way up my torso, licking and kissing as she goes, my cock comes to life, pulsing and jerking with the need to be pleasured. I try to tamp down my desire until she feeds, but she is making it so fucking hard.

As she ascends, she pauses, giving each nipple the same attention as she did my belly button, before continuing the climb back up. Reaching my neck finally, she gives a little suck before I feel the small pinch of her bite. Pleasure slams through me as she pulls my essence into her mouth, and I can't help but to grind my hips into her heated, naked crotch.

The torture is too much, so I undo my jeans and thrust urgently into her wet sheath. She moans at the force from which I take her, but she spreads her legs wider, taking me even deeper, "Fuck baby, you feel so good!" A crescendo of pleasure builds as she continues to feed from me and then my cock detonates, shooting liquid fire into her chamber. I continue to pump my cock until her pussy clamps down on me with her own release. By the time she comes down from her climax, I am drained of every drop of cum. She retracts her fangs and just lays across my chest, spent.

"Wow! I don't know what you did angel, but that was explosive for me! You always seem to amaze me."

"Well, don't thank me. These babies are the ones turning my hormones inside out. I am constantly horny every time feeding time is near."

"Do you mean to tell me that I can expect this for another three and a half months?"

"Please, don't sound too excited!" she laughs.

"The Compound isn't going to love it, but I'm going to take full advantage of it while I can!" I roll her underneath me and claim her lips. Reaching down, I grab the bottom of her shirt, and pull up, tossing it on the floor once it's off. Her bra goes next.

I am mesmerized by the sight of her as I slowly move within her tight sheath. Her eyes bright with desire, lips plump and tinged red from the feeding, and her glorious, rounded breasts, there for the taking, "Tell me angel, how do you want it?" I whisper.

"Take me any way you want, warrior. I am yours for the taking." She gasps each time I thrust in hard and pull out slowly.

I continue this tempo as I draw a nipple into my mouth and swirl my tongue around it before giving it a good suck. She is whimpering with need, but I keep the pace. Demanding her to look at me as I let part of my vampire out, my fangs extend, and I can see the glow of my eyes mirrored in her own. Keeping my eyes on her, I bite down right above her nipple and take the first draw, causing her to groan in pleasure.

She wraps her legs around my waist and matches my thrusts. "More... I need more!" she pants. I pick up speed until I am pounding into her and ripping her orgasm from her. As she comes down, I take one last big pull from her breast, sending her back in the whirlwind of desire. She screams my name as her walls clamp around me once more, taking me over the edge right with her.

We lay there for a few moments, and I realize that she has fallen asleep. I get up and cover her up with the blanket, then make my way to the bathroom to clean myself up. As I finish dressing, there is a pounding on our bedroom door, and someone is yelling for Jill to open the door.

I quickly go to the door before they wake Jill up, and I fling it open, ready to rip into the person on the other side. Alex is there, her fist raised ready to pound again, but she stops in midair as she stares at the anger oozing out of me. I step out of the room, causing her to take a few steps back, and shut the door behind me.

"If you ever come knocking my door like a mad woman ever again, especially when my pregnant mate is sleeping... I will end you!"

"I-I didn't know you were here or that she was sleeping!" she stammers.

"It does not matter, never pound on my door again! What is it that you need?"

"I need to talk to Jill."

"About what?"

"That is none of your business!"

"Let me get this straight. You come pounding on my door, demanding that Jill, my mate, opens the door and you are telling me it's none of my business?"

"Yes, I am." She pales a little once she speaks her words.

"Oh, little girl, you don't know who you are messing with here! And if this is about your little crush on your maker, get over it! It's not going to happen and no matter how mad you get at my woman over it, it's not going to change anything!"

"She needs to learn to keep her mouth shut and stop running to Xavier with lies!"

"Sorry to tell you this, but she hasn't said a word to Xavier. It was me! You want to yell at someone, yell at me. Not that it will do you any good."

"You are the one that went to him? Why?"

"I did. He needed to know about your crush. He feels responsible for you since he is the one that turned you and you took advantage of it. It is unnatural to drink from your maker, but he let it slide. You need to move on, little one, or we will have no choice but to turn you out on your own and that is the last thing that we want to do."

"You wouldn't do that, would you? Xavier wouldn't let you do it!"

"Taven is the only one allowed to kick you out and he doesn't like controversy, so if it comes between one of his long-time Elite warriors and a slip of a girl like you, who do you think he will choose. Hey, don't take my word for it. Do what you want, but just remember, come near my mate out of anger again, and you won't need to worry about getting kicked out!"

Alex stares at me a moment longer and then stomps off. I head to Taven's office to have a little chat with him.

Kole comes knocking on Taven's office door just as we are finishing up our conversation about Alex, "I hate to interrupt, but there is a situation downtown with some vamps. Cooper and Jayde just called in for some back up."

"I will go round-up the men. Send me their location and we will head over." Finally, a little action! It's been pretty dead around here lately since the warehouse raid and the men have been getting antsy.

I head to the weapon's room as I send out a mass text to all the Elite. Everyone arrives within five minutes and are suited up, armed, and ready to go in another five minutes. Kole had sent me an address to a local night club. Shit! I hate these. There is always a chance of being found out or we worry about the local law enforcement getting in our way. Hopefully tonight will not be one of those nights.

I have Ryder and Axel driving the Cargo van over and the rest of us hop in four different SUV's. I try to contact Jill through our bond, but she must still be sleeping, so I will try back later. I didn't want to wake her before I left, so I have Jax contact Cassie and have her let Jill know when she wakes up. Sometimes Jill forgets about the bond and so she doesn't open up like I need her to. We will have to work on that.

We pull up to the curb a block away from a night club called the Dark Zone. It's a popular club for those who like dark fantasy sci-fi, and also for Vamps who would rather drink fresh blood, but do not want to do it in public. It's a place where people play out their fantasies, especially with vampires, but do not realize that it is an actual vampire drinking their blood. Crazy, I know, but to each their own, I guess.

The club is one of our usual details to watch, because actual vampires hang out here, but we usually don't have any issues. I wonder what has brought us here tonight. We file out of the vehicles and head towards the club, a few of us at a time. Xavier, Jax and I are the first to enter. Women are calling out to us, as usual, begging us to take them in. The bouncer is one of us, so we get let in without the wait.

The atmosphere is dark, hence the name Dark Zone, with red lights placed minimally throughout the club and strobe lights on the dance floor. Cages are scattered throughout as well, with scantily clad men and women dancing in them. Fake bottles of blood line a wall behind the bar, but they also keep real blood bottled up for the vamps that do come in. The owner of the club, Felix, isn't one of us, but he knows us and has friends who are vampires. I'd say he definitely chose a good business to venture into, but nights like this, he would tell you different.

We head straight for the bar and order three beers, asking Drake, the bartender, where we could find our brothers. He nods to a corner booth, well hidden in the shadows. We pay for our drinks and head over to where Cooper and Jayde are sitting, watching the dance floor. Taking our seats, I ask for a report and Cooper informs us of the situation.

Apparently, a group of seven to eight vamps came in twenty minutes ago and started some bullshit with a few of the locals and are now on the dance floor harassing the women. Cooper said that Drake told them that he has never seen them in here before. It makes us wonder if they are just traveling through Augusta or if they are new fledglings. Either way, they need to tune it down a bit. We haven't even been here two minutes and we already know which ones we are dealing with.

We see Kaid, Dane, and Kai walk in and make their way over to us. Raven, Max, and the new recruits are positioned outside in case they are needed. Not wanting to make a scene, we wait until one of them walks over to the bar. Jax and I walk over and flank each side of him.

"Are you and your friends new to town or are you just passing through?" Jax inquires without looking at the vamp.

"What's it to you?" is the guy's only reply.

"Well, me and my friend here," Jax nods to me, "We keep the peace here in Augusta, along with our friends, and we got a call that you and your friends were being a little rowdy here tonight."

"We are only having a little fun, blowing off some steam."

"We are all for blowing off some steam. Hell, we need it ourselves time and again, but there is a difference between blowing off steam and causing trouble in a public night club." Jax points to the dance floor where a couple for the guy's friends are trying to sandwich a lady that does not want to be bothered, "Are you telling me that your friends there are only blowing off steam?"

The guy looks to his friends and then back to us, "We are only having a little fun, man. Give us a break."

"I'll tell you what, you and your friends leave quietly, and we will give you that break." I tell him.

"Fine! I'll see what I can do, but Frankie can be a little ass when he wants to be."

"However many of you leave peacefully, will be left alone. The rest will be taken in." I inform him, "Before you make your decision, look over at that table in the corner. You will see some of our friends waiting and there are more waiting outside. Just something to think about."

"Okay, okay! I will go talk to my friends!" He walks over to the dance floor and says something to one of the guys, who then looks at us and then over at the corner that the others are watching from.

His friend comes stomping over to us, "Who do you think you are, coming in here and telling us that we have to leave? We have every right to be here, just like everyone else!"

Jax straightens up, "You do have every right to be here… if you are behaving yourselves. You are harassing the women on the dance floor and that, is not behaving. That is why we are giving you a chance to walk out. Otherwise, we will take you and your friends down to Elite Headquarters."

"You are with the Elite?" the guy asks.

"We are. I take it you have heard of us?" I look between the two men.

"Yes, and we don't want any trouble with you, so my friends and I will leave."

"Smart choice. We always like resolving these issues without violence or taking anyone in. Thank you for your cooperation." Jax and I watch as they go grab their friends and leave the club.

"Do you think we will be seeing them again?" Jax asks me.

"You can count on it. Did you see the tick in his jaw and hear the tightness in his voice? He didn't like backing down, but knew they were outnumbered. We will be seeing them again."

The bartender thanks us as we pass the bar and leave the club. I am a little disappointed that we didn't get to see any action, but I have a feeling that we will soon enough with this group.

JILL

I'm sitting in the kitchen with Cassie and Liz, eating reheated chili, waiting for the guys to get back. I hate when they go out on these missions, because I don't know how dangerous they are, not that the guys can't take care of themselves. It's just stressful on my end. All I am doing is stirring the food around in my bowl, even though I am starving.

Liz gets up to go rinse her bowl out, "Good God Jill, why don't you just contact him and make sure he is okay? It's what I do with Jax." Cassie's annoyance with me shows.

Damn, why do I forget about that all the time? I need to remember to keep my mind open for him during times like this, "I always forget about the bond. It's just weird for me, but I guess I had better start getting used to it and using it."

I open my mind to Duncan and call to him, 'Ah, I see sleeping beauty is awake!' he answers me.

'Yes, I'm feeding my belly right now. How is it going? I have been worried.'

'It went well, no need to kill or bring anyone in, so we are headed back now.'

'Good. I hate waking up to you being gone.'

'Sorry babe, but I didn't want to wake you and I did try contacting you. You must have still been sleeping. I will be back in about ten minutes, love ya, angel.'

'Love you too, warrior.'

"They are on their way back, thank God." I turn to Cassie.

"I could have told you that, dork! Unlike you, I am in constant contact with my man."

"Piss off, bitch! I will get the hang of it!" I stick my tongue out at her and then turn my attention to my chili and begin to scarf it down just as Liz comes back to the table.

The next afternoon, Dominique, the seamstress, arrives with two other assistants to measure us for our dresses. Apparently, Cassie has given her an idea of what style of dress I would like, and Dominique has drawn up a few different sketches for me to look at. Her designs ware gorgeous! Cassie described the styles perfectly, simple white dresses, made of satin and lace. It is hard to decide, but I end up going with the one that I can see myself in the most. It is a satin dress with a very deep cowl neckline. The back is completely exposed, and it goes to mid-thigh. I choose to add a train to it, which starts by wrapping around my waist, leaving the front open. Even though I only have a little baby bump, I want to hide it as much as I can. The dress is simple, but elegant and perfect for a wedding on the lake.

I let the girls choose their own design for their dresses, because I want them all comfortable. My only demand is that they all need to be a teal blue in color. The longer the afternoon goes on, the more excited I become. Duncan tries coming in a few times but is kicked out by Dominique, giving him a few choice words.

About three hours into the fittings, I have to excuse myself for a bit to go feed. I contact Duncan to have him meet me at our room, but he is already there, waiting. I burst through the door and find him already on the bed, back against the headboard and legs straight out, butt ass naked. I give him an evil grin and rip my shirt up and over my head. My shorts are next, but I leave my bra and panties on, knowing that he likes taking care of that part himself.

I stand up on the bed, placing my legs on each side of his and look down at him. His face is level to my crotch, and I can feel the puddle forming in my panties as he stares straight ahead with hunger in his eyes. I take a step closer, so my pussy is only inches from his face. His nostrils flare as he inhales my desire that awaits. He moves in and runs his tongue over my panties, between my thighs. I grab the wall at the sensation that it brings to me. I look down and see that he is staring at me as he does it again, this time nipping my clit once he hits it.

He slowly pulls the lacey fabric down and has me step out of it. Hooking one of my legs over his shoulder, he gently opens the folds of my skin and pushes his tongue into my opening. He uses my wetness to lube my backside and presses a finger into me. Finding the bundle of nerves that drive me crazy, his other hand pinches and squeezes my clit while his tongue fucks my pussy, and the fingers on his other hand fuck my ass. His play causes me to throw my head back and groan as I feel the pleasure growing inside of me. His fingers then switch places with his tongue as he fingers me and sucks hard on my sensitive nub. I scream and render what he wants the most, my cum spilling over the fingers inside me.

Duncan grabs me and brings me down onto his stiff cock, pushing through until he is deeply seeded. Bringing my head down to his neck, I open up and sink into his jugular as I begin to move up and down on his cock. He moans in pleasure as I pick up speed taking deep pulls from his neck. I feel him bite down on my neck and my desire builds once again. We both are slamming into each other, keeping to the same rhythm, and building each other's climax until we tumble over.

It is in the middle of our orgasms when we hear a knock at the door and Liz calling my name. Duncan grunts as he pushes out the last of his seed and I cry out. Before I can answer Liz, I hear her on the other side of the door, "Um… never mind. It can wait.", and then it's quiet. I let a giggle slip past my lips at the thought of poor Liz hearing us orgasm. Duncan chuckles.

"They will learn not to come knocking at our door." He says.

"I love you, Mr. McPherson. Thank you for taking time out of your busy day to relieve a woman in need." I smile and press my lips to his for a quick kiss.

"Only if that woman is you."

"Ah, I see I've trained you well!"

"You have bewitched me for eternity, love."

Ten minutes later I head back to the ladies. Smiles on my wedding party's faces and frowns coming from Dominique and her assistants, "I am so sorry. I had an urgent errand to run." I explain to Dominique.

"Hey, it's your time and your soon-to-be-husband's money." She responds with a shake of her head.

Another half an hour and the seamstresses are packing up, getting ready to leave, "I'll be back in two weeks with the dress and a fitting."

"That's great! Remember to make it just a little bigger, you will need room to work with." I explain as I rub my belly.

"No worries. I have been doing this since before you were born!" she smiles.

We all say our goodbyes and I walk them to the door. I rejoin the women again and the first thing I hear is, "You little slut! Couldn't wait a little bit longer, could you?" Cassie jokes.

"No, I couldn't! When I want it, I want it." I smile.

"Well, we all want it too, but here we are, our vaginas drying up like age old grapes!" This coming from Liz.

I look at Cassie, "Okay, I am cutting Liz off from hanging out with you!" I laugh hard.

"You have to admit… that was a good one!" Cassie says as she winks at Liz.

"Yes, it was!" The room fills with laughter

Duncan ducks his head in to see what all the raucous is. He notices that Dominique is gone and strolls into the room, wrapping his arms around me. The girls all make gagging noises and disappear, leaving me and my warrior alone, to our own devices.

TWENTY-TWO

DUNCAN

It's only two weeks before the wedding and I am in complete wedding mode. Who knew that I, Duncan McPherson, would be nose deep in wedding planning? The things that I do for the love of my life and the mother of my children, but I had promised her that we would pull off this wedding in a month's time, and we are going to do it! The women and I have been busy hiring caterers, a DJ, a photographer, and florist. Most are wanting extra fees, since it is such short notice, but hey, money is no object for me.

As my Best Man, Jax has been recruited against his will. Since he did such a great job at his own wedding with the food portion of it, that is his sole job for my wedding. Once he learns this, then his whole attitude changes, and he jumps on board.

Jill is stressed out over her parents coming, and of how they are going to react when they find out that she is pregnant. Cassie and I are trying to keep her as calm as can be, but it's easier said than done. At this moment, she is waiting for the seamstress to arrive with her gown and last fitting. This morning she voiced her concern that the seamstress isn't going to make it big enough for this fitting. She has actually popped out quite a bit in the last two weeks, I love it, she's gorgeous! This morning as we laid in bed, I held her and the babes in my arms, and I couldn't help but think how beautiful she is with her protruding stomach. She definitely has the glow of pregnancy about her.

I am just finishing up a call with the travel agent for our Honeymoon to Scotland, when Xavier pops his head into the open doorway. I hold up a finger and motion him to come in. Making himself at home, he waits for me to finish up my business. I hang up the phone and turn to him, "What's up?"

"We have detail tonight, so I thought I would come and let you know."

"I thought I am off detail until after the wedding?" I crinkle my brows at him.

"Yeah well, another one just came up and Taven is short on warriors, so he needs you. Is that a problem?"

"Well, no, I can actually use the distraction after all this wedding planning. What time do we head out?"

"We leave at six forty-five sharp. Oh, and it's kind of like an undercover detail so dress in nice casual." Xavier informs me.

"That's weird, but whatever. I'll see ya then." I watch as he walks out, a slight grin on his face. Hm, what's that all about, I wonder.

I spend the rest of the afternoon with Jill, sating her "appetite", like I have done every day this week. It's a tough job, but someone's gotta do it, right? I inform her that I am going out on detail and that there will be blood bags with my blood handy, in case she needs them.

"But what if I need you as well?" she pouts.

Just the way she says it, gets my dick hard all over again! "Oh, I will be giving it to you one more time before I leave, no worries! If you do feel the need to have another release, just take your trustworthy toy out and contact me through our bond. I will talk dirty to you and get you off. I see her eyes light up and next thing I know, she is going down below the covers and sucking me off, "Fuck Baby, where have you been my whole life?"

I hear her muffled voice, "Mm, I love tasting myself on your dick!", and that was it. As soon as her mouth was back around me, I fill it up so full, she is having a hard time keeping up with swallowing it all.

I only have an hour before I need to leave, so I better make this quick. I grab her up and tell her to hold on to the bars on the headboard. I push her head down onto the pillow and whisper in her ear, "Keep your head down and ass up. I will take care of the rest. I mean it, don't move." I move in behind her and slide two fingers into her wet pussy, pumping them until they are lubed enough for her ass. Pushing one and then the second finger into her bud, I start finger fucking her ass as I shove my dick inside of her pussy. I don't go easy on her as I ram myself in and out, making her cry out in pleasure. My balls are slapping against her clit as I fuck her.

In no time at all, I have her screaming my name as she clamps down on my dick with her orgasm. I hold my own off, because I want to fill her ass with my cum. Once she is calm, I pull out of both holes and stick my fingers back into her pussy for more lube. I shove them back into her ass and pull them out again as I line my cock up with her hole. I inch in slowly as she is panting and gripping the bars.

"Are you okay, babe?" I ask her tenderly. She shakes her head yes. That a girl, always loves a good fucking! I keep pushing in inch by inch until I'm deep in her ass, "Are you ready for this?"

"Just fuck me already!" I needed no more coaxing. I pick up speed until I am slamming myself into her tight fucking ass, trying to hold off until she comes again. I reach around and pinch her clit sending her body into overdrive and her body spasms as she comes. I let myself go and thrust hard as cum shoots out. I pull out a little and thrust back in for another spurt and yet again for another.

I roll us to our sides, my dick still up her ass. I start pumping into her, this time biting her neck, causing her desire to build yet again. I lift her leg and start fingering her until she comes one last time. I pull all the way out of her and turn her head, so I can kiss her tenderly. Pulling away, I look her in her eyes, "Thank you, love. I am sorry if I was too rough with you, but you take it every time and I thank you. Now get some sleep, I love you." She smiles as she closes her eyes and tells me she loves me back. I slip away from her and cover her body up with the blanket.

Xavier pulls up to a club and tells me that there are some guys in there that keep coming back and they get rowdy as hell. There is also some party going on tonight and they wanted some extra hands to help out with security.

"So, what? Now we are bouncers? This is bullshit!" I go to call Taven, but Xavier grabs my phone.

"It's just for one night. Quit being a baby!" He jokes.

"Fine, whatever! Let's just get this over with!" I could be laying, snuggled up with Jill right now, but no, I have to babysit a bunch of horny men that don't know how to respect women! We walk into a darkened hallway and open the inside door. Music blares through the speakers and naked women are walking around with cocktails while girls are on the stage dancing.

There are a few men with their backs to us, right up on Sniffers Row, holding up cash. One of the dancers is giving a lap dance to a guy in their group. As we get closer to these men, I see the profile of the guy with the stripper on his lap. Is that Kai? Then out of nowhere I hear my name shouted and the group turns around. Every one of my Elite brothers are there, smiling at me.

Xavier grabs my shoulder, "Welcome to your Bachelor party bro!" He laughs in my face and then goes and joins the guys.

I laugh and shake my head. What the fuck are they doing? Of all places, they bring me to a strip club! Yep, Jill is sure going to like this one!

"Come on, Dunc! Come join the party!" Kai yells as the stripper shoves her tits in his face. Well, there is nothing to do now, but to join them, but I will be sitting behind them. I don't need no fake shit being rubbed on me, especially if it isn't Jill's.

An hour into the party, Jill contacts me, 'Hey babe, how is it going?'

'Damn, it's good to hear your voice!'

'Why do you say that?'

'There was no detail! These assholes that I call my brothers brought me to a damn strip club!'

'Oh, I know. It was my idea.'

'What!? Why would you have them bring me here?'

'Just to make sure you know what you have at home and what you won't be missing anymore.' She giggles.

'Oh man, you are going to get it later when I get home! I can't believe this!'

'That's what I am looking forward to! I love you, babe. Have fun, but not too much fun! Catch my meaning?'

'No worries there. These women have nothing on you!'

We break contact and I continue with the rest of the guys. They try their hardest to buy me lap dances, but I'm not going there. I know we don't catch diseases, but just thinking about another woman's pussy rubbing up on me, just doesn't do it for me. Not going to happen. I did enjoy watching Taven get one that I had bought for him. He didn't know what to do with his hands and looked so uncomfortable. Each Elite ends up with a stripper in their lap at some point. I notice that Raven and Jax aren't here though, and I question Xavier about it.

"Neither one wanted to come and thought that they would stay behind to protect the women. You forget that Mika is still alive."

"At least, they had the good sense to stay home." I shake my head and chuckle. I look back at Xavier and he has a weird look on his face, as if he is thinking about something, "Are you okay, buddy?"

"No, yeah. I was just thinking back to the night at the Dark Zone. Those guys that were causing trouble, two of them had looked familiar, but I couldn't place them, so I just dropped it. It just hit me where it was that I have seen them before."

"And... where have you seen them?"

"The night of the raid on the warehouse, when we had to save your stupid ass. They were there. I remember seeing them right after we loaded you up into the van. They weren't among the dead either. They must have escaped with Mika."

"Are you saying that some of the Hunters are now Vampires?"

"That is exactly what I am saying. That may be why they have been hanging low and we haven't had any more trouble." He replies.

"So, what? Mika is making vampire's now? The very thing he hates?"

"Maybe. Maybe he is making just enough to be able to take us out and then he plans on killing them afterwards."

"Wow, you could be right. We need to dig further into this though, before we start making assumptions."

"Yeah, I know. I hope to God that we are wrong, because if we are not, we have a bigger problem."

"What is that?" I look at him a little bit confused.

"Vamps can smell type O blood. You saw what they were doing with the women while they were human. It's going to be ten times worse!"

Well, this conversation just ruined the good ole time I was having, "Guess we better all get back to the Compound and start dealing with this right away." Xavier agrees with me, and we start gathering the men up to head out.

It isn't easy getting some of the men out. I am not sure how long the others had been here before we got here, but it takes a hell of a lot of liquor to get us vamps drunk and Taven, Max and Kai are wasted! I can't believe Taven had drunk that much, but he is looking uncomfortable. Maybe he kept drinking to try and loosen up, not realizing how much he was actually consuming; now we are left to deal with his bad decisions.

Cooper and I walk in the front door carrying Taven in while the others handle Max and Kai. Cassie and Liz peek out of the rec room to see what the commotion is all about and both gasp when they see us carrying Taven. Liz is the first to reach us, "Oh My God! Is he hurt?"

Taven lifts his head and smiles, "There's my beautiful girl!" he slurs. Cassie chuckles behind her hand.

Liz blushes from Taven's statement, "What is wrong with him? Is he… drunk?" She sniffs at him and wrinkles her nose.

"Nope," Taven says, "I don't get drunk." He tries to stand on his own, but then stumbles a little and Liz grabs at his chest to help steady him. "Mm, you smell good!" He says as he wraps Liz in his arms and shoves his nose in her hair.

"We had better get him back to his room." I tell Liz. Nodding her head, she follows Cooper and I as we take him back.

We lay him on the bed when we get there as Liz goes for a wet washcloth, "Too bad he won't have a hangover in the morning. That would be fun to tease him about!" Cooper chuckles.

"Do you really want to see Taven grumpy with a hangover?"

After thinking about it, "Yeah, you're right. That would suck dick."

Liz returns and sits on the bed with Taven, placing the wet cloth on his forehead.

"I think I'm going to be sick!" Taven cries out. I jump for his garbage can and set it down in front of him just as he empties his stomach. After a few minutes, he is finally done and must have thrown the majority of the liquor up, because he is almost his self again, "Fuck! I haven't puked in centuries!"

Liz looks at us confused, "Just a figure of speech." I explain.

Taven lays back and notices Liz sitting on his bed, "Oh man, you should not have just witnessed that!"

"Good Lord! I have two boys that have been sick. I can handle it a little throw up." She smirks.

"Well, thank you, I appreciate it." Taven grabs Liz's hand and gives her a small smile.

"Guess that is our cue to leave." I say while grabbing Cooper's arm, "We need to meet first thing in the morning, so don't keep him up all night!" I wink at Liz. She opens her mouth to say something, but I shut the door before she can.

We all met in the Conference room the next morning and Xavier explains why. We haven't heard from Mika for some time, but we know that we haven't heard the last of him either. If it is true that Mika is turning his men into vampires, then we will definitely have a war on our hands and we will need to do something soon, before they have a chance to hurt any more innocent people.

JILL

Duncan has me laughing so hard, telling me about Taven the night before, that I have tears in my eyes. Now I wish I hadn't retired early, but my warrior really wore me out before he left and by the time I drank two blood bags, I was exhausted. I am just glad that the guys had a good time, they need a night out once in a while. I also know that Duncan wouldn't have wanted to be around all those naked women and so he would be good, but at least they got out.

He also tells me about their meeting this morning and their thoughts on Mika. I am not sure how I feel about it. Mika really hated vampires… or maybe just the Elite. If he thinks he can control the vampires, then he may not be as averse to them.

Then another thought comes to me as I am taking my shower. What if Alex wasn't really attacked like we thought she was, and it was her plan to get changed to a vampire? There is just something about her that doesn't sit well with me. I walk out of the bathroom as Duncan is carrying our breakfast in.

"Duncan, I was just thinking back on what you told me about Mika and the vampires. Are you sure you saw Alex getting gang raped? I mean, really getting raped?"

"I know what I had seen, and I know what I had heard. Why do you ask?"

"Could it be possible that it was somehow staged? Okay, so what if they did see you at the first warehouse and knew you would come to the second one as well. They had to have known that back up would come. You said that Mika said so, himself, saying that I would come for you. What if they staged the rape in hopes that we would take the girls back to our Compound."

"I don't know if I am following you."

"What if Alex was meant to be brought here to spy and also to turn into a vampire? I mean, even you have to admit that she is kind of hostile. Oh my god! She is also the only one that refused to be checked out by Dr. Howard, even though she was the only one that was raped!"

"Hm, you do have a point. The thing is, you know how well my eyesight is and I saw with my own eyes that they were penetrating her."

"Yeah well, you know how bad she wants to get Xavier into bed. She's probably a little slut. Hell, maybe they pulled trains on her all the time, we don't know."

"Wow... just put it all out there like that." He laughs.

"What? I am not going to put anything past Mika or that little hussy! Someone needs to keep their head on their shoulders when there is a pretty face around."

"I have to admit, I think you may be right."

"Can you please say that again?" I smile sweetly.

"And... there she is! The smartass that I know you to be." He wraps his arms around me and kisses the tip of my nose. "Now eat, so we can take your crazy thoughts to Taven and Xavier.

We walk into Taven's office an hour later. Xavier is always there waiting on us, "You know, some of us have places to be. What, did you have to stop for quickie in a closet?" Taven teases.

"Fuck off, Tav!" Duncan scolds, but his smile takes the harshness away.

"Okay, seriously, what's this about?" Xavier asks, "I really do need to get to training; Alex is waiting for me."

"Well, once you hear my theory, you may not be in such a hurry to go help her." I start right in on telling them my thoughts about Alex.

They listen to every word I say, without interruption. Once I finish, I just stand there and wait for them to say something, but Duncan is the first to speak.

"I really think that Jill may be on to something. A few things don't add up with Alex. The only thing that we do know for sure is that she has formed a huge crush on Xavier."

"That is weird in itself!" Taven jokes, earning himself a grunt from Xavier., "That aside, it is a possibility. I will check her story out. I'll have Kole hack into the college records and the DMV and then go from there. In the meantime, Xavier, keep a close eye on her."

"For her sake, I hope you are wrong Jill. I have never killed a woman before, and I don't want to start now."

"I hope I am wrong too, but you guys always tell me to go with my gut, and my gut is telling me that something isn't right with her."

This is the last thing we need with our wedding being only two weeks away! Why can't anything go smoothly for any of us, ugh! "Oh my God! The wedding! She has been living here all this time, she knows everything about the wedding! What if that is when they plan on attacking?"

"Let's not get a head of ourselves yet, babe. Let Kole do his thing and then figure things out. Do not stress about this, okay?" Duncan holds my shoulders as he tries to calm me.

He is right of course; I can't stress about this right now. I may be wrong, but if I'm not, she had better watch her ass, because hell hath no fury like a bride-to-be having her wedding day ruined!

TWENTY-THREE

DUNCAN

We have been busy for the last two weeks, between the wedding, trying to find out more about Mika's plans and whereabouts, and last, but not least, finding out who Alexandria Murphy really is. Giving Jill reassurance, we beef up security for the wedding, bringing in more Elite Warriors like we have in the past, posting them around the whole perimeter surrounding the new Compound and its land. No one gets in without their specially made chipped invite. Anybody can make a copy of an invite, but when they don't know that it has a chip in it, they cannot duplicate it.

As for Alex, her college transcripts checked out perfectly, but unfortunately, the DMV records did not. The real Alexandria Murphy has red hair, green eyes and lots of freckles, whereas our Alex does not. Looking at facial recognition, we found a Miss Samantha Warner, high school dropout, with an arrest record for prostitution. So, the question now is, what is she planning and is there a specific reason why she has shown interest in Xavier? We haven't let it be known to her that we know that she is a fake, continuing on like everything is normal, but keeping a very close eye on her.

Jill's parents arrived two days ago but are staying at a local hotel. Jill wasn't kidding about her parent's feelings on her being pregnant before being married. They did, however, calm down a little once they learned of our wedding. Jill hadn't mentioned anything to them previously, because she did not feel the need to. I have been trying really hard to keep my mouth shut when her mother is around and is making snide comments about Jill's stupidity on getting knocked up before the wedding. I finally speak up, and in the nicest way possible, lie through my teeth, informing her that we were supposed to be married long before this, but I got injured and had to postpone the wedding and that we both made the decision to try having a baby. She scoffs at my excuse though and continues with her opinions. Since then, I turn and walk the other way when I see her walking in my direction.

The view for the wedding ceremony is unbelievable. I want it to be a surprise for Jill, so she has not been allowed to see it, but I know my Angel, she will be speechless. With a sunset wedding, the lake behind where we say our vows will be aglow with the setting sun. Seating is lined up for the guests, with an assortment of teal and white flowers, wrapped in teal ribbons. The arch that we stand under is decorated almost the same way, with tulle drapes. There are tents set up with decorated tables and a dance floor for the reception. I am thinking I did pretty well planning my first wedding. Of course, I had help, but all the final say was me, so I will take the credit for it.

As Cassie takes her place under the arch and my guys and I line up, I start to get a little nervous. Not because I have doubts of marrying my mate, but nervous over seeing my bride as she walks down the aisle. As the last guest takes their seat, the music starts, and the women begin their trek down the center aisle. Once again, Xavier is transfixed with Liz as she makes her way down the center and past all the guests, taking her place beside the bride's spot. The music stops and the guy I personally hired for this specific moment, begins playing Highland Cathedral with his bagpipes. It's a beautiful sound from my homeland and I hope that Jill loves it just as much as I do.

Jill makes her way down the aisle, her eyes never leaving me. I can't help but stare at the angel that seems to be floating in my direction.

She has a glow to her it seems, and the sight takes my breath away. I wait until she gets to the end of the aisle before stepping up and taking her hand. I see the tears glistening in her eyes, but they do not fall. We both step up to Cassie together and see that she has tears flowing down her face as well.

"Seriously, Case? Suck it up and marry us already!" Jill scolds jokingly in a whispered voice.

"Oh shit, sorry!" She wipes her face off as I shake my head and smile at her choice of words. She begins the ceremony and in no time at all, Cassie is announcing us as husband and wife. I grab my Bride and claim her lips, dipping her in the process and getting cheers from the guests in doing so.

"God, you look amazingly beautiful!" I tell her before I lift her back up.

"And you, warrior, are more handsome then ever... even in your kilt!" She smiles adoringly at me.

"How long do we need to stay at our reception?" I ask her hungrily. She ignores my question, but chuckles as she turns to face the guests and I follow suit.

"I now present to you Mr. and Mrs. Duncan and Jill McPherson!" Cassie announces. The bagpipes start playing as we make our way back up the aisle together.

JILL

Tears come to my eyes as I look over the scene before me. The set up for our wedding is truly amazing. Duncan has gone above and beyond my expectations. As I walk down the aisle to the beautiful sound of bagpipes, I stare at the man, the warrior, that has stolen my heart from day one. I didn't make it easy for him in the beginning, but he waited patiently for me and that, is true love. He stands before me, at the end of the aisle, dressed in a black tuxedo jacket with a family-crested sash across his chest. The kilt he is wearing does nothing to take the warrior out of him. If anything, it makes him look like a true Scottish Warrior. His muscular legs send shivers down my spine as I think back to all the times he has used them to hold me up while making love to me.

As my best friend has us recite our vows, I feel my eyes fill up, but the tears do not spill. I am marrying my other best friend and the love that I see in his eyes for me, shows me that I will be loved and protected for the rest of my long life. Cheers explode as he kisses and dips me, taking my breath away from the passion within the kiss.

Duncan is anxious to have me to himself, already asking me how long we have to stay at the reception. As much as I want him to take me away from everyone, we have to stay a few hours, but I think we can manage to sneak off for a bit. After all, I will need to feed soon, I smile to myself.

"Oh, my God, you are married!" Cassie squeals as she comes running up and hugs me.

"Yes, I am!" I stare up lovingly at Duncan, "He's finally made an honest woman out of me." I wink at him.

"Thank God for that!" My mother walks up frowning.

"Can you just be happy for me, for once?" I ask her.

"I am happy for you. I just wish it happened before the pregnancy."

"Well, it didn't, Mother, so get over it! If you can't be happy for me today, then please don't talk to me. This the happiest day of my life and I will not let you ruin it! I love you mom, but you need to get the stick out of your ass!" I grab Duncan's hand and walk away feeling exhilarated.

"I am so proud of you, Mrs. McPherson! I am really turned on by the way you handled your mother." Duncan nuzzles my neck.

I laugh out loud, "You are always turned on in my presence."

"Can you blame me?" He asks as I run my fingers through his shoulder length locks. I love it when he keeps his hair down.

"No, I can't." I take his hand and pull him around the corner of the building closest to the tent. I look around and see that it's some sort of shed, but it will do, and we slip through the door.

Duncan lifts me up and I wrap my legs around his waist. "Husband, I am going to feed, and I want you to fuck me hard while I'm doing it."

"I am pretty sure that I can oblige." He lifts his kilt and finding me already wet and without panties on, grunts and plunges into my already wet opening. I sink my fangs into him and pull long and hard. A few more big pulls and he has his own in my neck to cover up the roar that tries to break free as his cock explodes into me, sending my own desire crashing through me.

When he finally retracts his fangs and closes up the puncture marks, he pants in my ear, "God woman, you are definitely going to be the death of me!"

I have no words at this moment, and I feel as if I am drifting in air. A knock breaks the moment and Kole's voice drifts through the door, "I know you two are in there. Just wanted to let you know that they are waiting for you guys to cut the cake." We hear his laughter as he walks away.

"Can we get no privacy around here?" Duncan snickers.

"Not as long as we continue fucking in public places." I reply with laughter. We straighten our clothing and head over to the tent to feed the hungry guests.

DUNCAN

Jill and I spend two weeks in Scotland for our honeymoon and it is the best time of my life! There are days that we spend almost all day in bed together, learning each other inside and out and no one there to give us any shit about it. I show her the area where I grew up, but with the centuries that have passed, nothing looks familiar to me anymore. The best part about the trip, aside from being together, is that we are not looking over our shoulders every time we are out and about. Unfortunately, our private time together ends too soon, and it is time to head back to real life.

It is chaos the second we walk into the Compound. We hear screaming and swearing coming from somewhere within. Dropping our bags at the door, we run in the direction of the commotion and find half of the Elite in Xavier's quarters trying to subdue Samantha, A.K.A. Alex. Apparently, she has tried drugging Xavier and seducing him. Luckily, his metabolism burned off the drug she used within five minutes, and he caught her in the act. He awoke with his pants down and her half undressed. Saying he is livid would be putting it mildly. I have never seen Xavier as angry as he is at this moment. It is a good thing that a couple of the guys were walking by when they heard Xavier's roar and burst through his door or else Samantha would be dead now.

Cooper and Dane have her cuffed now and are leading her down to the Interrogation room. Xavier tries to follow, but I put my hand on his chest to hold him in place, "Whoa buddy. You can't go down there in the state you're in. You need to calm down before you can even be in the same room with her." I tell him.

"I want her executed!" He says through clenched teeth.

"We need to get to the bottom of this first. Find out why she has done all this, so we can be prepared. We both know that Mika is behind this."

"Fine! Just so you know, when the time comes, I will be the one to end her! I made her and I will be the one to take her out."

"I am sure nobody will have a problem with that, it is your right." I reassure him.

Samantha is in the Interrogation room for hours and we aren't getting anywhere. She knows that her time on this earth is over, regardless on if she tells us anything, so she refuses to talk all together. We have no choice than to have Jax retrieve the information for us. He isn't too happy about it, but he knows it is the only way and this all needs to end now.

Jax does his thing in two parts, the first part being, why she is here and so obsessed with Xavier. Jill's assumption is correct, Samantha was working for Mika... at first. They had staged the whole rape seen and got her into our Compound. She knew a few of us would be walking around the halls at the time of her "suicide", it was always busy at that time of day, and so she slit her wrists. Vampires can smell blood a mile away, if not more, so she wasn't too worried. She was hoping that she was correct in assuming that we would change her. She assumed right. What she wasn't expecting was to fall for Xavier the way she did. She truly believed that her and Xavier were meant to be together, and she thought that if they had sex, he would finally see it too.

As for the second part, we learn that Mika's plan is to make an army of vampires to try and take us out. He had captured a female vamp and tortured her until she gave him pretty much all of our secrets. That is how he knew so much about us and about vampire mates. Of course, he eventually killed the poor woman, just like I am sure he plans on killing the fledglings that he is creating. That is all we can get from her, all that she knows.

After we get all the information and Jax relays it all to Xavier, he decides that he can't go through with killing Samantha. He does, however, have no issue with throwing her into a cell, hoping that maybe some therapy sessions will help her get her mind straight. Then he will reevaluate the situation in a few months; I think it's the right thing to do, for now.

After an exhausting day and still having jet lag, I crawl into bed and snuggle up to my sleeping wife. She mumbles something in her sleep and snuggles in closer, her ass wiggling on my cock. I run my hand up and down her naked thigh before slowly sliding it to her sex and circling her nub. She moans and starts pressing herself into my hand, coaxing me to continue. I slip a finger into her dampening folds and slide it back and forth before inserting it. She throws her thigh over my legs, opening up for me. My hard on slips in between and I pull my finger out, replacing it with my cock.

"Mm, I love waking up like this." She mumbles.

"I wasn't planning on waking you, but when that tight ass of yours rubs against me, it leaves me no choice." I kiss her neck, "I am going to fuck you until you pass out, baby." Biting her earlobe, I increase my pace and the rhythm of her breathing changes, telling me that she is close, so I ease off. "I don't want you coming yet, love."

She whimpers at my words. I continue taking her to the brink of orgasm many times until, finally, I feel my own desire burning and I start thrusting harder and faster. I sink my fangs into her neck, and she screams like no other from the orgasm that rips though her. Her orgasm is drawn out with each pull that I take from her vein, until I decide that she has had enough, and I let myself go, filling her up with my own hot seed.

I am not done with her yet. I can never be satisfied with only taking her once, or even twice. Before I am finished with her, I take her doggy-style, using her vibrator in her ass at the same time, I take her again with her on her back and legs up over my shoulders. The last is when I fuck her ass and use the vibrator in her pussy with the clit stimulator working its magic at the same time. By the time I am done with her, both orifices are dripping with my seed, and I can't bring myself to wash it away just yet. Yeah, I can be a sick fuck sometimes, but she brings out the beast in me. Before I even pull out her, she is fully sated and passed out cold. I pull her into my embrace and fall into a deep sleep.

JILL

I can barely walk today after the way Duncan took me last night, but I am not complaining, I love it when he fucks me like that. I feel like a dirty slut in a porno and it turns me on like no other! Everyone I run into smiles or chuckles when they see me trying to walk normal and then laugh when I try chalking it off to being a beached whale from the twins. I am alone in the kitchen when Duncan finds me and starts molesting me, but I have to shoo him away, because I am too sore.

"Am I walking really funny? I know I am sore, but I thought I was hiding it very well. Everyone is finding humor when they look at me." I pout.

"Oh Baby, you have no idea how loud you were last night, do you? I had you screaming bloody murder most of the time. I am sure the neighbors heard you!"

"Oh my god!" I feel my face turn red and cover my face with my hands.

"Yes, you were screaming that too!" He chuckles as he nuzzles my neck.

"Why do you bring that out in me?"

"Because you love it and want it. I will give you everything you want in life, especially in the bedroom! I can't get enough of you, Angel! Luckily, we have an eternity together."

"I don't think an eternity will be long enough." I gasp as he places his hand between my thighs.

"I think sore or not, somebody is ready to go again. I know I can." He moves my hand to his arousal.

Max walks into the kitchen at that moment. "Oh, HELL NO! This is my domain and I've told you that stuff isn't allowed in here! Do I have to hang up the rules?"

"You know what? I really can't wait until you find your mate, so we can give you the same shit that you give us all the time! You will see how hard it is." Duncan exclaims.

I giggle on his last sentence, "That what he said."

Duncan chuckles at my comment, but Max tries glaring at me before he begins to smirk. "Get the fuck out of my kitchen, both of you!"

Duncan picks me up and carries me off to have his way with me... again!

EPILOGUE

THANKSGIVING

DUNCAN

The whole Compound spends Thanksgiving together. The women help Max with the meal while the rest of us sit in the rec room watching the football game. We are even thoughtful enough to let Jenny and Samantha join us for the meal. No one should spend the holiday locked in a cell, but they do have to wear ankle bracelets that will render them immobile if they step an inch out of the Compound. Jenny is pretty good company although her and Ryder spend a lot of time conversing together, but Samantha won't let her attitude go, so we all ignore her.

The meal itself is delicious and leaves us all sated, Kaid and Dane actually pass out in the recliners. The rest of us sit around the table playing Cards Against Humanity and laughing our asses off at each other's card choices. Taven and Liz have their own little conversation going at the end of the table and every once in a while, Liz will laugh at something funny that Taven says, which is really weird because he's always so uptight; maybe she will be good for him. Her own boys are on the couch playing video games together, yelling at the screen every time one of them dies.

Jill grabs my hand and whispers to me, "I think we had better call Dr. Howard, Babe."

"What's wrong? Are you having pain?" I go into panic mode. I had taken her in the laundry room this afternoon when I found her in there putting a load into the washer and starting it. I highly suggest fucking your girl on a running washing machine when it's on spin cycle! I didn't think I took her that hard, but maybe I did.

"No pain yet, but my water just broke!"

I jump up, knocking the chair over and causing everybody to look at us, "Jill's water just broke! Someone call Doc!"

"I'm on it!" Jayde responds.

"Calm down warrior, we aren't going into battle. At least not yet." She chuckles.

"Let's get her down to medical while we wait for the doctor." Raven suggests. I pick Jill up and start carrying her, my heart beating rapidly with excitement. My babes are coming! We had found out through the ultrasound that we are having twin boys and Dr. Howard gave us the result of the lab from Jill's miscarriage that we had lost our baby girl. Jill took it pretty hard, but she has now come to terms with the loss, not that she doesn't feel it anymore, she just handles it better.

"I call 'Not Me' on cleaning up this mess all over the floor!" Kai calls out as he points to the amniotic fluid under Jill's chair. I roll my eyes at him and walk out the door.

"No worries, I'll clean it up, big baby!" I hear Cassie tell Kai.

As we get to medical, Jill feels her first contraction come on. I lay her down on the bed that is set up for birthing and close the curtain, so I can help her undress and get the hospital gown on. Another contraction wracks her body just a few minutes after the first one and I become alarmed. They are too close together already. I holler for Raven and tell him my concerns when he approaches.

"Well, looks like these babies are wanting to be born." He smiles at me.

"They can't come until Doc arrives!" I really start panicking now.

"Don't worry, as much as I would rather not do it, I can deliver a baby Duncan." He chuckles and shakes his head at me. Then he instructs Jill to put her legs into the stirrups and has me help her scoot down further on the bed. "I need to check you Jill, I'm sorry."

"That's okay, I don't mind. I trust you Raven." She smiles until another contraction hits and she cries out.

Raven goes in to check her cervix, but his eyes widen, "I'm afraid the good doctor may not make it in time. At least not for the first one. I can see his little head, so I am going to need you to push on the next contraction Jill."

I help hold her up as she pushes. A few more and his head is out and on the next one, he slides right out. Raven has me come and cut the umbilical cord just as Doc comes strolling in smiling, "I see you were too impatient to wait for me!"

Raven moves out of the way and takes my son over to examine him. I hear a whale of a cry come from the little one and it chokes me up, bringing tears to my eyes.

"Duncan, can you come over and help your wife as she pushes?"

I hurry back over to Jill and grab her hand. She looks at me questioningly, "He is perfect!" I inform her of our first son.

Both of our boys are born healthy and only four minutes apart from one another. I sit beside Jill on her bed, we each hold a babe in our arms as everyone comes in to see the two new additions to the family.

"Oh, my God, they are so precious!" Cassie says as she reaches out to take the baby from Jill's arms, "So, what does this auntie get to call her precious nephews?"

Jill and I look at each other, "We named them after Duncan's father and grandfather. The one you are holding is Callum James."

"And this little guy," I say as I look down at my other son, "is Colin Joseph."

Congratulations are shouted throughout the room, startling my sons. I can't be mad at them; I am so happy at this proud moment. I squeeze Jill up against my side and kiss the top of her head. I can't believe that I finally have a family of my own, kids and all! At this moment, I am happy that I got turned into a vampire, because I could never imagine living a life without Jill in it. She has filled my heart with joy and has given me children... sons, who I can continue to pass the McPherson name on to. I will protect her for as long as I live. She is the love of my life, my wife, and the mother of my children. She is my Angel.

*Don't miss Taven and his mate's story in
The Vampire's Salvation, the next book
in the Elite series...Coming Soon!*

www.ingramcontent.com/pod-product-compliance
Lightning Source LLC
LaVergne TN
LVHW091637070526
838199LV00044B/1104